GRANT'S
Blaze

SHARK'S EDGE: BOOK SIX

ANGEL PAYNE & VICTORIA BLUE

GRANT'S *Blaze*

SHARK'S EDGE: BOOK SIX

ANGEL PAYNE & VICTORIA BLUE

WATERHOUSE PRESS

It's said that what's most important is not the destination but the journey. I think it's neither, but the person you choose to travel with. I would never have had the courage to pack my bags, let alone buy this nonstop ticket if it weren't for the encouragement, support, patience, and loving guidance of the best writing partner a girl could have. Thank you, Ms. Angel Payne. You've ensured all my memories from this trip are in bright, exciting, living color, and I love you for every single one.

—VB

Ms. Blue...this one's for you! Thank you for the fire, ferocity, and incredible constancy of your friendship: one of the most awesome gifts the Creator ever gave me.

—Angel

CHAPTER ONE

RIO

"In five hundred feet, you will have reached your destination. Your destination is on the left."

My Fiat's navigational assistant directed me to the Malibu address with efficiency. This wasn't a part of Southern California I was intimately familiar with, but my little car was perfect for the tight streets and dimensionally unusable parking spaces that had to be passed over by the larger luxury sedans and town cars that were more prevalent in this zip code.

Five days had come and gone since I arrived home from my Hawaiian vacation with Grant. Well, what I had rebranded as a vacation. In reality, the trip had been the man acting as my savior. Once again. When he broke me out of a mental health facility in downtown LA, I was in the throes of a crisis that no one in my life wanted to touch with a ten-foot pole. So instead of doing whatever they could to support me, they had me committed to Clear Horizons.

But Grant swooped in to save the day. My very own action hero—Christ knew he had the looks and the physique for the role—carried me out while my mind swam through a drug haze and then stole me away for the trip of a lifetime.

But that three-week pleasure cruise aboard a private yacht with one of the world's most eligible bachelors ended with my life's second-worst day. Late in the night, automatic-weapon-brandishing maritime pirates boarded our vessel and took Grant hostage.

Disbelief still twisted my gut. I pictured myself pitching this crazy bullshit to studio execs as the plot of next summer's biggest blockbuster.

If only I were making it up.

Back to reality, though, and the hulking house before me. I dug into my jeans' back pocket for my phone to make sure I had the right address. Never mind I'd just done the exact same thing before I parked.

Concentrating on anything for longer than a minute or two was proving to be a challenge. Even on an average day, it wasn't my strong suit. Throw in the trauma of the last week, and I'd become a real basket case again. Reminded me a lot of the days right after Sean's accident, only Grant wasn't here to pick me up every time I fell down.

I could not lose another man I loved. I wouldn't survive this time. I knew that declaration to be real with every breath I took. It was the thought that scared me into action every morning and terrorized me in my nightmares every night. I had to do everything in my power to bring Grant home.

That plan started right here.

"Focus, Rio," I muttered to myself and took a deep breath of salty air to let it center my wayward thoughts. The ocean had always been a balm for my frazzled nerves, and I hoped like hell when the agony of witnessing Grant's abduction wore off, I would again feel peace when I heard the familiar sound of waves breaking and watched seagulls dancing and dipping on the offshore breeze. Right now, the only things settling over me were fear, anxiety, and a lot of frustration.

I pressed the button at the solid wooden gate and waited. My gaze wandered over the meticulously crafted iron trim and followed the shallow gully it created up at least ten feet to the highest point on the fence. With an easy rock back on my heels, I could see the entire property was surrounded like a fortress. I took a quick look behind me, hoping none of the neighbors were watching me gawk like an obvious outsider while I waited for the homeowner to answer. Finally, a low buzz sounded, quickly followed by a click as the gate was unlocked.

With a fortifying inhale, I pushed my way inside and followed the pebble-finished sidewalk to the front door. I half expected a team of Doberman pinschers to bound around the corner with their teeth bared and hungry snarls set in place as they positioned themselves to defend their master's property.

Instead, Elijah Banks appeared at the front door. His bare feet drew my gaze down, and I admired his powerful, dark-denim-clad thighs on the way back up to the plain white V-neck T-shirt that stretched across his defined chest and arms.

Had this man always been so good-looking? His sandy-brown hair flopped carelessly to one side, and a few days of unshaven beard stubble complemented his olive skin.

Instantly, I felt guilty for checking him out so thoroughly. I darted my stare back to the ground and then casually to the landscaped apron around the front walk.

"Elijah, hey. You have a beautiful home, this location... wow."

Perfect. Now I was a tongue-tied basket case in front of Grant's best friend. Though between my sleepless nights, this larger-than-life house, and the man himself, who could blame me for having an utterly scrambled brain?

The castle-size front door swept inward, and Elijah stood

back and motioned for me to enter while saying, "Thanks for coming here to meet. I know it's a bit out of the way, but given the nature of the conversation, I just felt like it was the best choice."

Like an obedient child, I followed him once he closed the front door. The house was enormous, and my nervous energy flowed right out through a snarky remark.

"Jesus, Elijah, I didn't realize you ran a bed-and-breakfast. How do you find the time?"

He didn't even grace me with a glance back over his shoulder at the comment.

Ohhhkaayyy, not one for sarcasm. Got it.

We passed through room after room until we came to the kitchen. Instantly, I relaxed in the space where I felt most at ease in any home.

"Can I get you something?" he asked. "Coffee, tea, something else?"

"I'd love a cup of tea, actually. Thank you," I said quietly, trying to make sense of the crooked smile he offered between his words and mine. Was that a habit of his, or was he that relaxed about what was happening with Grant? Because I hadn't slept for days. My nails were chewed down to the quick, and I was wearing a path in my carpet from anxiety-induced pacing.

The light clatter of the cup and saucer against the marble counter snapped me out of my thoughts. My host slid my tea across the island and motioned toward it with a lift of his chin.

"Take a seat," he instructed, and just like that, I wasn't pondering his smile anymore. He issued the instruction in that same tone of voice that Grant always used. *That* tone. The timbre that always made my body move before I thought twice about what was happening.

Four stools lined the marble-topped island on the nonservice side, so I climbed onto one of the buttery-soft leather chairs and tried to relax a bit. I took a moment to look around the kitchen again, thinking everything in this room had been planned with a level of care that only came from someone who loved to cook.

With a bit of intrigue, I stared at Elijah as he moved— almost gracefully—around his kitchen but quickly lifted my tea to my lips when he caught me watching him.

"What is it?" the man asked. Nearly demanded, really.

"Hmm? Nothing." I shook my head a bit, wondering why this guy was making me so edgy.

"Bullshit. If you have something to ask, ask it."

A secret smile spread across my lips before I could hide it. "It's not really a question." I tried to distract myself by stirring my tea, but it was pointless. "You and he act so much alike. It's sweet how good of friends you are." When I finally dared to look up, Elijah's hazel eyes were studying me.

"Bas, Grant, and I have been friends most of our lives." Now Elijah was the one smiling wider. The expression had me entranced. Maybe memories were playing on a quick reel in his mind.

Finally, I asked, "Can I be really honest here?" As soon as Elijah nodded, I went on. "Why aren't you worried right now? I mean, no offense. This is just—"

"Honesty," he filled in. "I hear you, Rio. I get that."

"So what gives?" I persisted. "I'd be hysterical if my lifelong friend were being held hostage by a bunch of unknown bastards in some unknown place."

"Well, for one thing, I don't get hysterical." The man met

my stare with his newly serious one. "About anything. For another thing, I don't believe he's really in serious danger."

Before I could get a word of my mounting objection to that comment out of my mouth, the laidback guy held up a steady flat palm to stop me.

"Calm down and hear me out. I'm not saying they won't knock him around a little bit." He shrugged—actually *shrugged*—and then sat on the stool beside me. "But Grant's a big guy. Tough too. My man can take a lot before he snaps."

For a long second, I didn't say anything. I just watched as different facets of Elijah's heart projected onto the screen of his face. It was quite a privilege to experience. I suspected this man typically held his emotional cards close to the vest. I also suspected there was a lot more to this man than he let on to with his carefully cultivated exterior.

First, I'd noticed a flash of pride when I mentioned how similar he and Grant were. I knew all three men—Grant, Sebastian, and Elijah—had rough childhoods on and off Los Angeles's streets. While the city was a different place now than twenty years ago, those boys and then young men saw some hard times.

Finally, he said, "I have all the faith in the world that he's going to be alright, Rio. You just have to go with me on this."

But I still had a bothersome feeling Elijah was keeping something from me. And while I didn't expect we'd be braiding each other's hair or playing a few rounds of Never Have I Ever, I had foolishly—naïvely, I supposed—expected him to treat me with the same respect he always gave Grant. Honestly, I wasn't sure he would give me the answers I asked for at this point regardless, but I would never know if I didn't try. Otherwise, I would go home wondering and beat myself up for the rest of the night.

"I just feel like you're holding something back. Like you have information, but you think I can't handle hearing it." I studied his expression after I hurled my accusation, but he didn't so much as twitch. So I kept on going. "But you're forgetting, I was the woman lying in bed beside him when they dragged him from our cabin in the middle of the goddamn night!"

Yes, I was getting pissed, but someone needed to be outraged on Grant's behalf. Actually, somebody needed to be a lot more than that.

"I haven't forgotten, Ms. Gibson." The maddening man narrowed his focus more intently on my trembling hands resting on the marble counter.

I quickly clasped the traitors together in my lap.

Elijah continued in an even darker tone of voice. "Nor have I forgotten why he was on that boat in the first place. So don't hurl qualifiers in my direction right now, Rio."

"Is that what I'm sensing, then? You're blaming me for all of this? If he hadn't been on that boat with me in the first place, this would have never happened?"

"That's a pretty obtuse conclusion to draw. Even for you. If I didn't know better, I'd say someone's projecting." He raised one perfectly sculpted eyebrow in accusation.

"'*Even for you*'? What is that supposed to mean?" My voice rose in pitch and volume with each word that tumbled out. "And it sounds like I'm not the only one who's done some time on the therapy couch!" I gave him the raised eyebrow right back. God, this smug bastard was infuriating.

But what he wasn't was ruffled. Not in the slightest. Maybe a little amused, but positively not angry or upset in any way.

"All right, all right." He held both hands up as though

he were a holy man blessing his flock. "Let's just calm down before things are said that aren't meant. It was not my intention to offend you."

Well . . . okay, then. Even though it came from out of left field, I'd accept his apology.

"It's fine," I said. "I'm sure I'm overly sensitive. I wasn't joking when I said I haven't been sleeping well. While we were on the boat, Grant really helped me work on getting my sleep pattern back in order, and now it's shot to hell once again." I shook my head ruefully and mumbled, "He's going to be so disappointed in me."

"Rio," Elijah said quietly, but I couldn't meet his hazel stare. "Look at me, girl."

Well, that did it. Once more, that damn voice . . .

I slowly looked up to find those piercing hazel eyes looking through to my soul.

"He's not going to be disappointed in you over lost sleep. Especially while you're under so much stress." My host walked across his kitchen to the refrigerator for another bottle of water. He was downing them one after the other since I arrived, and I was biting my cheek to not make a joke about lowering his salt intake.

After gulping half the bottle of water down, Elijah said, "But while we're on the subject of disappointing that man, I think there's something else we should probably talk about."

"Well, shit, Elijah, I wouldn't have thought you capable of letting anyone down." Of course, I knew exactly where he was steering the conversation, but if I could derail his train, I would.

"Don't be cheeky." He scowled and finished the last swig of his fourth bottle of water, if my tally was accurate.

"I don't need a lecture, Elijah. Or a reminder. Or a pep talk, or any other branding you want to slap on your nagging me about something that doesn't really concern you."

Quicker than I could process what was happening, he was on my side of the island, invading my personal space until I could feel his breath on my cheek with each low, menacing word he issued.

"Listen closely, lady." He leaned back just far enough to get his arm between us and *thump* his thumb back into his own sternum. "It was me who took the phone call from my brother when he needed someone to trace your cellphone call from Clear Horizons." He studied my expression closely before going on. "And it was also me"—*thump, thump*—"who followed that same best friend out of a fucking burning building filled with innocent people. And here's the real kicker... You'll love this part... My best friend was carrying your ass the whole way because you were busy babbling like the corner hobo on a bad Molly bender. And that man loves you so damn much he literally walked over fucking fire to save you!"

By the time he finished that last bit, he had flared his nostrils to greedily inhale fresh oxygen. But when I tried to interrupt, he widened his eyes in reproach, and I instantly shrank back.

"And it is still me"—*thump, thump*—"Ms. Gibson, that covers your ass for the mess you made the night of your late husband's accident. Almost every. Single. Day. Our other best friend grills me. Accuses me. Attacks my character in one way or another. And all for the sake of saving your precious dignity and reputation. So do not tell me that your pyromaniac tendencies don't really concern me. Have I made myself clear?"

"Abundantly," I retorted. "But unless you want your dentist to have to extract your balls from somewhere behind your twelve-year molars, I suggest you back the fuck up, Mr. Banks, and get out of my personal space."

I drew an imaginary arc in front of me to exhibit where my personal space started and stopped. Not that he was even noticing.

"Okay, cut to the chase here, dude. Why did you agree to see me today? If you don't have any information about where Grant is or how much longer they will keep him prisoner? Hell, it doesn't even sound like you know who these people are. Maybe it's time to call the police. Get some professionals on the case." I knew I was goading him with the comment, but if it spurred him into actually doing something instead of just bullying me, then his ire would be worth it.

"Don't be a fool," Elijah scoffed.

"A fool? How is that being a fool? Sitting around doing nothing seems like the fool's bet here, Elijah."

"The police despise Bas. And just because you see nothing, or know of nothing, doesn't mean nothing's being done, Ms. Gibson."

"What does LAPD's opinion of Sebastian have to do with Grant?"

He tilted his head in a wordless *you can't be serious*. But I was serious. As a shark attack.

CHAPTER TWO

GRANT

Elijah, the stubborn bastard, finally gave up trying to have a conversation with me after the third time even though I could clearly hear him. He'd handed me a headset for that exact reason before the chopper took off from the small municipal airport on Santa Catalina, but instead, I just stared at my white-knuckled grip on the armrest beside me.

The flight was a quick one from the best-known Channel Islands back to Long Beach. I just wasn't ready to talk about what happened yet, and he would have questions. Roughly three thousand and twenty-nine of them, according to my best guess—and I couldn't stomach the thought of answering even one. So I took the pussy's way out and chose radio silence for the aerial hop back to LA.

Yet sadly, that wasn't the end of the entries in my *King Wuss* journal. Yeah, that was me, pushing his phone away when he offered it to me to call Rio. That was also me, glowering at his equally confused look when I refused to have him call her on my behalf. The only clipped explanation I could offer was something along the lines of "Not yet, man."

Fortunately, Elijah backed off with a firm nod. I don't know what that nod was supposed to mean, but I'd deal with it all eventually. Just not yet. Exactly like I'd explained. I wasn't a complex man. Not like him, at least. And sure as hell not like the leader of our little brigade—the guy who still had me on his persona non grata leaderboard—Sebastian.

But that was a different concern for a much different day.

Once we landed on the mainland, my best friend continued to eye me cautiously. Concurrently, I kept pulling in air through my flared nostrils, hoping he'd get the overall message. One more sideways glance when he thought he was being covert, and I'd backhand him. My hand-to-hand fighting skills had gotten a fast refresher course over the past—

Shit.

"Hey. How long was I gone?" I asked, my voice gravelly from shouting after such a long stretch of disuse.

"A little over a week," Elijah answered as we started across the tarmac. "Nine days today."

The information was both relieving and troubling. If he'd gone into months on the answer, I wouldn't have been shocked. Still, I'd just been robbed of nine goddamned days of my life.

"I'm so tired," I finally muttered. I still hadn't explained how I'd gotten to a private resort's beach near Avalon, Catalina's main port. I was sure Elijah already had some theories and was spinning up more as we left the terminal.

"All right, man. You sit here, and I'll get my car. I had to park at the end of the lot, it's just about noon and it's damn hot already. Gonna be a scorcher today." He tried to steer me toward a concrete retaining wall that was low enough to sit on.

I stepped back, raising my hands. "I'm fine, Banks. I'm tired. My legs aren't broken."

He huffed in frustration because we both knew *I* was being the stubborn bastard now. It didn't escape my notice that he slowed his pace considerably so my pussy ass could keep up. He hadn't been joking about the heat, either. Even as we entered the big parking structure, the shade was compounded by the compressed heat of the abnormally sultry day. Thank God for the dependable onshore breeze in Long Beach, always blowing no matter the hour of day.

Still . . . me and my damn prideful ways.

The parked cars began to morph into different shapes and shades while we lumbered up the incline, heading in the direction of Elijah's vehicle. I squeezed my eyes shut and opened them again when a nearby pickup looked like a melting ice cream cone. Christ, I needed water. I was dehydrated and overheating. Fast.

The first time I reached wildly for my buddy's arm, I got nothing but air. "Liii—" I desperately clawed his bicep to hold myself up while calling his name to make him stop walking, but the syllables came out in unintelligible grunts. "Shuuuh."

On the second try, I made contact. It was enough to grab his attention. He spun around, now seeming to get the full point.

"Holy shit, brother," he muttered. "You're in a world of trouble."

But somewhere between hearing him and comprehending him, my balance spun out of control. My knees buckled, and I crumbled to the rough concrete of the parking garage.

After that, things went by in woozy blurs. I was conscious of him swearing more and then helping me get upright again. But exactly where I'd ended up was a mystery. It was still shrouded in cool darkness . . . like the garage but so much more comfortable . . .

Just when I thought of dozing off into a sweet little catnap, the asshole nudged me. Hard. "Twombley, you stubborn motherfucker. Do not space out on me now."

"Space," I repeated in a daze. "Ohhh. Is that where we are? My favorite planet is Saturn. What's yours?"

"Shut up and sit up. You need to drink more, or these hallucinations will get worse." When I didn't respond, he gently touched my arm. "Hey. You still with me, man?"

I shook his hand off—or at least in my mind I did. Based on the quiet tone he still used when he spoke again, I hadn't been as successful with my menacing display of male power as I thought.

After cracking one eye open ever so slightly, I grimaced before asking, "Why are you naked, Banks? I thought I told you no the last time you tried this shit." I let both eyes fall closed again but could feel his body vibrate on the seat beside me with his chuckle. "Seriously, man, why don't you have a shirt on?"

"Your knees were bleeding. I didn't want that shit on my interior."

I weakly wrapped my fingers around the water bottle he put in my hand and had designs on drinking the entire thing, but the dickhead plucked it from my grasp after only about a third of the liquid made it down my desperate gullet.

"The fuck, man? My throat is so fucking dry and raw." Even to my own ears, I sounded like a whiny brat. Worse, I was too weak and pathetic to do anything more than that.

I forced my eyes open wide enough to try to buckle my seat belt. The smirking dude behind the wheel watched me struggle through several attempts before taking over and easily snapping the tab into the lock. "I'm pretty sure you're dehydrated. If you down too much, too fast, you will end up throwing it all up and doing more harm than good. So, for now, we pace."

"Fine. Whatever. Can you just be quiet now?" I decided to lead by example, hoping he'd follow suit. Besides, it helped me focus on other things—like breathing without fear.

I counted slowly to ten on each inhalation. Held for ten. Exhaled to the same count. The ultimate plan was to keep going until I fell asleep or was interrupted. I was strongly hoping for, but not counting on, the former. It had been a long time since I had to employ any sort of meditation exercise to deal with anxiety. But tried-and-true relaxation techniques, like old friends, were familiar no matter how much time passed between visits. And right now, I needed all the friends I could count on.

But nearly immediately, bad feelings from the past nine days came rushing in.

Really bad ones.

Loneliness and despair ran out in front of the pack. I was desperate to cope with them better by asking about Rio but had no right to do so in this crazy condition. That was what my twisted brain kept telling me, anyway. Besides, talking about her would make me miss her more. And missing her would make me ache to be near her. But being this close to her, right in the same city and not getting to hold her in my arms . . . damn it, not getting to fuck her . . .

I groaned inwardly. I needed to stop this self-torture right the hell now. I was only making things worse. Already, it was nearly impossible to resist calling her. But doing that would just be unfair, ultimately to us both, and I knew it with crushing clarity.

But fucking her would feel so good right now . . .

Okay, forget the inner flogging. I went straight for thumping my head against the passenger-side window.

Somehow, in some way, I had to get a goddamned grip on this stuff.

Had the experiences of the past week really reduced me to the level of my captors? I didn't doubt it. I felt like a barbarian with a lukewarm IQ, even though I was currently sporting a Balenciaga T-shirt and coordinating joggers. Fucking Elijah. But how did the saying go? You could put lipstick on a pig...

Yeah, something along those lines.

My rudimentary line of thinking and pathetically weak bearing hadn't changed how I felt for Rio Gibson, though. It might have made it worse if I let myself have a moment of honesty. I groaned, thinking of all the truths I didn't want to face right now. Perhaps because higher thought hadn't been an option for the last week or so.

"You okay, my brother?" Elijah asked in his smooth voice, darting glances between the freeway and me as we made our way home.

"Yeah, yeah, I'm good. Just need a long shower and a bed. I want to sleep for a week."

Elijah grunted. "Not a bad action plan, buddy."

"Yeah, but also not realistic. I'm sure Bas will have other plans for me right away. He'll demand me back at my desk first thing in the morning."

"Grant." The silence was accentuated with at least three me-windshield-me circuits of his glare. Finally, he huffed an exasperated, "Come on."

"'Come on' what? You know the man as well as I do, right?"

"Absolutely. But I'm telling you right now, he's been as worried about you as I have been."

I made a dramatic show of looking around the interior of

the car. "Yeah, I can tell. Worried sick."

"You're not being fair, but I'm not going to defend him. He's a big boy, so that's on him. But he doesn't even know you're back. I didn't tell anyone." He held out a hand like he was about to stop me from protesting. Maybe he was spot-on with the instinct. I wasn't really sure of my own reaction on that, so I couldn't blame him for the precaution. "I thought you might need some time to readjust."

Years of a brother-close friendship had planted Banks right inside my head. The bastard plucked thoughts from freshly sowed seedlings in my mind's garden like I didn't have a say on the topic at all. A lot of times, I was damn grateful for it. Today, not so much. Because this stabbed at my mental acuity—a position I despised being in, at all costs. I was just grateful Elijah not only saw all the bad shit going on in my head but was willing to cover my ass until I was at full capacity again.

Which all basically meant that I should be saying something by now. At the very least, giving him a grateful grunt. But instead, I was pissed off. No, not just that. I was a triggered basket case and apparently wearing it like a sandwich board. Step right up, folks. See the once-great Grant Twombley. Now, you will barely recognize the man.

What a difference a day really made. Or nine, in this case.

God, I was a miserable son of a bitch. Just another reason why I couldn't see my girl yet. I had no idea what the last nine days had been like for her, but she'd have to make it to ten. Maybe longer. I couldn't face her until I pulled my head out of my ass. She didn't need to see me like this, and she certainly didn't deserve to be exposed to this weak, muddled version of me.

"Honey, we're home."

Elijah's deep voice woke me from a fitful dream, confirming the old relaxation technique must've finally worked. I woke with a start from my drifting sleep, and just in time. The last thing I needed were more embarrassing leftovers from this fucked-up experience. It was bad enough I was going to have to deal with them myself. Others didn't need to know about it too.

My body hurt like I'd been in a street fight when I unfolded from my buddy's front seat. The distance between the car and the door to his luxurious Malibu home seemed to have tripled since I was here the last time, too.

Wait...

"Banks," I barked. "Why are we here? Didn't we talk about this? I really just want to sleep in my own bed, you know? Be among my own stuff." And goddammit, my king-sized shower.

I'd taken enough recent cracks to my skull to accept that confusion was a normal state of mind. But I did tell the big jerk to take me straight home. Might have even said it before he handed me the thousand-dollar workout shit. Or loungewear. Whatever the catalogues were calling it these days.

Elijah stood in front of his car, kicking at imaginary pebbles. "I'm aware of what you asked, man. But..."

"But what, damn it?"

"I'm worried about you."

I swung the passenger door closed. The panel barely made a pathetic slap, let alone the angry *whomp* I'd intended. "Well, don't be."

"You can say the words all you want," he snapped. "It's not going to make me stop caring about your well-being. You're dehydrated and exhausted, and I have no idea the last time you've eaten."

He wasn't wrong, but I had to speak up. "I'm sure Rio wouldn't mind—"

"Grant, come on."

"What?"

"I'm not convinced the woman is fit to take care of herself…or even that little cat." He pushed his front door open and followed me inside while he finished his thought. "Definitely not both at the same time."

"Don't be an ass."

"I think you'd be better off here with me for a few days while you get your head screwed back on in a decent manner. Take care of you before going home to her and ending up back in caretaker mode."

"Okay, whoa." I said it as much to my whirling balance as to him, while finding a barstool at his kitchen counter to conveniently drop onto. "Who said I was her damn—"

"Nope. You don't want to go there with me. Not right now. Whatever the semantics, we both know it's true. If you get within ten feet of that woman, your shit isn't going to get handled."

"So, what?" I couldn't help the sarcasm that spread across my lips. "You're going to handle my shit instead?"

"Now who's being the ass?"

We stared intensely at each other for a few more moments until my weary body screamed at me to lie down.

"Listen, man. I don't have the energy to argue with you on this," I conceded, rubbing the back of my stiff neck. "You're right. I'm exhausted. Just point me toward the room I can catch a few hours of sleep in, and then I'll get out of your hair. I promise."

"You can stay as long as you want, and you know it."

"Shower and bed?" I persisted.

"All right, all right." He splayed both hands in surrender. "See how you feel after some sleep, chief. I was thinking we could set you up in the room off the courtyard by the pool. I know you always like it out there. The sound of the water on the infinity edge—"

"No!"

I sliced the air with my hand, maybe a bit too forcefully based on his facial expression.

"If it's all the same, I don't want to hear water sloshing, lapping, rippling, dripping, or trickling." I winced just thinking about it. A physical shudder racked my body. "Yeah . . . no. Not in any way, shape, or form for a very long time. Maybe ever again."

"All right, all right," Elijah repeated. "I get that. I do."

"Thanks," I muttered.

"How about the blue room? You've been in there a couple of times . . . just not ever by yourself. But maybe the nice memories will help? Shit, what were the names of those two fine females we last had there?"

"Seriously?" I snapped. "I just want to lie in a bed that won't have rats running across it in the middle of the night." My body gave in to another shudder before I continued my thought. "And I don't want to be woken up by a boot to my stomach. That's probably not too much to ask in this palace you have here."

I forced a chuckle when the asshole factor of my words sank in. My friend was just trying to be accommodating, and I threw it all back at him with dickhead word choices.

"Hey. I'm sorry, man." I shook my head and dropped my stare to my toes after behaving like such a cad.

"Don't be ridiculous, Twombley. You've acted like a much bigger ass than this in our years. Come on. Let's get you cleaned up so you can get some sleep. You look like shit."

CHAPTER THREE

GRANT

After nearly eighteen hours of sleep, I felt like a new man. Well, relatively speaking, at least. I indulged in another shower before going in search of my host. With nothing but a white towel wrapped shamelessly low around my hips, I followed my nose back toward his large gourmet kitchen. The delicious scent of coffee steered me like the Pied Piper's own rodents before they ditched Hamelin.

Just before entering the kitchen, I heard Elijah's voice as though he was having a conversation. I figured it was a phone call because I only heard his voice. Only after coming around the corner from the back hallway and through the butler's pantry did I see the back of the woman he was speaking to.

Swiftly I shrank back into the pantry's shadows and just as quickly gave myself a mental *what the fuck?*

Damn it. This wasn't like me at all. But what exactly *was* me right now? My body had suffered a considerable amount of physical abuse over the past nine days, and I had the rainbow-colored bruises to show for it. I'd also been alternately starved and then fed, which put me on the brink of dehydration. That sort of abuse wreaked havoc on everything from sleep patterns to muscle tone and mass. All of that was definitely already showing as well.

And I hated it. With a deep vehemence.

It had been close to two decades since I'd been this self-conscious about my body. Nearly twenty damn years. But suddenly, I yearned to become invisible. Exactly the opposite happened when the icemaker in the spare refrigerator whirred, and I jolted.

At once, Elijah's guest spun around.

My inner profanities turned the inside of my brain blue. No way could I get out of her sightline fast enough, nor did she appear to want that. Elijah's visitor was actually a woman we both knew intimately.

Fuck.

Who the hell bought a backup fridge with an icemaker?

"Hey, Shawna." I looked around for our host, but he seemed to have pulled the magic trick I was fantasizing about.

None of that was lost on the pretty redhead.

"Looking for Elijah?" she prompted.

"Yeah, sorry. I don't mean to be rude. Just not feeling so great. Do you know where he went? I thought I just heard him in here." I couldn't meet her gaze, so I looked over her shoulder to the courtyard just beyond the windows. Sure enough, there was my target, speaking animatedly to a man servicing the pool.

"Anyhow...it was...umm...nice seeing you again. If you'll excuse me?"

No way was I waiting around to hear her reply. Instead I focused on beelining for the pool deck before Elijah was off to manage another household problem.

Still only in the bath towel, I stepped out into the late-morning sun. The warm rays felt so good on my skin that I surreptitiously gave the lounge chair deep consideration instead of having a conversation with my best friend.

Really, what was another lost afternoon at this point? No one knew I was back. I could lie there, just relaxing and pulling my shit together before going back to my place. It wouldn't hurt anything. Or anyone.

Well, maybe someone.

"Hey, there you are. How do you feel? Did you sleep well? I see you found the shower stuff I set out."

Elijah's smile was genuine, his questions sincere. They always were. The man never asked if he didn't really want to know. Each query's answer was a building block to the carefully constructed vision he had of a person. Banks didn't take friendships lightly. He gave all of himself to a relationship and expected the same in return. Unfortunately, there were times he ended up getting hurt because of it.

"Yes, Martha Stewart," I teased him. "The thread count on the sheets could be a little higher, though." I gestured toward the towel around my hips. "But seriously, do you have something I can throw on for the drive home? I don't think an Uber driver will appreciate my balls on their upholstery."

We both chuckled, especially as the pool guy whipped his head in our direction.

"Yeah, I can make that happen," Elijah said. "But chief, listen, we need to talk."

I cocked a brow. "About the fact that Shawna's inside and you're out here dicking with your pool filters?"

"No. About you going home. Are you sure that's the best plan?" He strolled around the courtyard to the far side where a set of French doors led back into the house.

I kept pace beside him, assuming we were headed to one of his walk-in closets so I could get into something better than a bath sheet.

"Why are you giving me so much shit about going home?" I asked, not hiding my frustration.

"I'm just worried about you, man."

"I'm fully aware. You don't need to keep saying it."

"Actually, maybe I do," he groused.

"Banks." I shifted my gaze to look at him in my periphery. "What the hell is this really about?"

"Shit." Elijah stopped at the vestibule of his master bedroom and faced me. "Maybe I should just come right out and say it."

I gripped two fistfuls of my disheveled hair before blurting, "Damn, I wish you would."

"Fine. I've just noticed, in glaring ways, that you have this...look...in your eyes. I don't know."

His words were coupled with an awful set of gestures. A small shrug combined with a slow head shake. His actions made me feel equally strange. Like he was my disappointed parent, giving up and resigning himself to my failure.

If that were the case, who was left to champion my cause? I was depending on Banks to support me through my self-pity and morbid introspection stage. And after that, I needed him to cheer me on through my phoenix-rising stage, and then to help me celebrate during my congratulatory phase. It was our truth, after all. The tidy roles we normally played. Elijah was the deep thinker here. And me? Well, I was...not trying to pinpoint that right now.

"What the hell do you mean?" I urged.

"I don't know, Grant," he repeated. "I don't know how to explain it. We've been friends for a long time."

I gave a curt nod.

"Do you know the last time I saw a similar look on your

pretty-boy face?" my best friend asked. When I didn't respond, he bulldozed through the silence. "Dude, it was the day we found your mom."

I shook my head. For a long moment, that was it. Because what could I really say? The man had always been incredibly perceptive. Even when we were kids, Banks knew when something was off with one of his friends long before the rest of the crew did. But how much did I want to saddle the guy with now? He didn't need to be weighed down with the grisly details of what happened on that damn cargo boat. Worse, he didn't need to know all the shit that had been going on in my head ever since.

What were my options, though? Go home alone and climb the walls? No thanks.

Option two: unloading all my psychological baggage at Rio's front door. She had enough of her own crap to deal with. To take on mine too? That would be another massive *no thanks*.

I was already skating on very thin psychological ice. Losing her on top of everything else I was dealing with... It'd be the final fissure in the frozen version of Lake Twombley. I'd fall right through to the icy waters beneath before completely drowning.

The only other friend I could call was Sebastian—but that was if the almighty Shark agreed to speak to me after tending to his biggest priorities: a brand-new baby and his fiancée. Still, this was the first time in our entire friendship that a squabble lasted this long, and it didn't feel good.

In theory, a relationship as deep and long-lasting as ours should be able to endure any tiff, big or small. But this shit... It was far beyond a tiff. Once someone did Bas dirty, they were dead to him. In his mind, that was exactly where I stood, and I certainly wouldn't be begging the man for an audience.

"Hey. Sorry I went there, buddy." Elijah's voice was drenched with deep concern.

I jolted, having forgotten he was still standing there.

"But are you good?" he asked.

"Nah, man, I don't think I am." I looked at him with worry, already feeling the thick, stinging flood waters rising. "But . . . I don't know what to do."

Oh, holy crap. They were going to crest and spill over any second. I looked up toward the ceiling, hoping like hell that would send the shit back where it came from, because I couldn't remember the last time one of us cried in front of the other.

Elijah wisely kept to his side of the conversation. I sensed how excruciating it was for him, holding back on delivering the hug and shoulder claps that were an ingrained part of his personality, but if he went there, I'd probably deflate one of his kidneys. Maybe both. I was barely holding on as it was. My hair-trigger temper was another thing I was still getting used to.

Finally, he settled for murmuring, "It's okay, man. Whatever it is, all or nothing, you know it's totally okay by me. You need a few things to break? An empty wall to punch?"

"No. Yes. Hell, I don't know." I pulled at my hair in frustration before continuing. "I . . . just don't know where to start, you know? Part of me thinks, ignore the shit. That usually works for everything else." I blinked rapidly and pinched the bridge of my nose, trying to cut off the hideous burning sensations in my sinuses. "It always works itself out. But this . . . is way heavier than normal." I thumped on the center of my chest. "In here, man. It feels really, really bad in here."

And fuck if the tears didn't spring right back up just when I thought I'd gotten the upper hand on that mess. God*damm*it.

"Have you given any more thought to staying here for a while? You know what I'm saying is true, right?" My friend's hazel eyes were nearly gray with emotion.

"I miss her, though," I managed to croak out. "You get that, right?"

"Of course I do. Probably more than you think," he replied. "And believe me, she's been a mess without you. I'm not saying you shouldn't see her. I'm saying maybe you shouldn't be her personal Dr. Freud for a while. At least not until you have your own shit worked out again."

"That's just it." I scrubbed my hand back around to my nape. "I never felt like I had shit like this to work out before now. How am I supposed to know where to start or what to get worked out?"

"What do you mean?" He moved deeper into the bedroom, absently rearranging items atop his dresser, as if to give me ample time for contemplation.

I huffed and shook my head. "It's hard to explain."

"Try," he all but ordered while disappearing back into the closet. "Seriously, just try. So I can be of some kind of help here."

I sat on the bench at the foot of his giant bed. I looked around the room for a long minute while he found something for me to wear. I noticed he'd painted the walls a warm gray in here, and I really liked it.

Maybe all I really needed was a little scenery change, and I'd be right as rain again.

And maybe Santa Claus and the Easter Bunny would invite me over for poker night next weekend.

Elijah finally tossed some clothes my way, so I stood up to dress.

"Okay"—he waved his hand through the air as he dictated—"finish your thought. You said you feel like maybe you have some issues to work out? Like what? Mental health stuff? Do you feel depressed?"

I shook my head. "I don't think that's it."

"No one would fault you for it," he asserted. "And I'm not prying about anything you're processing since those assholes—"

I shot up a hand. "Well, that's just the thing. It's really not about those assholes." I turned my hand over, as if examining my hand in Jesus-feeds-the-masses mode would lend me new insight. Instead, it had me admitting with even more confusion, "I'm feeling other things. Well, I guess *remembering* other things would be more accurate."

"Remembering?" he echoed, narrowing his gaze. "Okay. Remembering things like what?"

"Shit that happened when I was a teenager. Close to the time my mom died, I think."

"Ohhh-kaaay." He drawled it out this time, practically adding a smirk. The moment felt like a strange gut punch.

I sprang to my feet and gripped at my hair. "Okay?" I spat. "That's it? That's your idea of helping?"

"Whoa. Easy, Twombley. You look like you want to rip my windpipe out with your fucking fangs."

"Maybe I do!" I shouted—before catching a long look at my reflection in one of the large picture windows that looked out to the pool area.

Holy crap. The guy in that window was a madman.

The sight pulled me up fast. At once, I sank back down on

the bench. For a few long moments, I just sat there, my face cradled in my hands, willing my thundering heart to settle the fuck down.

Eventually, in a much lower volume, I said, "And I don't understand that bullshit, either. I've never felt so violent in my entire life. What's going on with me?"

I'd always prided myself on my even temper. One passionate powerhouse in our posse was enough, and Bas already had the engraved throne for it. But here I was, having to tamp down boiling rage over the slightest provocation.

Elijah still wasn't helping with a solution, continuing to study me with perplexed attention.

Now I knew what zoo animals must feel like. Trapped and stared at wasn't working well for me. I shivered.

"You want a sweatshirt, man? Or the heat turned on?"

I held up my hand again, adamantly stopping his mother hen bit. "It goes as quick as it comes," I explained. "I'm telling you, Elijah, I'm all fucked up right now. Apparently, all the way down to my body temperature."

I shook my head, because even though I knew damn well that being a hostage wasn't my fault, I was so disgusted with myself. So disappointed that I had let bullshit like this happen *to me*. It made me so angry. Angry and ashamed and sad.

After some appreciated silence, where my best friend and I just kicked back on his enormous bed, I mustered the courage to speak directly about the ordeal I'd just been through. Hell, I was tempted to relabel it already. An *ordeal*? Really? But what other title actually fit? Maybe going through it would lead to that answer . . . and others that I apparently desperately needed right now.

"I think they were drugging me with whatever bites of

food they gave me. It's the only thing that makes sense. There are too many symptoms, or whatever, to have all at once."

Elijah remained silent, actively receiving whatever it was I needed to get this mess "into the universe," as he always said.

"But these flashes of anger . . . damn it." I trailed off, throwing my forearm over my face. "What if I lash out at Rio in the same way? You already know how infuriating she can be."

Weirdly, I laughed out that last part. God, I missed that woman. I needed to see her again so badly. It was becoming a physical ache, but not in the usual places. For the first time in my life, the center of my chest throbbed harder for a woman than between my thighs did.

But then I lowered my arm and bolted my gaze back up at the ceiling. Without looking away from that comforting blankness, I sucked it up to ask the most terrifying question of my world. If I was looking at no one when I spoke it, then no one knew I was afraid, right?

"What if it's finally happening?"

I finally dared to peer over at Elijah.

His gaze was utterly clueless.

"What if I'm losing my shit?" I persisted. "You know. Just like her."

"Rio?"

Tamp down the rage. Tamp down the rage.

It wasn't a far stretch to figure out his assumption. I mean, the current "crazy" person in my life was that woman I was head over heels for, but the guy also went way the hell back with me. So if he had been a little more thoughtful with his guess . . .

But he wasn't, and there was the reality. I'd have to deal.

"My mother," I said through gritted teeth.

He sat up then, holding up his hands. Somebody had gotten the memo about how pissed I was. "That was insensitive, man. My apologies. But Grant, your mother was a drug addict, not insane. There's a difference."

I pinched the bridge of my nose between my thumb and index finger again. Christ, no wonder Bas made the gesture all the time. "I think she was both. *Chicken or the egg* fits pretty perfectly."

"You're probably right," he offered. "But damn, buddy. We were what—fourteen or fifteen when she died? Grown-up enough to think we ruled the world; young enough to screw up a lot of attempts getting there. So how does a kid understand complex mental health issues at that age?"

"Not saying I did. But have you ever remembered something from your childhood, and the more you think about it, the more you think that it doesn't really add up?"

"I guess so. I don't really know." My best friend let out a heavy sigh.

It dawned on me that maybe I'd crossed the line between tapping into his advice and overburdening him with all my dramatic woes. Yes, he was the one who brought me here instead of my own home. And yes, he was the one who kept encouraging me to stay a few days while I tried to get my head screwed on straight. But now, I wasn't sure a few days was going to be long enough—the same way I sensed that I had more to deal with than just the last two hundred and forty hours.

"I think I'm going to call Rio," I finally said, needing to change the subject. "I really want to hear her voice."

Like, right the fuck now.

"I think you should wait, but I've said my peace on the matter."

"Elijah, can you imagine doing that to the woman you love? Letting her worry even a moment longer than necessary? It's already shitty enough that I've waited this long to reach out to her."

"So don't tell her you waited. I'll call her and tell her you passed out from exhaustion the minute we got in my car. I brought you back here, and you've been sleeping ever since. It's not too far from the truth. You've only been awake some of the time. It's been what? Two hours? Three, tops?"

"And you know that so precisely...how?" I retorted, rolling off the bed. "Is this where I add creepy babysitter to the long list of your illustrious nicknames?"

My friend just chuckled as we left his bedroom through the French doors that led back out to the pool deck. I couldn't help but turn the spotlight on him for a few minutes. God knew I'd had more than my fill of centerstage for the day. No—the year.

"So Shawna, huh?" I knocked into him while we walked, throwing him off balance for a few steps.

"Don't read more into it than it ever is with me. You know how I roll," he answered with very little emotion.

"You think you'll ever collar someone again?" I asked randomly as we walked around the infinity edge pool toward the extensive guest bedroom wing.

At once, Elijah spat, "Hell no."

I almost scuffed to a full stop. "Wow," I blurted instead.

"What *wow*?" he volleyed.

"You just answered so fast, and with such conviction," I explained, stabbing my hands into the front pockets of his butter-soft lounge pants that he'd given me. "I'd like to feel that way about something. Shit—about anything—right now."

The path forked, and he led the way out toward the lookout point over the ocean instead of back toward my guest room. "You don't feel like that about Rio?" he queried, almost too casually, as we walked.

"Well, of course I do. I love her," I declared into the briny air. "I'd get down on one knee—hell, I'd get down on both—and straight-up beg her to marry me, but I know she's not ready. So for now, I have to be satisfied playing the sad puppy chasing behind her. I'll keep lapping up her crumbs, and I'll be grateful for it."

He grew still, as if literally comparing me to the big hound that galloped next to his jogging owner on the sand below us, looking more than happy with his crumb-filled life.

At last, he asked, "Is that really how you see yourself?"

"Kind of," I muttered. "Yeah, I guess I do. At least right now it is."

He didn't hesitate to turn and stare at me. Forget that—he was fully gawking as if I had three eyes and he was trying to figure out how he could get a third for himself.

Finally, I snapped. "What the fuck are you looking at?"

"You, my brother. Very definitely you." He didn't let me sputter anything as he rolled his shoulder and then arced a thumb over it. "Because, you know, I'm trying to figure out what happened to the guy."

I drew in air through my flared nostrils. "Okay, just spit it out, Banks. You already know I'm going to ask."

"Yeah, but humor me."

Goddammit. "Fine," I muttered. "What guy?"

"Oh, you know," he said with a shrug. "The guy who called me demanding I pick him up out front of SE to go storm the castle walls of some looney bin so he could rescue his princess."

I couldn't help but grin at his retelling of the story. If Rio and I had kids one day, I could hear Uncle Elijah in the other room telling them how their parents got together.

He narrowed his eyes and waited for me to focus. "Have you seen that guy?"

With pursed lips, I made a *hmmm* sound. "Yeah, I vaguely remember him. But last time I saw him, he was thrown into the Pacific Ocean between a couple of the Channel Islands after the water was primed with a bunch of bloody chum."

"Christ," the guy gurgled out before the sound developed into something rougher. "Grant, for the love of—" He pivoted hard and finally went for a hard grab on my shoulder. "Why didn't you tell me that when I picked you up? You need to see a doctor right the hell now."

I wrenched away with a wide step. "And I didn't tell you because I knew that was coming."

"Twombley—"

"Banks," I returned. "Listen. I'm fine, okay? I just want to talk to Rio and then take another nap. Or ten."

"And you're sure you don't want me to tell her you're crashed? Exhausted?"

"No. I should be the one to do it. If it's you, I guarantee that little firestorm will drive Kendall straight through your front door." The image brought me to an instant and undeniable smile.

My friend peered back as if wondering if he really wanted to know why.

"Kendall?" he asked.

"That clown car she drives."

"Her car has a na—" He held up his hand in a stop gesture. "Nope. You know what? I don't even want to know. I'm just going to answer a few emails that look like they need my personal attention, and I have a security issue to deal with for Bas. After that, I'll be working on my tan out by the pool. If you have trouble napping, you're welcome to join me."

"Yeah . . . okay." Jesus, I was going to have a mess to return to. The job that had been the center of my orbit had been all but nonexistent from my considerations for weeks.

Great, and I could just add that to the pile of guilt at my feet. Right now, I could step over the rubbish and keep pushing through the day. But I wasn't sure how much longer that would be the case if I dialed Rio's number.

I hadn't been able to force my fingers to punch the sequence of keys since my feet hit solid ground in Catalina. What made me think I'd be brave enough to do it now?

CHAPTER FOUR

RIO

"Okay, but this is the last one," I said.

It was those big eyes. Robert looked at me with those big round eyes, and I was a goner. I couldn't say no to him, but when I saw the little kitty gut he was sporting when he lay around the house these days, I knew we both needed a kitty-treat intervention. He was the junkie and I was his enabler, and our codependent relationship needed to change.

Yeah, I was losing it. I didn't even need a heartless asshole like Elijah Banks up in my face to point it out today. I could see the writing on the wall all by myself. Well, look at that! A gold star in the self-awareness journal!

My cell phone's ring stopped my runaway train of self-loathing before it careened off the mountainside. When I looked at the display, I didn't recognize the number, but with Grant still missing, every phone call could be an important one. I picked up the call without a second thought.

"Hello?"

The line was quiet for a few beats, but I could tell someone was there. Finally, a voice broke the still air. And then broke my heart wide open.

"Blaze."

It was all he said. But it was all he needed to say. His voice was deep and husky, like he'd just woken up.

"Grant? Is . . . it really you?"

"Last time I checked," he answered with a chuckle.

I shot to my feet. My free hand fluttered to my throat and then back down again.

"Are you . . . laughing about this?"

Because if that were the case, I was truly going to kick his ass. All right, so it would be a slight pleasure because his ass belonged in its own glass case in the world's finest art museum, but I'd still kick that fine thing to the Canadian border and back.

As if he'd heard that whole diatribe, he dialed back the mirth. "Only because it feels so good to hear your voice, baby," he said softly.

I gulped hard. Then even harder. It was nearly impossible, considering every drop of saliva in my mouth had been sucked dry by shock and elation.

I needed to stay calm. I wouldn't be useful to either one of us if I got hysterical. But my voice didn't get the memo on that sentiment yet. "Where are you? Do you need me to come for you? Can I see you?" I was on my feet, scurrying around the house, looking for things. Not sure what things, exactly. But things.

He chuckled again, and I decided to just stop and . . . enjoy it. God, it was so good to hear that sound again. His laugh was so much like him. Deep and meaningful and robust. I wanted to sob, thinking of how many times I dreaded never hearing it again.

But I didn't. Instead, I decided to try sitting down. Not for long. Just for a moment, to absorb the enormity of what was happening. That he was really back. Truly home and safely away from the monsters who'd abducted him.

Well, the best-laid plans...

In my dumbstruck haze, I misjudged the distance between my backside and the sofa cushion. I skimmed past the edge, landing with a brutal thud on the floor. I also split the rear seam of my jeans, but I didn't care. I just wanted to listen to his voice and know he was okay. Tears ran down my cheeks and dripped off my chin, leaving darker polka dots on the denim covering my thighs.

"Grant? Are you still there?" I worried aloud.

"Yeah, baby, I'm here."

"Where's here? Can I see you? Are you okay? Are you hurt? Do you need a doctor? A lot of them do tele-med stuff now, you know?"

At last, I comprehended how my nervous energy had me rambling like an idiot. I forced myself to take a breath. On the exhale, I whispered, "I'm so sorry. It's just that... my God, I've been so worried. So scared. I wondered if I'd ever hear your voice again."

"I've missed you so much, Blaze. Every single thing about you. Don't apologize, okay?" He was equally soft spoken, and I missed the self-assured dominant man I loved so much.

Whoa. Wait a second.

That thought wasn't the sole cause of my concern. It was a pile-up of other factors. The staccato edges of his breaths. The drag of his long pause, filled only by rough scuffs that filled me with nervous energy. A helplessness that I abhorred.

So I accommodated by going for my comfort zone. Grabbing the damn bull by the horns.

"I'm coming to you. Tell me where you are so I can put it in my nav."

"Yeah," he said slowly. "About that . . ."

"What do you mean 'about that'?" I was trying to keep my tone even, but I was barreling toward becoming the bull instead of just wrestling it. Already, I didn't like where this was headed. Not one bit.

"I'm so exhausted, so I'm just going to sleep the rest of the day," he stated. "It's really what I need. And then we'll see how tomorrow shapes up . . ."

"How it 'shapes up'?" I flung back. "Wait. And what do you mean, tomorrow? Grant—"

"But I'll call you later if I end up waking up again, okay?"

"No," I blurted once it seemed like he was done with the hurried—and rehearsed—brush-off speech. "That's not okay. Grant—"

It was all I got out before he cut me off. Maybe my tone was too plaintive for his preference or energy and comfort level.

"I'll talk to you soon, baby. Bye."

Like an ass, I sat with the phone to my ear listening to absolutely nothing for at least another minute. When I finally set the device on the table, the screen had gone dark. I was smart enough to add that unrecognized number to Grant's contact card though. That way I wouldn't foolishly let another call go unanswered like I almost had this one.

Time for more trusted behavioral defaults. In this case, my inclination to overanalyze conversations. In this case, I'd have to consider the few sparse sentences of the conversation I'd just had with the man I loved.

He missed me. I missed him. Nothing too controversial there. I was so thankful he was back. He was thankful to be back. Also pretty cut and dry. Either my deductive skills were razor-sharp today, or that conversation was a real snooze festival.

Option B seemed like the clear winner.

Everything was fine until I asked—in several ways, and at several opportunities—for his whereabouts. Head, meet wall. He'd been very deft about just changing the subject or reverting to dazzling me with sweet talk.

Dazzling me. In this case, a fancy word for diverting me.

Why was he being so evasive over where he was sleeping tonight? I knew he had a bunch of homes, and he'd never been embarrassed or awkward about the fact in the past. Hell, he'd even taken me to see the downtown property before he made the offer to buy the place. I remember feeling special, as silly as that seemed, that Grant asked my opinion about some of the kitchen upgrades he wanted included in the closing costs on that property. Something about the whole experience made the place feel more like ours when I started spending more time there after Sean passed away.

I forced myself to haul in a long breath. I nearly made it to Grant's magic number of ten before letting the air back out. And whether I wanted to admit it or not, I was calmer. There was no use spinning myself into hysteria about this, until I became the woman I used to be. I promised myself I was going to be a better version of myself when we got off that damn boat, and this was my first test. If he said he was tired and just needed to get some extra rest, then I had to believe him. He'd never lied to me before; I had no other choice—even if the truth hurt a little more than I was willing to admit.

So, great. Just damn great. My feelings were a little tender, and now I had a bruised ego to boot. And I knew I was being ridiculous. Grant was the one who had just been held prisoner by some nasty motherfuckers out in the middle of the ocean. But I wanted to be the one he turned to when he got back. More than anything, I wanted to be his safe harbor, the person he felt secure with. It should be my arms that held him and shielded him when he felt threatened.

Because Grant would be all those things for me.

He already had been.

So why couldn't I return the favor? Why wasn't I all those things for him? Why couldn't he count on me the same way I could count on him?

Again, the truth was right there. It stared me in the face when I looked in the mirror, shaking its recriminating finger as soon as I heard my mother's nagging, doubting voice in the back of my mind. I knew the answer already; I just didn't want to face it.

I wasn't reliable in most people's eyes. I wasn't stable or even sane as far as most of my friends and family were concerned. Hell, two of them had already called the necessary agencies and had me carted off to the funny farm!

So yeah . . . as much as I wanted to be the arms Grant ran into when he was returned home to Los Angeles, I knew why I hadn't been. But that didn't mean it hurt less. Hell. Understanding the reasons why might have made it hurt even more.

Cutting deep enough to make me start bleeding with new fears.

If I wasn't comforting the man, who was?

Another woman? One of the many he regularly entertained before he decided to tie himself down with the likes of me? Or perhaps someone new, ready to be the bosom he nestled into for welcome warmth . . . and more?

Somehow, I managed to suck in another breath. It stabbed into my sternum, making me push a trembling fist to the throbbing spot. "Don't go there," I ordered myself in a rasp. "Don't go there. Don't go—"

The cellphone's ringtone snapped me out of my spin cycle, thank God. I snatched the thing up off the sofa and accepted the call without looking at the display. At that point, I would have talked to a telemarketer if it meant getting out of my own damn head for a few minutes.

"Hello?" I rushed out.

"Hey there, it's Hannah." Her upbeat voice came across the line.

"Oh, hey." A big burst of air came out of me like a cough-laugh-bark combination. "I meant hi. Sorry." Who laughed, coughed, and barked at the same time anyway? That thought really did make me laugh. My God, maybe I *was* losing my mind.

"You okay there? Did I catch you at a bad time?" my sweet friend and Abstract Catering sous chef extraordinaire asked from the other end of the line. Her gentle voice had a soothing effect, even over the phone.

"No, of course not." With my free hand, I rubbed at the knot of tension that had gathered in my forehead. "I'm just laughing at my own ridiculousness. How are you, beautiful girl?"

"You're too kind, Rio. And other than missing you, I'm doing good. Are you well? You've been away so long, and the last time we saw you at the kitchen . . . ummm . . ."

"Not my finest hour. I know."

"No, no. That's not what I was going to say." She gave up

a delicate snort. "I was actually going to issue my two cents about how Abbigail wouldn't let up on you that day. But I guess we don't need to go down that road again, do we?"

My smile was so sincere, actual tears crested over my bottom lashes and spilled down my cheeks. "I hope I can meet your parents one day soon. I really want to congratulate them on the fucking exceptional human being they made in you, Hannah."

"Oh my God. That is the sweetest thing to say! Thank you!" She laughed a little more before saying, "I would love that. To introduce you to my parents, I mean. I would love to watch their faces, especially my mom's, while someone paid her a compliment like that."

"Oh yeah?" I returned, letting her hear my affectionate undertone. "That's so cool. My mother would likely accuse me of paying the person."

"Oh, grrr! So mean!" Hannah chuckled out but sobered very fast. She definitely picked up that I wasn't laughing with her. At all.

"Yeah, well, my mom wasn't the Carol Brady type, you know? But that's enough of that bullshit too. Tell me what you've been up to. Tell me something freaking amazing, Hannah. Right now! I insist!"

Nervous laughter came over the phone. Maybe my mood swaps were freaking her out.

Dial it down, girl.

"Oh! I'm getting ready to take the exam for my ballooning license!"

Well, that sure had me sitting up straighter. "Your license for . . . what?"

"Ballooning." There was a cute smirk in her tone. It had

me grinning too, despite my confused scowl.

"Okay, hold up. You need a license to make animals with latex balloons, but literally any person with a functioning dick can forget to put on a rubber and father a child? I don't know what more to say, Hannah."

After indulging more laughter than my line probably deserved, she chilled herself out with a long, breezy sigh. "So, when are you coming back to Abstract?"

Once more, I fell back against the cushions. Wasn't that the million-dollar question?

"You know, Hannah, I've had so much going on since that day, I haven't given it a lot of thought," I confessed. "But your phone call may be exactly what I needed at the exact right time." I opened my laptop while we talked because I was embarrassed to admit I wasn't even sure of the date.

"Oh yeah? How so? This sounds exciting!"

I joined her in another light laugh. Lord, this sweet girl. Hannah Farsey was truly sunshine personified, with a wholesomeness about her that was hard to come by in this decade. It was especially inherent in her voice, which had an alto and earthy tone to it, always making me think of bamboo wind chimes.

"It just may be," I offered with more enthusiasm than I'd felt in a while. "I've been a little rudderless, you know? But I think coming back to work is exactly what I need. To get back into a routine." I nodded while I spoke—agreeing with myself, basically, but that was okay. Someone needed to.

"Yay! I'm so happy to hear that. It really isn't the same without you there. Abbi has been away too—you know, since the baby arrived."

"Sure. Right." I couldn't manage more than one-word

mutterings around the subject of Abbi right now. Somehow, at some point, she and I had to see our way back to some semblance of civilized conversation with each other. But not now. Not when scars were still raw for both of us.

But knowing she was still staying away, consumed with her man and her child as she needed to be, made it easier for me to think about physically returning to the kitchen. There was a lot of my heart and soul in Abstract, and I missed the creative challenge of reaching for new culinary horizons.

"How have things been going with the temp we hired?" I queried then. "Has she been doing a decent job? From everything I've been reading on her reports, it seems like you guys are handling everything just fine."

Oh yes, the more I thought about this, the better I felt. This was exactly what I needed to do. Refocus my energy on something positive. What better place than the business I cared for in so many ways?

"Definitely," Hannah assured. "But we're only following a great blueprint. You and Abbi have everything down to a science. It's just a matter of us executing the daily tasks, reordering supplies, and then handling any problems with the clients as they come up."

"Have there been issues? I haven't seen anything on that front that I can think of, but I figured I was being insulated from it." With a hearty chuckle, I added, "Then again, I think Abbigail tries to keep me away from clients as much as possible."

"Rio," Hannah chided, though the soothing quality of her voice didn't waver. "Why would you say that? No, never mind. If you wanted to tell me, you would've. But no, there really haven't been any issues with the clients. I mean, that Viktor

Blake is one creepy dude, but he's always more interested in what Abbi has personally going on than our food service." She let the comment hang in the quiet air between us for a few moments but then wrapped the topic with her typical diplomacy. "But that's nothing new, from what I understand."

"Yeah, that's a long story. One you're better off not knowing. Just trust me on that. In fact, you should probably stay far away from that guy."

"Yeah, I hear that. Well, I'll let you go. I'm glad we had a chance to catch up a bit, and I'm really glad you're considering coming back."

"Hey, Hannah?" I asked quietly before we hung up.

"Yeah?"

"Thank you for calling. You have no idea how much I needed to hear a friendly voice tonight."

"Of course! I'm glad I did too. And you know, my phone rings too. So anytime you need a friend, you know where to find me."

"All right." I just smiled for a few moments, consciously holding on to the warm feeling I had. "Talk to you soon. Bye."

After we hung up, I remained where I was. I sat and simply passed my phone back and forth between my palms. I never let go of my blissful—and thankful—little smile.

Hands down, Hannah was one of the best additions Abbi and I ever made to our business. If she ever decided to move on, we would be devastated. But it was a possibility for which we had to be prepared. She was a shining star in our industry, and we couldn't hold her back. I'd likely be the first to push her on toward new frontiers. I'd miss her, for sure, but not just in the kitchen. Most importantly, I would desperately miss Hannah's friendship.

It wasn't easy for women like me to make friends, especially with other women. I never felt like I really fit in anywhere, and women were tribal by nature. If a girl couldn't follow the posse's guidelines, they were pretty much recast as a lone wolf. It never bothered me much before because I'd always had Sean, and we'd gotten together so young. I hadn't cultivated a lot of people skills when we'd moved to California. But at the time, all I'd needed was the attention of my brand-new husband.

Now that he was gone, though, it was glaringly evident how few friends I had. It was one of many side effects of being a widow, and it always hit me at the strangest times. Times when I didn't want or need to feel so damn lonely.

A tiny mewl had me jolting out of the brood. Very well aware of the way Robert popped his head in to look at me, then around the room, then back to me, I fell over on the sofa and hugged my knees to my chest. When I was a little girl, I thought if I could make myself into a ball small enough, I would turn inside out and *poof* into thin air. I'd tried and tried and tried, but it never worked.

It always seemed like a solid theory of physics, though, at least when I was five. I never dared ask my mother if something like that would work. The woman took great pleasure in destroying my fantasies. Yet my dad would've certainly indulged me. He would've added to the tale, even. I got my dreamer's creativity from him, which was probably why my mother disliked me so much. From the first hint that I took after him more than her, despite all her best training and brainwashing to the contrary, nature was simply nature. Nobody got to choose whose genetic material had a stronger echo in their DNA.

But as I lay on my side, thinking of my dad and beating myself up for not calling home as much as I should, I force-fed myself some resolve. I was not going to waste another night lying here crying. That ship had already sailed, and I didn't need another cruise around the harbor.

Metaphorically, if emotions were a body of water, I truly enjoyed every sea condition known. I liked rising tides, stormy, tumultuous seas, raging white-water rapids, lazy winding rivers, whirlpools, natural hot springs, geysers...all the sweeping glory of it. Emotions were meant to be felt and, a lot of times, to be shared. Feeling meant I was living and experiencing—not sitting on the sidelines playing it safe.

And I was ready to live again.

To move forward, at last, from having all my days defined by Sean's accident.

I decided to go all-out on a luxuriously steamy shower. I gave myself the full spa treatment, starting with a copper and clay facial. After cleaning up my eyebrows, I indulged in a foot scrub too. When I was out and dry, I felt like a new woman. Still, I lotioned and buffed every inch of skin to perfection. I was dewy and glowing and smelled like a confusing bomb of citrus, gardenia, and vanilla. It shouldn't have all worked, yet somehow it did.

"Oh shit!" I yelped, and poor Robert went from peacefully licking himself to red alert in the span of one second. "Sorry, baby. Mama's sorry. But how haven't I thought of this before?"

I leaned closer to him to give him some kitty sugar, and he licked my forehead a few times. His tongue was so rough, the feel of the sandpaper texture on my deeply moisturized skin made me giggle. I grabbed my robe off the hook in the bathroom and headed out to the living room where I presumably left my phone.

Since I'd been living alone, I'd gotten in the habit of walking around the house naked. Why not? No one else was here for me to offend, and I kept the temperature exactly where I liked it, so that wasn't an issue either. Neighbors looking into my windows didn't pose much of a threat. Most of the homes surrounding mine were one story. In my older neighborhood, unless a home had recently been renovated or was right on the sand, houses were typically one level.

Scrolling to the phone log from earlier, I easily found the call with Grant. From the unfamiliar number, I assumed he was not using his old phone. But that wasn't my primary interest right now. I was only interested in seeing the location services, hoping against hope they were still enabled. On most phones, the default setting was on, forcing the user to purposely disable the service. If Grant hadn't bothered—or, as he'd claimed, was just too exhausted—to think of doing it, then I'd know exactly where he'd called from with a few simple keystrokes. If he didn't want to tell me, that was just fine. But that didn't mean I didn't have to know.

Fingers crossed. Fingers crossed. Fingers crossed.

Yes! It looked like it was going to work when a map populated my phone's display. It was easy enough to recognize key landmarks across the Southern California area, but those were always subject to change. The one unmistakable constant that wouldn't steer me wrong was represented by a swath of brilliant blue down the left side of the screen. The Pacific Ocean was always to the west.

"Goddammit," I muttered and scrolled until the "you are here" balloon disappeared off the edge of the map, letting the program find the signal for Grant's new phone number a second time. The map snapped right back to the location it landed on initially: Elijah's enormous house in Malibu.

I wasn't extraordinarily surprised. Nor could I necessarily be angry with him. But I had very mixed feelings toward Elijah at the moment. In fact, I had no trouble with the anger percolating in my blood at that guy right now. None whatsoever.

I got the fact that he and I weren't close friends. Hell, we were barely friends at all. But it was deceitful to mislead me if he knew damn well he was going to be hosting Grant at his home. Did he think I was another version of Abbigail, turning the crocodile tears on and off when it suited me? The man wasn't stupid. And I didn't delude myself to think he necessarily respected me. He must have been able to ascertain the sincerity of my concern—screw that; my full-on anxiety— about Grant's well-being. The conversation in his pristine kitchen was a bit of a blur because the guy didn't do much to set my nerves at ease, but I might have even used the L-word.

But if he'd still lied to me anyway? Well, I certainly didn't appreciate it. And fine, that was putting it mildly, but since he was one of Grant's dearest friends, there was sa part of me that was trying to give the man the benefit of the doubt. And another part of me not at all sure why I was.

Well, tomorrow I would just head back to Malibu and demand Mr. Banks let me see my man. I could kick up quite a scene if provoked. Something told me Elijah wouldn't want that taking place in his fancy-pants neighborhood either.

CHAPTER FIVE

GRANT

"Jesus Christ," I muttered, bending forward until my torso was parallel to Elijah's kitchen floor. The display on his fancy coffeemaker was so small I couldn't visually isolate one number from another or tell the difference between an eight and a three and so on.

"Do you need help?" The soft female voice came from behind me, interrupting my quest for the perfect cup. I startled and wheeled around.

Shawna must have been spending the night quite often if she knew how this overly complicated machine worked. Maybe I needed to ask Elijah about the seriousness of what he had going on with the woman in a different way than I had the first time. His response did come pretty fast and a little too easily. I wondered how often he'd been seeing her. Not that it was actually any of my business, but if he was going to make my business his, shouldn't the pendulum swing both ways? Only seemed fair.

More than all that, I worried about my friend. I knew he would deny it, but he'd been looking for his other half ever since things fell apart with Hensley. He could deny it to Bas and me until his face turned blue, but every time he claimed the opposite, the harder I was convinced. He was subconsciously searching for someone—hell, anyone—to fill the stark void after that woman wrecked him.

Deeper concerns for another time. Like when I was officially and fully caffeinated.

"This may require a doctorate to operate," I said while moving out of the way to let her get closer to the machine.

"Well, you're in luck," Shawna returned. "Did you already put milk in the steamer?"

"The steamer?" Confusion had to be broadcast across my face. "And what do you mean, I'm in luck?"

"Were you trying to make a latte or cappuccino?" Shawna asked instead.

A laugh escaped at that concept. I was proud of myself when I mastered the pod in the single-serving machine setup. "Really, I just drink black coffee. Sometimes I'll add cream or sugar. Maybe both if I'm feeling exceptionally daring."

"Not both!" she mocked.

"Now you're just making fun of me." I slid the grin in at the end of my comment, confirming that old habits died hard. All it took was a pretty girl to show up, and all my moves just came out of storage like a treasured winter coat.

"Well. Just a little bit of fun," she drawled while getting busy with my coffee. "But it can't be helped." She tossed over a casual glance. "Did you have strict parents?"

"No."

My answer was brief, if not terse. I hated this moment, but inevitably it came whenever I talked to someone new. Someone who didn't already know our story—mine, Sebastian's, and Elijah's—and then having to explain it in the most concise way without garnering pity. Of course, there was the juggle of keeping my dignity intact too. The ordeal was one of my life's crosses to bear, I supposed. I should have been really used to it by now, especially because a question like hers would've normally been no big deal. But what was "normal" about having to stare back at my interrogator, attempting to size up their eventual reaction? Wondering if she'd form a new opinion about me on the spot, based solely on the actions of my drug addict mother.

But was I really afraid of that now? I was protected against that shit, right? I'd made sure of that. It took me years—and a lot of therapy bills—to build up the shell I wore, so no matter what anyone said, intentional or not, the shit just rolled right off.

Fine.

I was perfectly fine.

I could repeat it and believe it now. I was solid about that. My mother's decisions didn't affect the man I was today. My decisions did. I was responsible for me. No one else was.

See? Look at that. Cured.

Perfectly. Fine.

"Grant?"

"Hmmm? What?"

"I said your coffee's ready." Shawna tapped a turquoise-painted fingernail on the counter beside the steaming brew, and something about that gesture really aggravated me.

But instead of being an asshole, I said kindly, "Thanks, hon."

And don't fucking tap your talon at me ever again.

I turned and hurried out before the threat actually made it to my lips. Jesus, what was wrong with me? Why was I still debating whether to go back and apologize to the woman for a private thought? Because that bullshit wouldn't make me look like a bigger ass, right? But seriously... *hon*? Where had that come from? I never spoke to women that way. Even in the height of my douchebag days, I was still a decent guy. At least I thought I was.

Between my hair-trigger temper, quick-to-release smart mouth, and tendency toward violence as a first choice to solve a problem instead of a last resort, something was really wrong with me. That last one concerned me most, as it should. This was behavior of my past. Behavior that took years to curb and then change completely. Relearning phrases and mannerisms that were acceptable in regular society, not in the street culture. I wasn't a thug anymore, and I had no interest in going back to that life or lifestyle.

Those not-so-glory days aside, I had to keep looking at this in big-picture terms. A massive portrait that included Rio—but how did I expect to be around her, acting this way? At the moment, I wanted nothing more than to see her. Hold her. Be inside her. I needed the physical connection as much as the emotional one.

Maybe after I reconnected with her, everything else would fall into place. I had to hope that was the answer, because I didn't think I could stay away from her for another day. But I couldn't show up in this volatile state.

After I went back to the room I was staying in, I gathered what I needed for a shower. I noticed Elijah had left more clothes for me outside my bedroom door after I'd gone to sleep the night before, so I grabbed that stack and headed in to do some serious thinking under the hot water spray.

By the time I got out of the bathroom, dressed and bearing a plan under my belt, I felt more like myself. So much in life really was about a personal attitude and what a man did with it.

So much rested in properly approaching the problems on your plate. In retrospect, I decided this one wasn't as bad as I was letting it seem. I couldn't let it gain wings and take over, or that was exactly what it would do.

Not acceptable.

Over the past decade, I'd been busting my ass to make a comfortable life for myself. I wasn't going to slide backward to where I came from because of a handful of kidnappers and a few dead bodies.

Christ. The bodies.

Perhaps it had been more than a few . . .

Shit. No!

Why did I have to let my mind go there? After slumping down on the end of the bed, I cradled my face in my hands. My skin was still warm from the shower because I'd cranked that sucker as hot as it would go, like I had every time I had showered since I got back from that nightmare. I never wanted to feel cold flesh again as long as I lived. Not mine, and definitely not someone else's.

With a brisk shake of my head, I stood up again. What the hell? I'd just said I wasn't going to do this to myself, and I'd lasted less than five minutes.

I gave the bedding a half-assed straightening and threw the pillows to the end against the headboard. Elijah's fussy standards couldn't be met if I tried, so he could come in and do things his way when I left.

Now where had I put that phone he'd lent me? I'd messaged Rio back last night before I went to sleep. I'd just told her to sleep well and that I hoped she dreamed of me. Uncharacteristically, she hadn't responded. I chalked it up to her already being asleep when I turned in, but without all the technology I was used to on my own cell phone, I had no way of knowing if that was really the case or not.

Normally I could log into the app for her security system and see if she had armed the system for the night or if she was still moving around the house, but all of that would have to be reloaded once I got a new phone.

Suddenly, I stopped. Everything.

My body. My breath. My thoughts.

It was like thinking about her manifested her voice. If that were the case, I was truly losing it. But I could've sworn . . .

It was her.

I heard her talking somewhere in this house.

As quietly as possible, I opened the bedroom's door and listened. All right, Elijah really was talking to someone. But now they'd both lowered their voices, and I couldn't hear who it was, but I could still tell it was a female. More than likely, it was Shawna. But it had been almost two hours since I'd seen her in the kitchen, and from what I witnessed the day before, he sent her home as early as possible.

"I know he's here. Cut the shit, Banks."

A grin spread across my face until it physically hurt where I still had bruises. My Blaze was storming the castle walls, and from what I could make out, she was looking for me. I walked farther down the hall but did it slowly so I could catch as much of their conversation—definitely a loose interpretation—as possible before being discovered.

"Just calm down," Elijah said.

Poor guy. I wanted to feel a tad sorrier for him, but the chance to witness my Blaze in action without being her actual target . . . well, that was something special indeed. Selfishly, I went for savoring as many minutes of it as I could.

"Seriously, Rio. Right now. You've got to breathe, woman."

I pushed my lips together to keep from snorting in delight. Christ, he really had no idea who he was messing with.

"Don't tell me what to do! You're a liar, Elijah Banks. I don't take orders from anyone, especially liars."

A seething grunt leaked from his locked teeth. "Okay, I don't appreciate—"

"Just save it," Rio spat. "I don't care what you do or don't appreciate. I know he's here, damn it. I tracked the phone he's using. Either go get him, or I'll start yelling for him. Believe me, he'll hear me. Your neighbors probably will too."

She'd make good on that threat. Fortunately, Elijah seemed to comprehend that too. Very fortunately, so did I— and I didn't want to test her willingness about it anymore.

With steady steps, I emerged into the living room. The front door was about twenty feet away, and now we had a clear path to each other.

"Oh my God. Grant!" She dropped whatever she'd been holding—it looked like some sort of purse or bag—and started toward me. At first, she was slow and hesitant about it. She walked so carefully. No, it was really more of a stumble. But she gained speed as she neared. Lots of speed.

By the time she reached me and I swept her up in my arms, she had some good momentum behind her, and she nearly knocked me to the floor.

All I could do was bury my face in her neck and inhale over and over like there was a short supply of oxygen and I was trying to store up for all future breaths.

"God damn, I've missed you, Blaze. So much."

I leaned back to look at her, only then realizing that I'd swept her completely off the ground. I grinned, feeling as mighty as a Titan, but I bent forward to set her back on the floor.

Her arms were surprisingly strong as she gripped me tighter around the neck.

"Don't you dare put me down, mister. Not yet." That last part came out in a shaky whisper, but then she found strength in her intention again. "Not ever."

I raised a brow playfully, and shit, it felt so good to be lighthearted about something. "Ever?"

"Never." With a solemn chin dip, she declared it to be.

And so it was.

Elijah cleared his throat, making us both turn to glare at him.

"Way to ruin a moment, man."

"Really? You're going there?" he volleyed. "Christ. All that sap is going to be hard to get off my floor, and I just had these redone." He scuffed the slate tile with his sock-covered toe.

"Yeah, I noticed when I got here the other day," I countered. "Wait, was that yesterday? No. Two days ago? Shit, I'm clueless. I don't even know what day of the week it is. Regardless, floors look good."

I walked over to my friend with my hand outstretched, and he took it. We did our usual combination of shakes and ended it with a brotherly hug.

"Thank you. For everything. I'll get the clothes back to you."

"Pfffft. Don't stress about it. I'm not going to," Elijah said.

"Do you stress about anything? Ever?" I teased.

"Nope. Not really." He chuckled and held the door open for Rio and me.

Once we were outside Elijah's gate, I stopped abruptly and

turned to the incredible woman clutching my hand. Rio looked up and quickly shielded her eyes from the early morning sun, until I stepped one foot to the side and blocked the glare for her with my stance. I would throw my body into oncoming traffic if it meant making her day—a moment—easier for her.

"What is it?" she asked with genuine concern. "Did you forget something inside? Are you feeling okay?"

I threw my head back and laughed. It was a relief, easing some of the tension on the smile that was so big it hurt. "Do you have any idea how happy I am to see you this morning?" I circled her waist, reveling in how she truly felt like a radiant fire after the dark forest in which I'd been trapped for so damn long. "Do you know how happy I am that you came here for me?"

Her eyes sparkled with tiny gold flecks. Her chin jogged up at the same time as her gorgeous lips. "So . . . I'll make you a deal, Tree."

"Name it."

Her pout was so full and sleek that I barely remembered she was propositioning me. My God, with that kind of an expression, she could've asked if I'd help her rob a bank, and I'd have been her eager accomplice.

"Don't you want to hear the stakes?"

"Nope." I thought of myself robbing a bank. It was still feeling like a hell of a lot of fun. "Whatever you want, it's yours."

"Hmmm, in that case . . ." she said, now throwing in a devilish tilt to her glossy lips. "I was thinking we probably should get a bigger car. I think Kendall is a little too small for someone your height. And the plumbing in the bungalow is really acting up. I was thinking about putting it on the market, but I'm not sure it will pass inspection. And—"

While she recited the wish list, we were power walking toward her car. Her frenetic energy was buzzing all around her, nearly at an all-time high. I didn't stop her. It was all too addicting. Too magnificent and familiar and beautiful. And absolutely perfect—until suddenly she stopped in the middle of the sidewalk and nearly pulled my arm from its socket.

"Shit, baby. A little warning if you're going to stop, yeah?"

"I was waiting for you to interrupt me!"

I shook my head. "Why?"

"Oh, Tree." As she pushed against me and pressed a hand to my face, a salty wind blew some of her cute spikes against her own cheeks. "I would never expect any of it from you."

I took a second, searching her face. Those sweet, full contours were better than my first sips of water after getting off the helicopter with Elijah. "But why not?"

She gave me a solid double take. "I was teasing you, Grant. None of that was what I was really going to say!"

"But don't you know I'd give you the world if you asked for it? And what were you really going to say?"

"You're ridiculous." She batted my cheek but was still grinning.

"Pretty sure that's not an answer. How is that ridiculous?"

She dropped her hand, though not far. With her slender fingers planted on my chest, she whooshed out determined air from her own. Damn it. I knew this move well. It was her one-size-fits-all for feeling overwhelmed, whether it was a slew of last-minute lunch orders or a string of my uncomfortable questions when she was on a yacht with nowhere to hide.

"Let's just go home and lie in bed," she husked. "I've missed you so much, Mr. Twombley."

I bent and kissed her softly. "Not as much as I've missed

you, Ms. Gibson." And I let her avoidance slide, because in one swoop, she gave me back at least one memory from the cruise to be cherished instead of burned.

"I just want to feel your body next to mine," she whispered against my lips. "I've been so alone, and you know how well alone and I play together."

I huffed. "As in, not at all?"

"He's selfish and doesn't share any of his toys."

"Wait." I jerked back an inch, displaying the depth of my new distress. "What about Robert? Did those assholes do anything to your cat? Because I told them, if anything happened to you or him—"

"Hey. He's fine, baby." But her tone was as if she were just confirming that she'd picked up groceries on the way home. So normal. So wonderful. So perfect. "But he's missing you as badly as I was, so why don't we get going?"

I grinned and quickly pecked her smooth forehead. So maybe everything would be okay after all. Pretty soon, all this shit would be ugliness of the past—a good thing, since all I wanted to think about was the future with this incredible beauty.

"Sounds like a perfect plan," I told her with lazy ease. "But damn, woman. Where the hell did you park? Zuma?"

She snickered at my reference to the famous surfing strand at Malibu's north end before popping up on her toes to see over the tops of the other cars parked along the street. "It's not too much farther. I can see Kendall from here, I think." She leaned out into the oncoming traffic lane to look. "Ugh. This is a beautiful neighborhood, but I think this parking situation would get really old, really fast," she finally summarized.

"Well, residents have garages and driveways. They don't

have to worry about finding street parking."

"But every time you have a guest, you'd be apologizing about the parking situation." She gave up a new shrug. "I know I would be, though I can't imagine Elijah Banks apologizes for anything. Whether he's at fault or not."

Now I couldn't help but laugh fully. She wasn't that far off the mark. Elijah lived without apology. I'd said those exact words on more than one occasion.

Once we made it to the car, we quickly decided to go to my place downtown. The condo was close to everything, including Rio's prep kitchen in Inglewood, her Seal Beach bungalow, my office at Shark Enterprises, and several of my other homes. For today, it made the most sense.

When I walked in the front door, it felt like it had been months since I'd done so. For once, I didn't second-guess the sensation. This one made sense. The last time I was here, Rio hadn't been committed to Clear Horizons. I hadn't raced to free her, leaving the place burning to the ground in our wake. The charter yacht in Marina del Rey was nothing more than a prick in my mind, waiting as a possibility for a wild vacation away with her sometime. It had become so much more.

Life itself had.

"Do you want to take a shower?" Rio asked, scooting up from behind to wrap her arms around my waist. "I can make you some lunch while you do that."

"No need," I said, rubbing my hands over hers. "Everything I want is right here."

But I suddenly needed to do more than tell her.

I had to show her. In the fullest sense of all those words.

In one hell-bent-for-passion swoop, I turned around and swept her off her feet. As I secured her in my arms, she yelped and giggled. There was more sweet laughter as she locked her arms around my neck, thinking I was going for playful Prince Charming, but when she got a look at the heavy-lidded lust in my gaze, she sucked in a sharp, deep breath.

"You good, Blaze?" I worried she wasn't going to exhale again. "I don't want to push you."

"No. I mean, yes! Yes, baby. I'm good. We're definitely good. So, so good. I've missed you so much..."

I was just a couple of steps into my direct course for the bedroom but stopped in my tracks. When a woman started spritzing tears with her words, that was as good as a stop sign.

"Oh. Hey," I murmured, even wondering if I should set her down all the way. "Blaze. What's going on? What's wrong?"

Her brand-new giggle had my brain flashing neon words. *What. The. Hell?*

"Nothing's wrong." She leaned up and peppered my cheek with fervent kisses. "Not a single thing, my love."

"Errr...huh?" I muttered.

"I just mean that I'm done fighting this, Grant. I'm done fighting us." She threaded her slender fingers through my hair, scraping her fingernails along my scalp as she went. Shivers ran up and down my spine—as fireworks and angels chased back and forth through my senses. Yeah, they smashed the neon sign. And no, I didn't give a fuck.

Barely believing what I'd just heard her say, I whispered, "Rio. Oh. God..."

I pressed my forehead to hers, savoring the seconds in which she held me even tighter. Nothing else came to mind but her name, again and again, like the litany I'd been praying to utter for so long. I couldn't stop repeating it, as though she would disappear if I stopped calling out to her.

"Rio." Kiss. "Rio." Sigh. "Rio." A kiss, longer and openmouthed, my tongue finding and dancing with hers. "Oh Rio, baby."

And finally, letting her say something too.

"I was so scared, Grant. So scared you wouldn't come back to me."

The frantic race of her words became intense kisses from her gorgeous mouth. She gripped me with violent need, pulling my hair at my nape. It was more than her usual lust, filled with a dark kind of desperation and a needy sort of command. I didn't mind the extra pricks of pain—to be honest, they were welcome distractions—but I grew concerned by the intuitions from her rising energy. She wasn't passionate anymore. She seemed . . . frightened.

"Baby?" I tried to pull back a little. Not very far at all. But she dug in her fingers, forcing my face close.

"No," she rasped. "No, Grant. Stay with me. Don't go. Please, don't—"

"Baby. Hey. I'm not leaving, okay? You couldn't make me leave if you tried." I finally made my way to the sofa and lowered to it, not letting up on the cocoon of my arms. She felt so small there. So shivery and frail.

Shit.

That was when the full revelation struck me.

She'd been backsliding. Not to the point that she'd set half the city on fire or anything but enough that her psyche was bruised, her heart unsure. I could feel it as if it was tattooed across her forehead. The ways, small but accumulative, in which she'd abused herself in the days I'd been missing.

Damn it. After all the hard work we'd put in during the cruise.

Well, I was no stranger to hard work. Not doing it myself or delegating it to another. In this case, it was a mix of both. A journey we'd just have to start all over again.

And what better time than now.

With that determination behind my every move, I laid her down beneath me on the sofa. At once, Rio began to soften for me. Expose herself to me. Also at once, I showed her my gratitude for her vulnerability. After bestowing a long, sweet kiss across her mouth, I let my mouth continue on to the delicate skin of her neck. She mewled with delicious abandon as I gently sucked.

"You taste like heaven. I missed this skin." I kissed her neck again, ending with a little bite. "And yeah, these lips." I moved back to her mouth, kissing her again, but pulled back when she clutched me and tried to deepen things. When she whimpered again, this time with urgent protest, I chuckled. "Greedy little kitty. Patience, patience. I'm worshipping you, woman. Just enjoy it."

"Can't," my beautiful girl whined. "I want all of you right now. I don't want to wait. I've been waiting for too long."

I didn't give her a laugh, soft or otherwise, for that one. Instead, I slid to my knees alongside the sofa. She cried out again, but there was method to my madness. I wanted to survey her entire body, reacquainting myself with all its mystery and angles, stretched out before me. "Hmm. Now, look at this gorgeous little girl who needs worshipping."

"Well, you got the *need* part right."

As I soaked up every drop of her adoring gaze, I took on new strength. Fresh desire. And even better, a surge of something that felt like . . . me. The man I used to be. The lover who reveled in a mantle of complete control . . .

Especially when it was given by a formidable female like my Rio.

"So . . . which end should I start with?" I tapped my chin with my forefinger in playful contemplation. "I think I need a solid plan here . . ."

"Grant!" She squirmed like a kitten batting at a yarn ball. "Come on! Please."

"Please what, baby?" I crooked my finger, turning the movement into a slow and elegant tease. She nearly undid me by licking her lips, but that shit was on me. I was extending this fun foreplay, not her. "What do you want me to do?" I murmured then. Having to focus on words was always a good way of setting boundaries for the gang below my belt. At least for now.

"I—I don't know. Just something other than sitting there, looking at me like I'm a Playstation on Christmas morning."

I chuckled. It just couldn't be helped. "Rio Gibson, you are better than a thousand Christmas mornings."

She wriggled again. But there was less frustration to it this time. This was also more her—the sexy, free-spirited siren that had risen from her emotional depths to expose herself to me during our time on the ocean waves.

"Okay, then. Why don't you come and . . . unwrap me, big boy?"

I laughed harder, attempting to summon a matching accent to give to her Mae West flair. But my John Wayne and Gary Cooper impressions were pitiful. Elijah, who excelled at both, was fond of reminding me.

"Soon," I promised her instead. "But first, a question."

She huffed. "No, I can't tell you how many ounces are in three quarts without a converter, okay?"

"All right." I leaned in, tilting my head. "How about an easier one? Like . . . are you wet for me?"

A gulp made its way down her throat. "Wha—?"

"Don't be shy now. Two seconds ago, you were Little Miss Bossy. So yes or no, Rio? Are you wet for me?"

She opened her mouth, but nothing emerged except an awkward gurgle. "I—I don't know."

"Bullshit."

"Grant!"

The little black band T-shirt she was wearing was thin, almost threadbare in some spots. From the hem, I pushed the cotton up over the swell of her breasts, slowing to unhook her bra—one of the pieces I'd purchased for her on our trip, which kicked my smile higher—before taking the mounds in my hands and teasing her with some small squeezes.

"Fuck. Your nipples are so perfect, lady. Just look at these pert little beauties." I smirked as she gasped, reacting to how I scraped my thumbnails over both her erect little nubs. "Are you telling me now that even with such hard, throbbing tits, you have no idea what state your pussy is in?"

Rio whimpered as I rolled her red nubs between my thumbs and forefingers. When I gave them both a deliberate tug, she finally cried out, "All right, all right! I'll tell you!"

I rewarded her with an approving growl but took a second to pluck at her angry peaks once more.

"Grant! All right, I'm wet! I've been soaked from the second I saw you at Elijah's." She cut herself off with another whine, high and achy and beautiful, that nearly derailed my efforts to get her shirt up and over her head.

Impatiently, I tossed the garment onto the floor beside me. At least that was where I thought it went. My gaze didn't rip an inch from the half-naked nymph before me, already making it hard to remember my breath. Who was I kidding? I was just hard, period. Everywhere. And getting harder by the minute.

"You are so stunning," I finally managed to say. "Do you know that, Rio? Do you get even half that truth when it leaves my lips? Every damn time I say it? Do you have any idea how much I—"

Whoa. Watch it, big guy.

I commanded it at myself, just to make sure every cell of my brain got the message. I needed to keep my head fully in the game or I was going to say something I regretted—aka something that overly scared her. Yeah, she'd been hearts and flowers and swelling orchestrations about declaring she was ready to go public about our relationship, but that was before I saw the thin glass beneath her bold trumpets. She wasn't necessarily ready to go down the I-love-you path with me.

"Grant? How much you what?" she prodded. My bright little minx hadn't missed a second of my slip, of course.

"How much I need you, Blaze." Quickly, to get her mind back on what was happening here and now, I leaned over and kissed the sweet swells of her breasts again. And then traced along her collarbone with my tongue.

"Look at this perfection," I murmured into her succulent skin. "You are flawless, woman."

She gasped and arched her back. "Only for you, mister. Only with you. Always…"

"I need to remember you exactly this way," I uttered. "Will you let me take your picture? Lying here like this?"

She opened one eye. Then the other. "Ummm…"

I laughed again. Once more, it wasn't intentional. I'd

spoken from my heart, but she'd also reacted from hers, and it was so damn adorable that I simply busted up with joy.

"Okay, why are you laughing now?" she groused.

"Sorry, baby," I said sincerely. "I guess you had to see it all from my point of view. But I'm serious about the pictures. I want to have you near me all the time."

"But you don't even have a phone right now. Are you using one of Elijah's?"

"Shit," I muttered. "Yes, you're right. Well, when I get a new phone, I promise you my first shots won't be of Robert."

She took her well-deserved turn with the mirth, erupting in a giggle that didn't stop until I swept in again, covering as much of her nipple and breast with my mouth as possible. Before she could gasp, I started to suck. I didn't stop even as she fought to both push me away but hold me close. Simultaneously, she begged me to stop and never stop. She moaned and panted, telling me how aroused she was by scissoring her legs.

When I finally eased off, smirking at the certain mark I'd left that time, her whole body was racked by shudders. She fluttered a hand up to her neck and clutched her throat.

"Jesus, Grant. What the hell was that? And why did that feel so good?"

I flashed my finest panty-slayer grin and said, "Ready for the other side?"

For the next second, she seemed to have a battle with herself. And she seemed to snap together the truth: that it truly had felt good. Why would she deny herself pleasure?

"All right. Do your best, Tree."

Fucking hell. My cock swelled at once from her sassy answer. It was always the surprising things with this woman that sent me over the edge. That was just another thing I loved about her.

And hell yes, I said loved. I could admit it to myself, at least. I was absolutely, irretrievably, in love with Rio Gibson. I'd known it for some time, actually. I might have even known it, in some crazy and deep place, the day she came kicking ass into my world in her fourteen-hole Dr. Martens, jeans that looked like she was waiting on or wading through a flood, and a black Psychedelic Furs T-shirt.

Before then, I had long figured I'd end up with someone who was safe and boring, or more likely than anything, that I would never fall in love with at all. Needless to say, all of this was a stunner of a revelation—so, waiting to tell her felt important. It had to be worth the wait. I just hoped I didn't slip up in the heat of the moment like I almost did again today.

I wanted Rio to be my one and only. So when I did finally feel safe enough to tell her my whole truth, I wanted it to be the perfect setup. The perfect location, the perfect music playing in the background, the perfect everything. Like she was for me. I wanted her to know in that moment that I was in this for the long haul. That I was her forever guy.

CHAPTER SIX

RIO

"I'm going to..."

I sucked in as much air as possible between declarations and moans, all while thinking I hoped these walls were really damn thick. Otherwise, we were really giving Grant's neighbors an earful this afternoon.

"Yeah...give it to me, baby," Grant encouraged with a raspy quality to his voice that just added to my arousal. "Come for me, Blaze." He looked up from between my thighs, his lips and chin glistening in the afternoon sunlight that was coming in through the slider. Even the tip of his nose was wet, and I gasped again. He was a beast today, and I definitely wasn't complaining. God, I'd missed him—and, I freely admitted, his powerfully talented tongue.

When I settled from my climax, I held my arms out to him and made a squeezing gesture with my hands. It was something I did on occasion when I wanted him to hold me or hug me. Anything that involved me in his arms. It was such a move forward for me though, wanting to be held and touched by someone. It had taken a long time to get to that point with Sean, so to already be that comfortable with Grant said a lot about how much I trusted him and how connected we were.

He prowled up my body with lust and hunger in his eyes.

"Take these off," I said, tugging at the joggers he continued to wear. "Give me what I want, Mr. Twombley." His erection was making an obscene tent in front, and I wondered why he was still wearing the things at all.

"Holy shit, woman. I can't wait to be inside you," he said, playfully capturing my hands and pinning them above my head. "You okay here?" He glanced pointedly up to our joined hands, then back to check in for my response.

"Yes." I nodded quickly. "Fine."

The kiss I received for that answer was slow, seductive, and teasing until I was whimpering with need. Again. He was getting really good at reducing me to wordlessness.

"My God," I gasped when we parted. "What are you doing to me?"

"Turning you into a slut, apparently." His eyes were the blue of a tropical bay. Fun, magical, and promising all at the same time.

"But only for you."

"Ahhhh. Right answer," he said through his sexiest grin. Then came another rewarding kiss, this time clear about his climbing urgency. Not that I wasn't aware already. The erection pressing into my belly was so incredibly hard, I swore I could feel his heartbeat throbbing through his length.

A simple thought, but it made me a thousand kinds of ready, as well. I wasted no time giving the man a saucy eye roll before bemoaning, "What does a girl have to do to get fucked around here?"

Grant's blues gained new fire. That didn't stop him from instantly supplying, "Well, baby, that girl has to beg."

I gasped in mock surprise. "I'm sorry, sir?"

"Beg me," he reiterated. "And make it good, Rio. Your

very best begging. You know the way I like it. Keep your hands where they are, but I want your eyes right here on me while I undress for you."

The heat in his gaze blossomed, already telling me what he hadn't put into words. That he craved this connection as much as me. That in some key ways, this control returned what he'd been stripped of for so long.

Now, I was damn determined to give it all back to him. I couldn't help heal his body, but maybe this part would be the salve he needed in his mind.

That thought flooded the forefront of my mind as Grant knelt up off my body. He scooted back enough to disrobe, starting with a clean whip of his shirt over his head.

At once, I gasped.

Of course, he anticipated my reaction. His tight expression told me so. He already knew that bruises still peppered his body from where those bastards had beaten him. But also across his features, there was the clear stamp of determination. That he refused to let the rainbow of his damage define what we could create in the sunshine of now.

"Baby, ssshhh. Stay here with me. They're old, okay? They don't hurt, and I don't want to think about any of that bullshit right now. I want to feel your skin on mine. All of it. But I can put the shirt back on if it's going to be an issue."

Shaking my head, I gave him my answer before my voice would cooperate. Finally, I was able to say, "No. Please don't cover yourself. I want to feel you touching me too. I've missed it so much, Grant."

I watched, completely enraptured, as he took his pants off next. His erection strained toward me like it knew the way home. With open legs, I welcomed him. My arms were still stretched high above my head in his verbal bondage, and as he moved over me once more, he took his cock in hand. I was mesmerized as he stroked himself roughly and tightly.

"Please fuck me," I said softly. "Put that gorgeous cock in me and make me feel like only you can. Grant...oh, God... I'm begging you, please." I wriggled with anticipation because it seemed like it had been an entire month since we'd been intimate even though it had only been ten days.

"More." My lover growled, and I responded with a confused expression. What did he want from me? Because if I knew, he'd have it right away. My surrender. My worship. My heart. Every depth of my soul.

"Give me more than that, Rio. When I tell you to beg me, do it and mean it."

"But...I do mean it," I whimpered.

"Yeah?" he teased while rubbing the dark head of his penis through the slick flesh at my core. "Okay, so tell me. How bad do you want this cock?"

I threw my head back. "Soooo bad. So fucking bad. Please."

"In your mouth?"

"Yes. I'll take it there."

"You'll take it there what?" he growled, seeming to be impatient now.

"What?" Confused again. I was trying to play along, but he really had his dark flag flying, and I wasn't completely sure what my part in the game was. "Ummm...please?" I squeaked.

"Is that a question?" He leaned back on his bent legs and smacked my mound with the pads of his fingers. The arousing sound of flesh on flesh completely overshadowed the pain he'd just zapped across my pussy.

"Shit!" I jolted. "Grant!"

"Put your hands back above your head, girl."

His tone was still ferocious, but the truth glittered in his gorgeous blue eyes . . . and seeped from the slit at the top of his cock. Physically, the man craved me in so many equal measures. Mentally, he needed another punch of domineering power. Which maybe meant that he wanted me to toy with the dynamic too . . .

Or maybe I was taking creative liberties of my own.

And maybe that would be some fun too.

I lowered all the way back to the couch's cushion. But instead of complying with the arm position, I slid my hands to my nipples. "Or what?" I taunted, circling my stiff peaks with my fingertips.

"Or no dick for you," he declared as his pupils betrayed him by growing wide with arousal. "It's that simple."

But then . . . he shrugged.

The man fucking shrugged. Like he could take or leave having sex after a separation that had been damn near my undoing.

Well, two could play that game.

"I've changed my mind." I tried bucking him away by lifting my hips, but he outweighed me by a hundred pounds at least. "Did you hear me, Twombley?" I growled from between clenched teeth. "Get off me."

"No."

"Tree, I'm serious. Get." Squirm. "Off." Buck. "Me."

"No. Stop being a brat."

He reached down, grabbed my wrists, and then pinned them above my head again. Though I was fighting him with all my might, he easily held me in place with just one of his obscenely large hands.

"Grant, I swear I will knee you in the balls if you don't let me go."

"Don't you dare," he warned in a menacing growl. His voice was barely recognizable. And damn it, my body responded at once. With suffusing heat. With rising awareness. With depleting strength, now even less effective against him than before.

I wanted to scream as loud as possible because I was so frustrated. But again, what would the neighbors think? Worse, who would they call? I wasn't interested in being on LAPD's radar right now, in any way, shape, or form.

A more troubling consideration than that? The slow, sexy grin he actually did give in to then—which dissolved my ire and immediately reignited my fury.

Damn it.

Just . . . damn it!

Within seconds, this man was capable of stirring so much in my blood. Like a master mixologist, he made a cocktail of desire and anger, tossed in a pinch of fascination and a squeeze of passion, and then topped it all off with a twist of love.

But I wasn't about to confess that to him.

He bent low to kiss me, but I turned my head so he made contact with my cheek instead of my mouth. I held my conviction firm even as he kissed a path back along my face to my ear and kissed me there too. With warm, heavy breaths, he tickled the sensitive skin just below that . . . before beginning to bite me in all those perfect, pulsing places.

He delivered little nips at first, starting under my ear, growing in intensity as he moved down my neck. By the time he reached my breast, I was writhing beneath him. My pussy was soaked and ready with arousal. If I could angle myself just right, I would be able to get his cock inside me. Not far at first, but just enough. If I could manage that, he'd surrender.

"Grant. Please, baby. Please fuck me. Fuck me so good. I've missed you. I need this. I need you. Please."

My words worked their spell on me first. By now, I was beyond crazy with desire for this man. I let that need compel me to wrap my legs around his hips and hold on as tightly as I could. Using that leverage, I cinched myself even closer to him. Then I caved, turning my head to kiss him back with an open mouth. I wanted to sob in elation when a long growl erupted from deep in his throat.

"That's my good girl now," he murmured as we parted to suck down fresh air. "Oh God, yes, Rio. Your cunt feels so good. You're so warm and wonderful, sliding on my cock like that. Are you ready for me, baby? I can't hold off any longer."

I released a breath of joyous abandon. "Hell yes," I offered, thanking myself for being bold. "Yes. Please!"

He maneuvered into position, making room for himself deeper between my thighs. "My sweet Blaze. I need to fuck you right now."

"I'm ready. I've been ready."

But still he teased, entering me with agonizingly slow carefulness. Of all the times to treat me like a fragile doll, of course it was the one time I didn't want to be. That wasn't true, though. During sex, I never wanted to be treated gently. He knew that, so this slowdown was intentional.

But thank God, our rhythm built quickly. The sensations were exquisite. Every nerve ending in my body came alive, singing an aria of need at the same time. Grant matched my energy with all his dark, decadent harmonies. They were so perfect. So good. He buried himself so deep in me. Then deeper still.

"Grant. Oh my God. I can feel you. I can . . . feel you . . . It's like—"

"My God, woman," he chuckled out. "Finish a thought."

"I can't." I huffed. "I can't think straight."

"Then don't bother thinking. Just feel. Right now, it's your job to just feel."

"Oh. Okay. In that case . . ." A laugh bubbled out, despite my full awareness of his *I am caveman, heed my grunts* tone. "In that case, I'm going to get a raise, because I can really feel you. And shit, man. You feel so good. So . . . damn . . ."

My words were choked off because he made a movement with his hips that took the air right from my lungs.

"Yeah, it does feel good, baby," he grated roughly. "And yeah, I am. Now flip over. Raise your ass in the air for me."

He slid out, and at once I missed his fullness. But I scurried to my hands and knees, exactly as he'd dictated. Once there, I waited with shivering anticipation. Being vulnerable to him like this . . . it took me away from how exposed I felt to the rest of the world. Being this open for him made it easier to think about trusting others in my life. And of course, getting an orgasm at the end was the perfect perk to the process.

But soon, it seemed like his anticipating pause had gone on for a whole month. I finally gave up and dared a look over my shoulder—only to meet his disapproving scowl.

"What?" I blurted, fully aware—and disturbed by—how he remained back on his heels.

"I said raise your ass." He motioned to my position like an intolerant ballet teacher correcting a student's crappy plié.

"What?" I snapped. "And in case you didn't notice, I—"

"This is not just your ass, is it? This is all of you."

He gave my ass a resounding smack with his very large palm. The sound bounced around the high-ceilinged room a time or two before settling in the sexually charged air between us.

"All right. Tell me what you want me to do," I whimpered, pressing my forehead down into my folded arms on the edge of the couch. I just wanted him to fill me again. "Just tell me. Please..."

"There you go, girl. You know what I like. I haven't been away that long. Come on now."

His next two swats came in quick succession. My moan was just as loud as his smacks, but it couldn't be helped. My skin stung like a fresh sunburn, and it was divine. I decided to tempt him—more accurately, taunt him—by suggestively swaying my backside from left to right.

"Well, someone wants a red ass today." He said it almost under his breath, and even with an inflection of savoring humor, but it was a warning to me, and we both knew it. He communicated as much with the solid sweep of his hand, coming down on the left side of my ass with a startling *crack*.

I jerked a little but recovered in time to drawl, "Mmmm. Thank you, Tree. Feels so good when you tickle me like that."

He chuffed. I couldn't tell if it was bringing on another laugh or a heightened growl.

"Oh girl, why are you going to do that?"

Okay, it was the latter. And I was secretly delighted. But he probably knew that already, even as he spanked my other ass cheek just as hard but quicker than I could even process. Still, I managed a stunned little grunt before he flipped me around to my back again. My head arched back over the top of the cushion, turning me into his exposed little prey as he pushed my legs back so far my knees were beside my ears.

And then he was inside me.

Not just a little anymore.

He was swollen and huge and stretching me until I gasped, driving his cock deep into me like he was a fully sparked piston. He ignited a hundred different flames—all more brilliant and beautiful than anything I'd been able to create with matches and kindling. The pure, dazzling brilliance of it had me crying and then laughing and then bawling again, which likely made me into a bigger lunatic than he'd ever encountered in our travels. But my wild sanity swings only spurred him on more, causing him to pump harder and faster. Thank fucking God.

"Do I amuse you, Ms. Gibson?"

"N-N-N-No," I stammered. "No. Oh, holy shit, Grant!"

I wasn't going to be able to walk when we were through here. I was totally sure of it—and beyond fine by it. I could take one for the team. More than one, if we had to go into overtime.

Please, Jesus, let there be overtime.

"Open your eyes, baby. Look at the man who fucks you so good."

"Grant—"

"What, baby?" he murmured, leaning in to kiss me hard. "What is it? You okay?"

"Yeah." I shook my head and pressed a hand to his face. "Just make me come. Let's go over together, okay?"

And as we did, I fought to hold on to the release as long as possible. How badly I wanted it to all keep going. To just let go, for once and for all. To just be free from the guilt I still held on to from the recent past. From losing my husband and falling for another man so quickly. For finally finding my soul mate when I thought I married him years ago. I wanted to let go and scream from the tallest building that I loved this man. This man whose body, mind, and soul fit so perfectly inside mine.

It was really that simple. I was in love with Grant Twombley.

And I had been for a long time.

★ ★ ★

We indulged in a long shower together, during which I insisted on inspecting every inch of Grant's body for injuries. I even looked for damage he might not have been aware of, though according to him, I'd have to bow out of that hand. Still, my poker face got a chance to really flex when I told him I was okay with all of it, pretending like everything was fine until he went to do some catching up in his home office. I offered to make us dinner so we wouldn't have to go out, and when I was sure he was tucked behind the closed door of his study, I instantly dialed Elijah.

"Banks." There it was, right on time. His regular perfunctory bark—no more, no less.

"Elijah. Hey. It's Rio."

"How can I help you, Rio? Is Grant okay?"

"Yes, he's fine." With a deep inhale, I tried to calm down. This guy made me so uneasy, and I didn't want to spend too much time trying to figure out why that was. "I was hoping you and I could meet somewhere to talk? Maybe tomorrow or the next day?"

Instead of an answer, he offered me the tension of a long and nebulous pause. And then finally, "Does Grant know you're calling me right now?"

The frown in his voice was as glaring as a bat signal in the sky.

"No," I answered with embarrassing haste. "But what does that have to do with anything? I really just wanted to apologize for the sneak surprise earlier today . . ."

"Accepted," he stated. "Is that all?"

"Well . . . no. I also want to say . . . I just think we've gotten off to a bad start. I know—"

"I think we should leave it at that," he said with a rough edge. "I don't like doing things behind my best friend's back."

I sighed until it was almost a snarl. "Well, it's not really like that. I mean, you're making it sound sordid, and that's not my intention. At all."

He let out a long sigh.

I clamped my lips shut, afraid I'd spit out some snide line about wasting his precious time, and again took a deep breath just to keep my cool.

"Then what is your intention?"

"I just wanted to talk with you." I tried to add some sugar to my voice without turning it into a verbal diabetes attack.

"We can talk now," he leveled.

"Well, no. I can't talk right now. And I'd really rather talk to you in person. If you can't meet with me this week, maybe early next week?"

"I'll check my schedule and have my assistant contact you with my availability."

"Oh, okay. That sounds great." But it didn't sound great. Not one damn bit. It sounded rude and like an easy brush-off, but I'd play the man's high-and-mighty game. I'd already struck out with one of Grant's best friends, and I was determined not to with the other one. "I'd really apprecia—"

Beep. Beep. Beep.

The dreaded three in a row blared in my ear, letting me know I'd been hung up on. Profanity brimmed at my lips, but why bother? This guy was an asshole of stunning proportion and didn't deserve that much of my energy.

I know he had a stellar reputation with the ladies, but outside of his good looks, I just wasn't seeing the appeal. And yes, I knew some women liked asshole dudes, so maybe this was all part of his schtick? Clearly, I wasn't in that camp. He'd be lucky if I didn't kick him in the nuts when I did eventually earn an audience with him.

After looking through Grant's freezer, I realized a home-cooked meal wasn't looking promising. Shit, I was striking out everywhere I turned since getting out of the shower. I decided to deal by going to find my man in his office.

My man.

I let out a girlish giggle as I walked down the short hallway to the bedrooms, one of which Grant used as his home study at this place. I could hear his deep voice coming from behind a closed door, so I paused before knocking.

"How's fatherhood treating you?"

There was a pause then, giving me room to recatch my breath. Oh, damn. I assumed, for a lot of obvious reasons, that he was talking to Sebastian Shark. I wanted to walk away. Seriously, I should have. It would be the right thing to do . . .

But that was not what I did. And I gave karma a shameless middle finger about it too. Grant was the most important human in my world. What affected his heart, soul, and mental outlook was the same important shit in my book. Especially right now.

"And how's Abbigail doing?" Another few moments

passed, and then Grant murmured, "Oh, that's good. I'm glad she's doing so well. Yeah, Dori seems nice. I mean, I didn't really talk to her much, but I'm glad Abbi has help and trusts her."

It was a little odd only hearing one side of the conversation and trying to imagine all the things that were said on the other end, but so far, it was a pretty basic conversation. Regardless, feeling like twenty kinds of a creeper, I raised my fist to knock on his door. I was just going to peek in and say I was headed to the market on the corner for some essential groceries—but then he said my name.

Creeper stalker girl right here at your service, fellas.

At once, I dropped my hand to my side again and just listened.

"Rio's great. Yeah, she's making dinner right now."

He paused again, probably listening to Sebastian's typically "pleasant" reaction. I was ready to indulge a private laugh, but Grant's next words had me back on full alert.

"Don't be a dick, Bas. I was totally cordial about Abbigail, so you can do the same." All too quickly, and for far too long, he was silent again. "Listen, I'm not going to argue with you, especially about her. I just wanted to let you know that I'm coming into the office tomorrow. I'm not sure how it will go, but I'll put in as much of a day as I can. I may have to work slowly up to full speed. I think Elijah is dragging me to a doctor in the morning. Or shit, maybe that's the day after tomorrow. To be honest, I'm having trouble with my short-term memory. I think that's why he's making me see this guy."

Wait. What? I straightened, jolted physically as much as I was mentally. *His short-term memory?*

How was this the first time I was hearing about this?

Why were they keeping me in the dark about something so significant? And how short-term was he talking here? A few hours? A day? A week? The past year? Had it occurred to anyone that if this shit exacerbated, he'd actually forget me? What if I was suddenly not the woman for whom he'd fought so hard over the last month but a naked stranger in his bed who needed to leave right away?

Well, that last one really did the trick. Now I was just pissed off.

After another extended wait, he said, "No, she doesn't know." Then cut in on himself with a huff. "Nah, most of it." There was a heavy beat or two. "Eventually I will, but I think we should probably get to the bottom of what's going on first, don't you?"

At that point, I'd heard enough.

He was keeping something from me. No. Not something. Everything. Probably all that had happened to him while he was held prisoner on that boat. I didn't get to hear the details, but fucking Sebastian Shark did? What was that shit all about? Hadn't I proven myself loyal at this point?

Wait. That wasn't it. It wasn't my loyalty in question at all.

It was my sanity.

Grant was afraid I wasn't strong enough to handle this. That if I knew what was really going on, the sky would be filled with flames and I'd be in a fetal ball on the couch. Or worse, some other kind of breakdown. No matter what, I'd be more trouble than he could handle at the moment.

So what did that mean for us? Was this how life would be between us from now on? If we agreed to try this relationship thing, would he always hide things, thinking I was too fragile? Always assuming I couldn't handle the going when the going got tough?

In the span of thirty seconds, I moved from pissed to livid. That might be a new record for me. But hell if I was celebrating.

Back in the kitchen, I started gathering my stuff. Fuck dinner. Fuck the groceries, and, well, while I was on a roll, fuck Grant Twombley too. He could go over to Casa de Shark and see what Dori the superhero was fixing everyone for dinner tonight.

Chuckling at the thought of Abbigail's personal assistant in her cape and mask, I quickly searched the countertop for my phone.

"Goddammit!" I growled.

"Hey, baby?" Grant said, braced in the doorway that led back toward the bedrooms. "What's going on? Why are you so worked up? I know there's probably not much here to cook. Do you want to go out? Or order in?" He stopped to finally look me over from head to toe, including the purse I'd slung across my body. "Why are you leaving? Oh, to the market on the corner, right? Give me a second. I'll get my wallet and phone, and we can—"

"No."

"No … what?"

"I think I'm going to go home."

He caught the gist of my tight tone. He took in every detail in my expression, and the next second, awareness dawned in his. He'd been way off the mark and now knew it.

"Blaze—"

"Don't."

"Don't what?" He slammed his hands to his hips, which would've normally bulged his muscles against his black T-shirt. But the loose hang of both sleeves were another reminder of how his world had become a different place over the last ten days. A world he was no longer letting me into. "Shit," he snarled. "Are we really doing this already?"

"Are we doing what, Grant?" I folded my arms, slapped on a plastic smile, and jammed a hip against the counter. "Go ahead. Brief me. All the details. Bring 'em on."

"Running away."

I laughed. Well, I meant for it to sound like a laugh, but it didn't emerge that way. "Ohhh, no," I snarked. "We aren't running. You know why? Because we're lying."

He frowned. The look was gaunt and harsh—and looked way too well-practiced. "Excuse me?"

"Well, you see, the beautiful man of my life—the one I've just spent the past week and a half crying for, every single night and day, scared to fucking death that I would never hold in my arms again—has been keeping things from me. Seriously key things, you know? And here I was, thinking I was the person he cares about. The person he claims to want a relationship with. Now, he'll probably say that it wasn't intentional, and that he was being strategic about protecting my feelings, and a lot of other lines that might look real great on paper—but you know what? Holding shit back . . . that's still considered lying in my book."

I gave him an artfully careless shrug before continuing to look for my phone, but then remembered I needed to get past him and into the bedroom, where I'd likely left it after our shower.

"Excuse me," I said, trying to wiggle past him in the doorway. But the giant motherfucker wouldn't budge.

"No," he intoned. "You are definitely not excused."

"Grant. Just move so I can get my phone. I think it's in the bedroom."

"If you go near that bed, woman, I'm not letting you out of there for the rest of the night. Do you understand me?"

He finished with glittering sapphires in his stare and a defined uptick at one side of his mouth. Why? Because I gave him full access to what that bossy alpha shit did to me, as my whole body tremored from the center out. Traitor! My fucking traitor pussy and all the tingling bits it kept claiming without mercy. Zinging and zapping in all those fantastic ways how traitor pussies zinged and zapped . . .

"I'm not interested," I still forced myself to bite out. Of course, with about half the venom I intended, which didn't help my effort to push past him again. All too easily, the towering man caught me around the waist and then used his ungodly long arm to pull me against his body. With my back now to his front, it was equally effortless for him to bend low and speak into my ear.

"Now tell me what this is about."

My first inclination was to pull away from him. Correction: to beat at his arms as hard as I could and then squirm until he released me. But didn't I promise myself I was going to give this a real go? I'd given myself hours' worth of pep talks that I was going to be better at this shit, to show up for all the lows as well as the highs, and not screw things up with this amazing man.

But how amazing of a man was he if he was lying to me? How thoroughly was he showing up for things in return?

"I heard you on the phone," I croaked. Tears were welling up in my eyes, giving me the craziest inclination to laugh. How many times had I been frustrated with Abbigail for her waterworks, only to be here pulling the same bullshit at the first sign of difficulty? Where was Rio Gibson, the badass non-crying warrior now?

Apparently, getting karma's giggling payback for my earlier diss. Damn it.

"When?" Grant charged. "What are you talking about? Just now? With Bas?"

I replied with a lame dip of my chin. I didn't want to speak and let him hear the emotion in my voice. The betrayal. At least that was what it felt like at the moment.

He'd gone behind my back. To Sebastian fucking Shark, of all people.

"Blaze." Grant sighed it out before putting some space between our chests without letting me out of the circle of his arms. Maybe he thought I'd still bolt if he did. And maybe—probably—I still would have. I wasn't sure where my head was at, to be honest.

When I only stood there, silent and still, he sighed again and kissed the top of my head. "Can we sit down and talk about this? I'm exhausted and hungry, and standing here is making me dizzy."

Well that set me into motion, despite my total unsurety if he was pulling some sort of tactic. But Grant didn't typically play games like that, so I had to follow my heart and care for him. Because I did care for him. Probably much more than I wanted to admit to myself.

"Yes, of course. Let's sit down over here. Do you want to order in? If not, I can at least make you some oatmeal. I did see that in the cabinet. Why isn't there more food here? Literally, all you have are coffee pods and some nasty powdered creamer." The questions were appropriate but also just nervous rambling. He knew it. I knew it. If he had a goldfish, it would know it too.

We made ourselves comfortable on the sofa, but I kept a full cushion of space between us.

"You're forgetting, I hop between seven different places," Grant said, resting his head back on the low cushioned back of the sofa. "Getting groceries just ends with me throwing out a lot of spoiled food."

He finished the explanation with his eyes closed, as if he would nod off at any moment. The observation was a double-edged sword. If he slept, I could sneak out with smooth ease. But if I did that, concern and worry were going to be my new shadows. I wouldn't stop freaking out that he'd never wake up again and would die alone on this couch.

"You're right," I said, and then mumbled, "as usual."

Grant surged back to being fully upright but looked pale for being so abrupt. "What the hell is that supposed to mean?"

"Oh, for Christ's sake, Grant." I huffed. "Can we talk about the real issue here instead of splitting hairs over groceries that don't even fucking exist?"

I'd gained some volume by the end of my question, and he reared back like I was at a full scream. I dragged in a long breath and leaned forward to rest my elbows on my knees.

"Listen. It doesn't make sense to argue right now. Let me make you some oatmeal, okay? If you're getting dizzy, you probably need something in your stomach. Please, can I just care for you in that way? In any way possible?"

His posture went stiff. "You do care for me, Blaze. In all the best ways."

"Right. Sure." I couldn't—and didn't want to—hold back on my scoff. "I mean, I'm not Elijah, who apparently makes doctor's appointments for you. And I'm not even fucking Sebastian, in whom you'll confide what happened to you at the hands of Captain Hook and his high seas Lost Boys. But I can make some fucking instant oatmeal."

"Rio—"

"Oh, yes indeedy. Don't everybody drop your jaws at once. Fragile, psychotic little me." I thumped on my chest with both palms. "I can make oatmeal."

"Rio. Damn it! You're getting it all wrong."

The new adamancy in his voice impacted me like a double-edged sword. It was a tone I'd never heard from this normally strong, virile man. It was the sound of complete and utter defeat.

And it nearly broke me.

"Wow, imagine that. Me, getting it all wrong," I rasped.

"That's not what I meant, and you know it."

"Really? Because your stare is saying a whole bunch differently. You're not going to set me off, Grant. I'm not that broken. I'm doing so much better since I've gotten back. I know it went really sideways for us—and for you in ways I don't even understand. But that trip you stole me away on? It did what you hoped. It helped me pull my shit together. I mean, I'm not saying I'm magically all fixed now. Yes, I still have shit to work through, but I'm not ready to light your building on fire because you've been lying to me all day."

His gaze bugged wider—until it didn't. He started leaning forward but clearly reconsidered at the last second. "Goddammit. Listen to me. I haven't been—"

I held up both hands, palms out. "Cut the bullshit, Twombley. At least show me that respect, okay? You just need cut the bullshit at this point."

He surged to his feet in anger but then plopped right back down. "Fuck!" He rubbed his forehead while dropping his head back again. Finally he muttered, "I'm trying to spare you from the fucking nightmares, Rio. Why won't you just let it go?"

Deciding it'd be wisest not to answer, I did the rising on behalf of us both. Still without a word, I went into the kitchen and found some bowls in the cabinet. By the time I found a spoon, the microwave sounded. I wrapped a dish towel around the hot bowl and then prepared the instant oatmeal.

"Well, it's not my carbonara you love so much, but it will have to do until we can get some groceries. Please sit up so you can eat." I was careful to make my voice as businesslike as my stance as I went to stand beside the sofa.

"Thank you, baby," Grant mumbled. "Will you sit here with me, please? I'm really sorry that I upset you. Once I have some food in me, I'll be more myself."

By the look on his face, he and I might have both been thinking the same thing after he made that comment.

This man might never be himself again.

CHAPTER SEVEN

GRANT

My head was spinning, and it wasn't from being hungry. Well, my empty stomach was partly to blame, but that was just the half of it. Judging by the skeptical frown on my woman's face, she knew it too.

My woman.

A stupid schoolboy grin spread across my face. I already knew she would grill me about that too—and I couldn't wait.

"All right. What's that smile about, Mr. Twombley?"

I quirked my lips. Did I know this girl or what?

"I was thinking about how I'd rather be eating your pussy than this oatmeal right now."

Her expressive, whiskey-colored eyes went totally wide before a glassy sheen washed across them like a filter applied to a digital image. Only the sight of her here, so close and clear, was so much better. That much more mesmerizing. I couldn't tear my eyes off her.

"Ooohhh." She dragged the word out across a few beats. "You're just too smooth for your own good, Tree. You've been hanging around Elijah Banks too long. And that man's not good for anyone around here. That I can say with certainty."

I *tsk*ed. "Elijah is a good man. He's been my best—"

Rio held up her hand, palm flat toward my face. "Yeah,

yeah. I know. You've been best friends for as long as you can remember. He's had your back through thick and thin. Blah blah bl—"

Quicker than she could track, I tossed my empty oatmeal bowl onto the coffee table in front of us. As the spoon clattered around in the stoneware, I thought about backing down from this confrontation—which I was probably way too tired to tackle right now—but I obeyed my strange instincts and surged forward anyway.

At once, I covered her small body with my much larger one. The furniture's soft cushions gave way beneath our combined weight, but that was only half of what grabbed my irritation and started turning it into something else altogether. Something that flowed deeper in my veins as I fit my lips to the hollow below her ear.

"What did you just say, Blaze?"

The woman never backed down from a challenge, and this time was no different. I was fully counting on it—and then reveled in it as she met my hungry stare with her ferocious one.

"You heard me."

I pressed my lips to hers. Once. Twice. On the third time, I swept in to deepen the connection by twirling and twisting my tongue with hers in the way that had become so wonderfully familiar and fiery for us.

When I finally pulled back, I asked her, "Do you still want to go to the store? Today, I mean?"

"No. It can wait until tomorrow," she replied, her tone draped in the same dreamy tint as her gaze. "Unless you're still hungry?"

I shook my head, conveying my instant disapproval of her venturing far from where she was. "I'm good, my love. The oatmeal hit the spot."

"Okay," she said, stroking my bottom lip with the same tender intent. "I can go in the morning, as soon as I wake up. And what time did you say your appointment was? Well, not to me, of course. But what time did you tell Sebastian?"

I narrowed my eyes, already letting her know I caught the dig. Her sassy mouth enraged my mind yet engorged my cock, and she was playing in dangerous territory with both now.

"I don't know," I finally said. Just as quickly, I halted her impending rant before it started. "I'm not being evasive," I defended. "I really don't know. I have to text Banks about what time the appointment is. He was trying to get me in with a buddy of his who's a neurologist."

"At Cedars-Sinai?"

"I don't even know," I admitted. "Elijah said he would handle the details. I think he's overreacting, honestly."

"Why?" she returned. "I'm asking honestly and openly. Why does Elijah think this is necessary? And why aren't you pressing him more about that? Will you share at least that with me?"

As her voice changed from challenging to desperate, so did her demeanor. Her posture went from defiant and confident to her rounding both shoulders and resigning herself to one hopeful question.

Instantly, I felt like a giant dick. Well, bigger than the one I'd apparently already been. "Rio," I sighed out. "Baby, I didn't tell you because I simply don't want you to worry." I swept her hands into mine and kissed her knuckles, one by one by one, while she looked on. "You've got to believe me. I just know there's so much on your plate already, and I don't want to burden you with this bullshit."

"Which isn't bullshit to me, okay? Don't you realize a lot of this by now? That by keeping me in the dark, my mind just fills in the blanks with all kinds of fantastical stories?"

She knocked at the side of her head, and icy fingers ran up my spine. I fucking hated when she did that, so I grabbed her hands again. I knew she didn't like when I restrained her in any sort of way, but God, the self-harm habits were the worst thing I had to bear witness to.

"Please don't do that to yourself. I'm begging you."

"You're missing the point," she snapped. "Damn it, Grant, it's a runaway train in here." She managed to yank one hand free and used it to knock her skull again. Thankfully, it was more of a tap this time. "And none of the tracks connect. They all careen over mountainsides." She waited for me to find her gaze again. "All of them," she emphasized.

In a decisive sweep, I stood up. It was a relief when I held my hand out and Rio unquestioningly gave me hers. After easily tugging my little pixie to her kelly-green Converse-clad feet, I looked down into the lush angles of her beautiful face.

"Thank you for coming for me today at Elijah's." I couldn't hold back a grin from escaping. "I will never forget hearing you giving him hell like that for the rest of my living days."

"I needed to be with you," she murmured. "I mean, knowing you were home, right in this town...yeah, I just couldn't sit still. And I was getting more and more pissed at Banks and his high-handedness."

"Whoa now, slow your roll—"

She was ready with a firm hand in the center of my chest. "I'm just stating my truth, not prepping to go set off a five-alarm at his obnoxious mansion. I just seriously don't appreciate how he assumes he knows what's best for you. For us."

"Just out of curiosity, how did you figure out I was there? At his 'obnoxious mansion' in Malibu, I mean?"

"Whatever app you were using to text me last night didn't have the location service turned off. Your daddy didn't think to check all those things before he gave you that phone to use, apparently. So I took a chance and checked if you were broadcasting your whereabouts." She smirked. "What do you know? Bingo."

"Very resourceful, Ms. Gibson."

She shrugged, but a devilish little grin played with her lips. "I do what I have to do." But then her pride faded. "I'd been there a few days before that, as well. I'm not sure if he told you that. He's not always the most forthcoming person."

"No, he told me. He was pretty clear about it the day he picked me up. What made you go see him that first time?"

Oh shit. Shit. I should've never let that slip. She would never let it go now. Well, maybe for five seconds, tops.

"Picked you up where?"

Fortunately, I didn't put money down on the estimate. That was three seconds on anyone's clock.

"Fill me in on what you've been up to." *Please take the bait. Please take the bait. Please take the bait.* "Seriously, what made you go see Elijah?"

"Grant." She just stared at me, confirming the bait might as well have been a pile of two-week-old garbage, before huffing at my purposefully blank look. "I'm crazy, not stupid. I know what you're trying to do. And it's not going to work."

I dragged a hand through my hair. *Well, fuck.* If she'd only kept talking about us in that cute little croak. If only her indictment didn't make me instantly defensive.

"I'm not trying to do anything," I bit out. "Why are you

getting so confrontational?"

Rio reared back. "Confrontational? Okay, you remember it's me you're conversing with right now, yes?"

"I just want to talk about something else other than everything I've just been through." I bellowed it and already hated myself for it. Didn't stop me from pushing on. "It was hell, okay? And it's not worth dredging my brain through it again. Is that so fucking hard to understand?"

I inhaled deeply through my nose, rubbed the back of my neck, then tilted my face to the skylight.

Can somebody give me strength?

Silence stretched across the room. I wasn't picking up more tension from Rio, but that didn't tick down the stuff she was already carrying. I wasn't about to buck the odds on a premature détente.

"Picked. You. Up. Where?"

I growled. Okay, maybe I'd bucked. Just a little. Clearly too much. Christ's sake, this woman could be like a dog with a bone. I'd already explained I didn't want to burden her with the bullshit details of my experience. Why wasn't that enough? Shouldn't that be enough? Apparently, even losing my temper wouldn't get her to break her stride, though.

Instead, she stood there and continued to glare at me. The little hellion had gloriously great glaring skills. When the expression started edging toward a glower, I debated tossing her over my shoulder, stomping back to the bedroom, and fucking every last ounce of sass from her perfect body and warp-drive mind. Maybe then we'd have a sliver of hope of getting one good night's sleep under our belts before starting back on dealing with both our nightmares.

With every passing second, I liked that idea more and

more. So maybe a version of the truth was the way to go. It would keep her at bay but not freak her out. Damn good plan— except I could do with some more time to work on the details of said plan. Which parts were worth telling her? Which got held back? Some were obvious, but others were necessary for the whole thing to be believable.

"He picked me up in Catalina. In a helicopter. Well, he didn't personally, of course." I rolled my eyes dramatically and then inwardly winced. That was probably one step too far, and I probably just blew my scam with one mistimed eyeball movement.

"Of course," Rio mocked.

Yeah, blew it for sure.

"But yeah, Catalina," I offered again and then waited to see if she'd push for more.

"So how did you get there from the boat that those monsters transferred you to? Clearly it wasn't some grand schooner or anything. I mean, not that I saw the whole thing. But not that I didn't try. It was so dark that night. But I could hear it. A lot of it. A lot of everything."

She waved dismissively, like that wasn't the important point of the conversation.

I was inwardly glad because her rambling was confusing the hell out of me. But maybe that was a blessing in disguise too. Obviously she'd mentally replayed the details of my abduction a million times—a connection that had me feeling like the world's greatest dick again. Hell came in a lot of different forms. The one she'd just been through was different from mine, but shitty all the same—as evidenced by the questions she was machine gunning at me.

And she deserves answers, asshole.

"But I'm still just not getting the logistics," she went on, waving her hand around again, which brought me a moment's worth of a grin. This habit of hers was truly adorable. I appreciated that more now. "I mean, it was days until we got to Marina del Rey from where that . . . incident . . . occurred. So for you to get all the way to Catalina . . . Did they take you to a larger boat after that, or what?"

As quickly as it had come, my mirth wilted. Bile rose in my throat the moment I allowed even one splinter of a memory to get under my skin. And now, with every new question, Rio was driving the traumatizing shard deeper.

Thankfully, she noticed something deeper was happening here. I was grateful when she reached up to place a tender hand on my stubble-roughened cheek. All traces of her aggression from just minutes before were gone.

"You know what?" she soothed. "Never mind. Or at least, you tell me when you're ready. You've made it abundantly clear that you're not ready, and I just keep pushing anyway. That's not fair to you, and I'm sorry."

I didn't know what to say other than the obvious. "Thank you," I said with gravel-covered emotion, turning my head to place a reverent kiss on her palm. I kept my gaze locked with hers, which brought my system to an entirely new dilemma.

The way my cock stared to twitch again.

The pressure was instant but insistent, a defined reminder of how I wanted to spend the last part of this day. At the same moment, my system absorbed the oatmeal like it'd been three energy shots and a speedball. I was ready to conquer the world.

Better yet, I was ready to master her.

The plan was effortless enough to start, as I tugged her small frame right into my chest. Rio sighed in sweet bliss while circling her arms around my waist. After she burrowed even closer, I kissed the top of her head and simply savored the feel of her body for a few long moments.

"Baby?" I asked it quietly, not wanting to break the magic spell of tranquility that had settled over us.

"Yes?" She said the word directly into my body. The warm puff of her breath made me shiver in all the best ways.

"I know it's early, but how do you feel about bed?"

She giggled into my left pectoral. "As an overall concept, or in place of reunion sex on your couch, or . . ."

"Any or all of the above," I chuckled back. "But generally, as a destination right now. We can just talk or watch a movie or whatever, but right now, I want to lie with you more than anything else I can think of."

She quit the snickering to lean back a little, far enough to catch my gaze with her mischievous one. As she raised one inky brow, the same side of her mouth lifted. In an instant, the same invisible puppeteer yanked on my marionette string too. I mirrored my crooked smirk to hers.

And then nothing could stop me from slamming my lips over hers.

The kiss was rough and roguish and completely awesome. Yeah, I knew I'd just suggested a movie—*dumbshit!*—but consoled myself with the surety that we'd be fucking within twelve minutes of getting horizontal on my mattress.

When I finally let the woman up for air, she offered, "If you give me some basic instructions, I'm sure I can close up out here."

My grin turned into a full smile. Her brandy eyes twinkled with lust, but here she was, still offering to help. This woman—fuck, this woman—she hurt my heart in ways I didn't know possible.

"No, I'll do it. Go get ready for me—uhh, ready for bed."

"Hmm. Ready for you works just as well, mister."

Before I could respond with half an aroused growl, the saucy little imp turned on her toes and started to sashay toward the hall. But reflexes kicked in, at least for a few seconds, and I pinched her ass with commanding force.

"Treeee!" She yelped and hopped, but there was definitely more sway in that sexy little ass now. I watched, with a dry mouth and a slack jaw, while her clothes started littering the hallway floor. My dark groan and deep inhale were the only soundtrack she seemed to need for the striptease.

After making love a second time, we passed out for the entire night. I just wasn't back to my pre-vacation body weight, and staying hydrated continued to be an issue. I was tiring quicker than normal and could only guess Rio's heightened stress level was part of what was wearing her down.

At least that theory helped with setting my priorities for the next morning. First thing, I wanted to meet with Bas and Elijah about how much I could share with her and not compromise Sebastian's safety. My two best friends and I still weren't sure what we were up against with the thugs who kidnapped me, but we agreed it more than likely had something to do with Sebastian. It always did.

Regardless, keeping stuff from my girl wasn't sitting well with me. It was no proper way to start a relationship. I knew at least that much.

Because holy mother of God, that was really what was happening. Me and her, really taking a stab at the "us" thing.

The thought had me indulging a face-splitting grin while toweling off from the shower. Those wall-mounted jets and the enormous rain head above felt even more magical this morning than they did yesterday. I would never take my luxurious lifestyle for granted again.

I came out of my closet knotting a patterned mint-green tie, then fussed with it for a minute in the bathroom mirror. I scowled, wondering what direction to take the floppy mess on top of my head that was trying to pass for hair. It was way too long for my liking. I made a note on my smart pad to have Reina call my stylist to schedule an appointment as soon as possible. In the meantime, no amount of product could save me. Not that I didn't try.

I was just waving a white flag in that battle when small hands started exploring my waist, just above my ass. I hissed in pleasure as they slid around to rest above my belt buckle. Rio pressed her cheek to my back, answering my primal sound with a low hum.

"You smell good enough to eat, Mr. Twombley. What does a girl have to do to get some of this perfection?" She slid one of her nimble hands over the fabric of my dark-brown slacks and caressed my hardening cock. I watched in the mirror, enraptured by the sight and curious as to her plan. Since I was more than a foot taller than her, I could only see her arms from her perfect elbows to her slim fingers and neatly manicured nails.

"Keep talking like that, for starters." I spun around so fast, she nearly fell on her ass. Quickly I grabbed my baby by the elbows and held on to her until she was steady again. She pouted a little when I slid on my suit coat, conveying there wasn't going to be a morning quickie today, but I distracted her with conversation while I put my wallet and handkerchief in my two back pockets.

"What do you have planned for today? Soap operas and bonbons?"

"How'd you know?"

She squinted at me while planting both hands on her hips. The little boy shorts she wore were such a gorgeously naughty distraction, I had to turn away. If not, I'd be tackling her there in the middle of the damn room, making me late on my first day back.

But damn it, there was no hiding my painful hard-on by now. Not that I was going to mount a war about that part. Most of the time, I knew when to pick my battles. And this time, judging by Rio's heavy-lidded perusal up my body, wasn't even a moment for politely rearranging the family jewels.

"Dude," she breathed, allowing her stare to latch again on my crotch. Her dark-honey regard wasn't helping a goddamned thing, and I didn't care. "Are you sure I can't talk you into a speed round?" She finished with a long lick of her lower lip before doing some little shimmy thing with the lower half of her own body.

In response, I growled.

Correction. I moaned.

Fucking. Moaned. Out loud.

In two strides I was on her. With efficient movement, I threaded my fingers through the hair at her nape. Rio's hair had grown out too, and it was finally just long enough to grab on to. I cranked her head back and kissed her so roughly she whimpered. From there, I made my way down her neck and left a sizeable mark on her skin that was already bruising. Damn straight it was.

I stood to my full height. With a shaking breath, I leaned to admire my handiwork. In this case, the artwork of my lips.

I didn't feel bad about it. Not even by a drop.

Mine, it screamed.

I stepped back over to her. Leaned in. Beside her ear, I growled, "Put some fucking clothes on before you make me late. And ditch those fucking panties today while I'm at work."

We were both grinning and a bit winded when I went out to the kitchen and she ducked into the closet to grab some pajama pants.

I unlocked the screen on my phone . . . and then just stared blankly at the thing. I had no idea what I was supposed to be doing.

Shit. Okay. This could not be that difficult. I told myself that, but the exhortation didn't register. I just kept staring.

What the hell? Why was this what was hanging me up?

I stared at my phone again as if the answer would flash across the screen like a Wall Street stock ticker. But of course, it wouldn't be that easy. I could remember something like the fucking Nasdaq index but not the next step to get out the door to work.

Red-hot rage bubbled up from nowhere, and I pulled back and then hurled the phone across the room with all my might. Like a star going supernova, the device burst into a trillion tiny shards upon impact with the marble mantel.

I roared at the walls, unseeing and uncaring about them. Right now, I could only comprehend darkness. Not just any abyss. It was that one goddamned hole, surrounded by those cold steel walls and the others in it with me . . .

The others.

No. Goddammit, no!

Fucking barbarians! They did this to me! One too many cracks to the back of the head with the butt of a gun and you have a head injury, ladies and gentlemen. Short-term memory loss? Check. Hair-trigger temper? Check. Fatigue? Check.

I just hoped this wasn't permanent and things would get back to normal on their own. I didn't have time in my day for monotonous therapy or even be bothered by some sort of lame home-exercise program just so I could remember how to do basic things. I definitely didn't have time to rest in order to recover, either.

Then there was that ugly truth. The events that played on repeat when I finally did fall asleep were insidious. No one needed to hear about that shit. If I had my way, no one ever would.

CHAPTER EIGHT

RIO

From the master bedroom of Grant's downtown condo, I heard a thunderous crash. The sound came from the living room, so I ran in that direction.

There wasn't much distance between the master bedroom walk-in and the open living area, so I was at Grant's side in a flash. The pants I'd been pulling on were left in a forgotten heap somewhere along the way.

"What the hell was that?" I nearly shrieked. "Are you okay?"

I gave him a quick head-to-toe scan and found no external damage, thank God. The tall man seemed to fold on stiff, rusty hinges when he collapsed onto the sofa. Currently missing from the scene was my confident, strong, and capable boyfriend. A Grant Twombley imposter slumped on the couch in front of me, refusing to meet my worried and expectant stare.

"Grant?"

I did my best to modulate my voice to something that sounded calm and in control. If he had suffered some kind of breakdown, even a minor one that would be done and forgotten by the time his ride pulled up, I owed it to him to be supportive. My God, after the countless hours the man had given me, it was the least I could do. Plus, I wanted to help him.

Watching Grant suffer wasn't something I'd allow. If he tried to ignore what happened while he was gone, that was one thing. But I wouldn't sit idly by and be the spectator of that sport. No way.

"Will you tell me what just happened?" I asked quietly, but he didn't seem to realize I was still here in the same condo, let alone the same room. The look in his eyes was stark and unfocused—and outright scary.

Maybe even more than that.

What if this hadn't just been a temporary slide or a delayed reaction to exhaustion? What if he was suffering something worse, like a seizure or blackout? If something were that seriously wrong, I couldn't even think of anyone I could call for help. Did the tried-and-true 9-1-1 still work? I thought so ... maybe ...

But that whole thought process should probably concern me on some level too. How had my own world shrunk down to this one human I currently shared a sofa cushion with? After Sean passed, I swore to myself I wouldn't keep such an isolated existence. Yet I hadn't done anything to change my situation. I'd simply swapped men I was utterly dependent upon.

Rio, Rio, Rio. Is this healthy? Are you right enough to be taking care of him now? What if you're not? What if you screw this up? What if you lose your shit? And if you do, what will happen to the guy you're supposed to be taking care of?

But now was not the time for my daily self-doubt and flagellation. There would be plenty of time for that later. Right now, I needed to make sure this incredible friend of mine was okay.

"Grant?" I said his name a bit louder then and put my hand on his forearm.

He startled, jerking away from my touch, but the sequence of actions seemed to shake him from the stupor he'd slipped into.

Sluggishly, the man turned to look at me. Caution filled his eyes, and tension lined his face.

"Hi," I said and, for some dorky reason, gave a little wave. I wanted to burst out laughing at my own absurdity, but the last thing I wanted was Grant to think I was laughing at him. Instead, I flowed my awkward embarrassment into a small, caring smile. Still keeping my voice gentle, I asked, "Babe, what happened?"

"I'm so sorry, Rio" was his verbal response, but the actual answer came in the gestures that went along with it. Grant's stress tell was him gripping the back of his neck. Today, it came after he scraped his hand back through his hair—obscenely sexy but also a clear invitation for concern—before I tried to figure where he'd go from there.

His neck rubs usually took one of three paths. Sometimes he squeezed his nape with his whole hand. Others, he'd brush up the back of his head and then briskly rubbed his close-cropped hair—which was rather nonexistent right now. The third entry in the neck language book was the grip-and-hold. To my interested eye, it always looked like his version of breath-holding. When he was tense or angry, this was the go-to move.

Which meant it was the gesture I watched in full now.

I gulped, struggling for composure. The torment etching his normally gregarious face was heartbreaking.

"Will you tell me what happened?" I softly asked. "If I had to guess by the cell phone carnage, maybe you took a call that didn't end well?"

"Oh, shit," he blurted. "Let me get that before you cut yourself. I'm pretty sure the screen shattered." He surged to his feet, but I was right beside him, trying to block his path.

"No. Let me worry about it. Your car is probably waiting downstairs. If they have to wait too long, the doorman will probably make them leave."

"My what?" He had the most bewildered look on his face, and I couldn't understand what part of my comment he wasn't following. "I don't have a car, baby. That much I know."

"No, I meant your ride. Have you already called the service?" I waited, but he just continued to stare at me like I was speaking a foreign language. "Grant, why are you just looking at me like I'm—"

But then it made sense. The pieces of this little puzzle clicked into place, and the outburst with the broken cell phone was the final shape. The question now, however, was what was the best way to proceed? Act clueless that he might be experiencing short-term memory loss and couldn't piece together what to do next in his routine? Or did I reassure him that according to the quick reading I'd been doing on the topic, he would likely be fine in a few weeks, a couple months at the most? Did I go as far as servicing him with platitudes like "What doesn't kill us makes us stronger"?

At once, I ruled out the last one. Terrible, horrible idea. Even I could hear that once I repeated it in my head.

The decision was taken from me in the next moment anyway, as the man spun and stalked toward the front door but stopped when he got to the foyer closet. He returned bearing the broom and dustpan, efficiently wielding them on the shards of plastic and glass that had flown to more places in the room than I'd imagined.

I watched him with a terse frown, still attempting to navigate the emotional wreckage of the situation more than his shattered electronics.

Or whatever the hell this was.

Because right now, it appeared Grant's chosen method of dealing with this was to not deal with it at all. At least not with me. As deeply as that panged, I clung to the bit of comfort in knowing that Elijah had him booked with a doctor sometime soon. Maybe even today.

I would give that asshole a call later and talk to him about what happened here this morning. Maybe if I was extra sweet and gave him lots of compliments to feed his ego, he would agree to keep me in the loop with how the appointment went.

Grant stayed busy with the mess, giving me private space to wring my hands in my lap. What else was there to do besides that? I just had to come to terms with what Grant had decided right now. That for the time being, he was choosing to keep me out of all of it.

But all of it isn't all *of it.*

The certainty blared in my brain, steadier than a dropped bassline in a packed nightclub. There was so much more going on here than even my imagination could conjure. I'd had a lot of downtime to think about this. Nothing had been random about what those dickheads did to my man. The arrogance they'd displayed coming aboard our yacht . . . the way they'd all but known who Grant was even before he'd confirmed their intel . . . and then the absolute commando act they'd pulled when motoring off into the night . . .

I suppressed a shudder. I couldn't relive that horror again. I refused to. But cataloguing those thoughts had definitely led me to another.

There was more to consider here now—namely the phone call I overheard last night. The things that hadn't been said with Sebastian, in addition to what had been vocalized...

I grimaced hard. I mean, I truly wanted Grant to mend his friendship with Sebastian, but at what price? The days of him being under Shark's control...were over, as far as I was concerned. If Grant went right back to being the tyrant's yes-man, I wasn't sure how I would handle it. It would hurt my heart. I knew that much. Regardless of how much better I'd been about coping with becoming a widow, I could not simply forget why I was a widow in the first place.

Someone wanted to hurt Sebastian Shark, and my late husband had paid the debt instead. With his life. Our life. But as long as Grant was in my world, I'd have an inexorable tie to my late husband's killer.

The sour taste of betrayal rose up from my churning stomach. This morning had already been an emotional bumper car ride, and this was my awful takeaway thought. The damn thing was stuck on repeat as I watched Grant shuffle around the condo getting things in order and picking up the mess he'd made with his phone.

"What are your plans for the day?" Grant finally turned his attention to me after re-storing the dustpan and brush in the entryway closet. "You want to come back here tonight?"

My favorite tree asked it while tugging me closer until our bodies were pressed against one another. I cranked my head way back to look up at him, and he chuckled the same way he did every time I had to strain to see his face when standing in my stocking feet. How did he switch gears so fast? Did I even want to know?

"Let's touch base after lunch," I offered. "I'm going to

head into the kitchen at some point and see how things are going there."

Grant raised one sandy brow as a way to underscore his skeptical glance.

"What?" I asked, hearing the peevish tone in my own question, but I wasn't sorry. In that one look he might as well have said, "I don't have faith in you."

But I was too tired to fight right now, and dealing with my insecure crap was no way for him to start his day. If Grant didn't think I was ready to return to work, that was something he could deal with. I'd already gone over it enough times and felt like I was.

Today, after I checked in on Hannah and the rest of the Inglewood staff, I'd head south to Seal Beach. My neighbor had been looking in on Robert for me, but he looked sad in the picture she sent last night. He was probably missing his cuddle time, and honestly, I was missing our special time too.

Grant kissed me at the door, and then he was gone.

Maybe I was just being silly? There was a strong possibility I was feeling hypersensitive because of everything that already happened this morning. When I looked at my phone for the time, I realized it was just coming up on seven thirty a.m. Yeah, this day had gotten off the starting line with a real bang.

Or was it more of a crash?

I snickered at my own dumb joke. Well, no one else was here to enjoy my lame sense of humor now, anyway. At least the little spurt of laughter released some of the tension that had begun to strangle me. Watching the man I cared so deeply about fall apart and then shut me out so steadfastly . . . it was still stinging deep. All I wanted to do was lend support to the one person who stuck by me when no one else had.

Seeing that look on his face over and over in my mind, though? Yeah, it stung like a bitch, as a matter of fact. Unlike Grant, I wasn't capable of turning on an emotional dime. This was the exact reason I'd gone so many years with protective walls up around me. Impenetrable, sky-high emotional walls that no one could breach. If no one got into my fortress, no one could hurt me.

The plan used to work like a charm. Then I met Grant—the tallest, most handsome tree in the forest.

I pulled out the overnight bag I kept in the closet in the master bedroom since Grant invited me to keep some things here. Even though I felt a heavy sadness in my heart, I smiled while I folded the clothes I took out of the dryer. Carefully putting Grant's items in his drawers, lining up the corners and folded edges just the way I knew he liked. I missed taking care of someone in these domestic ways. Little gestures that would let him know I took my time to do things, especially for him. If I had to pick my love language, these thoughts and my love of cooking landed me solidly in the service category. However, when folding my own clothes, the stuff got the most basic fold in half, then half again, and stuffed into my bag. I would use greater care when I got home and put my things away where they belonged.

Before I left the condo, I sent a message to Hannah to see if she'd already started on the lunch deliveries or was still at the prep kitchen. She answered right away, and we made arrangements to meet for lunch before I went into the kitchen.

As I made the twenty-five-minute trek southwest to Inglewood, I realized how excited I was to see my friend and catch up on how things were going with the whole Abstract Catering crew. We'd amassed a team of eight now, and even though that was still a pretty small operation, it was leaps and bounds above what Abbigail and I had ever thought possible.

I needed to set a solid plan in motion for my return to daily operations. Hannah had quickly become the head chef in the kitchen. Other than that, I didn't know who was handling what. I was embarrassed and ashamed that I had let my personal drama get so out of control that every other aspect of my life circled the drain too.

Right now, I needed something to focus on and direct my energy toward. If there were any hours left in the workday when I got home this afternoon, I promised myself I'd finally start looking for a therapist. Since I wasn't entirely sure what was going on with Grant, it didn't feel fair to lean on the man to the degree I had been.

Even that acknowledgment said a lot for me and my mental health's stability. The fact that I could recognize behavior in myself that had the potential to sabotage something as pure and good as our budding relationship and course-correct gave me hope.

I really looked forward to the day that my anxiety and panic disorders didn't enter the world before me. These two diagnoses were like mean, ugly bouncers that cleared a room before I arrived. With the events of my recent history, people were uncomfortable to be around me in fear they'd set me off. I'd trained many people how to walk on eggshells with skills akin to Cirque du Soleil acrobats. It sucked a lot of energy out of friends and family always being so concerned about me.

I arrived at the restaurant about ten minutes early, so I put my name in for a table before going back outside to enjoy the weather. In April, when I'd hosted Abbigail's baby shower for Kaisan, the days were already hot, and I thought we were in for a really scorching summer. But now that the season was almost here, Mother Nature seemed more relaxed. Cool nights and onshore breezes were still keeping things reasonable.

Hannah waved to me as she pulled into the parking lot. I swear, this girl had fallen off a rainbow made of candy sprinkles. The air around her practically shimmered from her good nature—to the point that at first, my bullshit meter was vibrating at a billion megahertz a second. But by now, we'd been working with Hannah for many months, and the meter was on ice. I knew her kindness and generosity were genuine.

"Hello, gorgeous!" I said to my young friend as she walked up. Her hair was down and loose in a beautiful blond waterfall that cascaded down her back. "I don't think I've ever seen you with your hair down, and girl, I have to say that you're more beautiful than the last time I saw you."

"Hey, Rio." She smiled with the greeting. "Talk about looking beautiful!" She stepped back from me while still clutching my hands, at once giving over an approving sweep of a stare. "I'm not sure what Mr. Twombley has been doing to get you to look so good, but tell the man to keep it up."

I smirked. "That man never has to be reminded about keeping anything up, I'm just saying. But that's probably why I look better. Happiness does funny things to your physical appearance."

Hannah blushed from my blunt sexual innuendo, officializing one of my developing theories. The woman really was an angel walking among us mortals. Corrupting her could be so much fun—or downright tragic. Probably the latter because so few really good people were left on this planet.

"I put my name in about ten minutes ago when I got here, so we should be seated soon. Hungry?"

"I am, actually. Surprisingly so. Do you ever just not want to eat after feeding other people all day?" We waited by the host's stand for the cutie to reappear. He must have been seating other patrons, because he was nowhere to be found. Hannah continued chatting. "Most weekdays are like that for me. I know it's a terrible habit, but when I get home at night, ugh. The thought of one more pan, dish, or even cereal bowl makes me want to cry. What? Don't tell me I have something in my teeth?"

She chuckled that last part out, responding to the way my expression tightened. I persisted in asking her, "Is it getting to be too much, Hannah? Are we working you too hard?"

My questions came out as quickly as I could pronounce the words because I was suddenly terrified she was priming me for her resignation. But she stopped me and my anxiety from spinning off into the next county with a firm hand on my forearm.

"Whoa there, boss lady." Her smile was warm and sincere. "I love my job at Abstract. I guess I was just indulging a bit of hyperbole. I'm sorry."

"You don't have to apologize. And seriously, I'm not that big of a basket case. I mean, let's face it, I *am* a basket case. Just not that big of one."

We both giggled, and I bumped my shoulder into hers as the handsome host strode up to us.

"Ready to be seated?"

"Yes, please," I answered for us because Hannah looked like a deer caught in very bright headlights. It was adorable to watch her and the surfer-cute host give each other flirting glances as we were shown to a table on the patio. I think the guy walked us around the entire restaurant twice just so he could keep checking over his shoulder and sneak peeks at her.

When we were finally seated and he walked away, I held my menu in front of my entire face so the poor girl wouldn't be embarrassed by my snickering over what I'd just witnessed. But just my luck, she flicked the back of my shield with her thumb and index finger.

"I know what you're doing back there, boss, so you can just put it down," she teased.

"How? No, really," I persisted when she rolled her eyes. "I'm usually slicker at playing that kind of stuff off. I even got pretty good sleep last night..." After Grant had ensured I'd seen the stars a few times. The real ones, beyond all the light pollution...

"I have four sisters, remember? I know every move in the book when it comes to girlfriends."

Unexpected emotion flooded me, and I darted my eyes from left to right and then past Hannah to see where the closest exit was. If I had to make a break for it because I was about to humiliate myself, I needed to know the quickest escape.

"Hey. Rio? Hey there. What's going on?" My employee leaned into the table, her voice low and even. "Why are you tearing up?"

"Oh, just ignore me," I said, pressing a hand to my throat. I could feel the heat crawling across my skin, and not because it was a warm summer afternoon.

"Not a chance." She nudged my shin with the toe of her shoe beneath the table. "Everything okay? Was it something I said or did?"

"No, no. Well...yes, I guess it was. My emotions are just a bit raw these days. I'm so sorry, honey, really. When you mentioned being girlfriends, you have to understand—" Holy shit, this was so embarrassing, but I could almost hear Grant's voice encouraging me to be honest and direct with Hannah. Just "put it out into the universe" as he always said. "You have to realize, other than Abbi, I don't have many girlfriends—" I tick-tocked my head. "None, really. So, it's nice that you said that. That you think that. Although now, after this, I wouldn't blame you if you never wanted to hang out again." I gave a painfully forced laugh because I knew I was rambling. "But again, I'd also be perfectly fine just leaving this here by the side of the road and driving away, you know?"

"I will do whatever makes you most comfortable and happy."

I dropped my head and studied that damn menu like it contained the most fascinating four salad choices, six burger combos, two chicken entrees, and a tiny kids' section. But damn it if the junior hot fudge sundae didn't rivet itself into place as numero uno choice for my emotional stampede. I even bet that host hottie could put in a good word and let me break the twelve-and-under rule for it. But just in case, I eyed everything else again. At least ten times. If Hannah didn't start a different conversation soon, I'd be memorizing the descriptions of everything as well, not just the clever names of the offerings.

Our waitress was the hero who relieved me of the hot seat post. Hannah and I chose the same thing from the salad list and giggled about that too.

"Either we're both super boring, or we both have incredible taste," she remarked.

"Oh, it's definitely the latter. Definitely."

"Agreed." We clinked our water glasses together and grinned, but then Hannah's face grew solemn. "I just want you to know you can talk to me about anything, Rio. I know I work for you, but I also would like to think of you as a friend. I assure you I'm capable of separating the two."

"Oh, honey. I know you are. And I want to think of you as my friend, too." I took a fortifying swig of water and backed it up with a long, deep breath. "I would like that very much, actually."

There. I said something about my feelings—out loud and to another person, at that! And unbelievably, I survived it. Baby steps, right?

Which, right now, felt like more than enough for the day. But while the ball was in my conversational court, I decided to steer the focus to her. "So that guy up front... He's pretty hot."

At once, my gorgeous friend's cheeks were an adorable shade of pink. "Well, you would not be wrong."

"You saw that he was nearly tripping over himself to check you out."

"I guess," she mumbled. "I mean, he was probably just being nice."

I tilted an incisive look across the table. "So there's no game plan for follow-up, girl?" I asked. "Still no man in your life, right? Or do you have something new to fill me in on?"

"No!" As if realizing how panicked her answer sounded, she spread out both hands in a diplomatic gesture. "I mean, nothing new going on in my love life. I've been on a few dates, but I think I'm too picky. And I'm in love with my job, remember?" She stuck in the last of it while the waitress placed her salad on the table.

"I don't think there's such a thing as too picky when it comes to finding a person you're compatible with." I gave up a cocky smile as the waitress inserted her approving hum of the statement before departing. "I don't think we should ever be asked to dial back our expectations."

"That's such a better way of looking at it, instead of blaming myself all the time," my young friend said, letting her shoulders fold forward toward the table.

I narrowed my gaze. "Are you using one of those dating apps?" I asked it out of curiosity more than anything. "I never really did, but I've heard good things and bad things..."

"I've tried a few." She scrunched her face up and continued. "But so many of the guys are just looking for a hookup."

"Really?" My astonishment was real. "I thought just the one was like that."

"Not anymore." She shook her head. "And I can do that on my own. I don't need an app and three hours of bad dinner and a worse movie for that. Right?"

We both laughed, and I offered her a fist to bump. "I'm sure there is no shortage of suitors coming around your house with five beautiful girls inside. Are any of your sisters in a relationship?"

Hannah squinted one eye as if running down the roster in her memory. "Yes, two of them are at the moment. They're both really nice guys. My youngest sister is in high school still." She snorted softly before remarking, "Now there's a girl we could all learn from."

"How so?"

"She has the most carefree spirit I've ever seen. And she has this motto, much to my parents' chagrin, 'take no shit, give no fucks.' But it works for her. No one will ever take advantage of Miss Clemson Farsey, that's for sure."

I wished I had been that way at that age. I wondered how many things in my life would've ended up differently. I pushed my salad plate back a bit so our server would know I was done if she came by.

Pointing with her fork, Hannah said around her last bite, "That was really good." She nodded a few times and then continued, "Oh, yes. I'd eat here again. In my family, that's how we judge if a restaurant was good or not."

"Seems like you guys are pretty tight," I submitted. "Your family, I mean." Though the observation seemed like a no-brainer, I hoped it opened her up a little more. Already I was envisioning the Farseys as what I'd fantasized the Gibsons would be—before realizing, much too late, how far off the mark I'd actually been.

Hannah popped her head back and forth a few times before confessing with a smile, "We are. It's . . . nice."

I had no idea how to interpret that strange little pause in her reply, and something told me there was no more room for exploration either. Instead, I filled in, "This is my treat, okay? I can write it off, so don't argue."

She held her flat palms up in surrender. "All right, since you put it that way."

And we both laughed again. Wow. I'd laughed more times on this short lunch outing than I had in the past week and a half.

Out front, we hugged, and I reminded her I'd be seeing her back at Abstract in just a few minutes, but I thought it was important the rest of the team didn't know we were hanging out off the clock. At least until I knew the new crew better. The restaurant we lunched at was only about five miles from the Inglewood location, so we vowed to do this again soon.

The kitchen was relatively calm when I walked in. Music played in the background, and everyone there was busy doing something. But they all stopped their tasks with unnerving abruptness when the door hinge squeaked and announced my arrival.

"Hi!" I said cheerfully, and the three staff members we had hired since Abbi went on maternity leave came over to hug me hello. This really was a great group we had assembled, and the more I thought about it, the more confident I was that it was time to return to work. "I just wanted to check in with everyone and tell you all in person that I'm coming back to work starting Monday. So be ready to have your asses run ragged."

Hannah came in the door just then, and I plastered on a smile. "Hey there! I'm so glad I didn't miss you. I was just telling the rest of the team I'm returning to the grind on Monday."

"Oh my God, Rio! That is awesome news."

She hugged me in celebration, and then I went right into business mode. "I was hoping we could go over the pantry and walk-in inventory so I can get back on track with purchasing. Do you have time for that now? I know I should've called, but I was in the area having lunch, so I decided on a whim to come in instead."

"Yes, absolutely. Let me set my stuff down and wash up, and we can get down to it. Also, since you're here, I wanted to run some menu ideas past you and get your approval."

I spent the rest of the afternoon dipping my toe back into the pool of my own business, and it felt so satisfying to be back. As the sun dropped down behind the buildings in the distance, I felt like my mind, body, and soul were realigned. All the bad shit that had happened to get to this very spot—to have the exact feelings I had right then—was about to be put to rest. Harmony. Peace. Contentment. Yes to all of the above.

Now, if I could get my home life with the program, I would

be on top of the world. Even with those unsettled thoughts rattling around in my skull, I felt better than I had in a very long time. I made my way south to my home in Seal Beach. I knew a handsome black-and-white boy kitty who would be very glad to have his mama in bed with him tonight.

And I knew one very tall, handsome, blond, overgrown boy who was not going to be happy when he realized I wasn't going to be in his bed tonight.

CHAPTER NINE

GRANT

I tossed my new phone on the coffee table and stretched out on Elijah's sofa. It was hard to remember the last time I felt so exhausted after only a half day of work.

The afternoon was even less fun.

For close to three hours, I was poked and prodded at a doctor's office on the campus of Cedars-Sinai Medical Center. I didn't care that Dr. Jeff Mallory was the head of the hospital's neurology department or one of Elijah's college buddies. I only knew that I felt like a massive piece of meat during the appointment, which included an extensive CT scan and several other evaluative tests.

After that, I met back up with my best friend in the hospital's cafeteria and then joined him for a stroll across the massive property to the professional building off San Vicente Boulevard. Most of the resident doctors had offices at this location and saw non-emergency appointments here.

When we arrived, the waiting room was deserted. Even the receptionist had her desk cleared off and was ready to depart. I gripped the back of my neck like a life preserver—all under the unyielding scrutiny of my best friend.

"You doing okay, man?" Elijah asked calmly.

"Yeah. Yeah. But would you mind sitting in on this

appointment? I'm terrible at remembering this medical stuff." I exhaled in a *whoosh*. Just asking the question lessened the muscle tension immeasurably. Even if he turned me down, I felt better just admitting my vulnerability aloud.

"Not sure I'm much better, but yeah, no worries."

"Thank you for setting all this up." I fiddled with the new cell that Reina had plunked on my desk just before lunch. Reinstalling my favorite apps was a perfect diversion for ignoring my slashed nerves. "Damn." Forget the apps. "Really wish Rio were here too."

"I'm not enough for you, big guy?"

Even before I glimpsed his upturned mouth, I knew he was joking. And I was damn grateful. This guy was the most steadfast friend I had. The only time I could remember him being even slightly disagreeable was when all the shit went down with his psycho ex, Hensley Pritchett. But Santa Claus would've been pissy if he had to deal with that woman and her drama. Elijah had been a saint, given the games she'd played with his emotions. No one blamed him for losing his temper every now and then.

At the moment, though, I was getting the side-eye every time he saw me checking my phone. What the hell had happened between him and Rio while I was missing? I couldn't imagine he would care if I had a steady woman in my life. He hadn't given Sebastian a hard time when Abbigail came along. Hell, he and I had pushed for that relationship's success from the moment we caught wind of it. It had changed our friend in a lot of good ways.

"Maybe she's getting her nails done or something," he offered, and I spurted out a laugh. The only time Rio wore nail polish was for special occasions. Since she was handling people's food all day, she insisted on keeping her nails short and unpolished.

Whatever the cause of Elijah's stress, the mystery would have to go on a little longer. The nurse took me back to meet the doctor and hear what conclusions he'd drawn from today's test results.

Dr. Mallory was very friendly and seemed incredibly intelligent. Still, by the end of the appointment, I was more frustrated than before. He informed me that I had suffered a series of concussions from the blows to the head by my captors. Because of that, some brain functions had been interrupted, and he didn't have a clear idea of when—or if—they'd be returning.

Which wasn't the answer I wanted to hear, but damn it, it was the one that made the most sense. No matter how thoroughly I hated the memories that brought me to that conclusion.

One of my assailants in particular had been keen on smashing the butt of his rifle, shotgun, or pistol into the back of my skull. There were a few times he was brave enough to use his fists and heel of his shitkicker. Of course, the coward would only come that close after I was nearly unconscious and no threat to him whatsoever. Otherwise it was the non-business end of his weapon.

I swore to myself every single night—and yeah, in this moment too—that if I ever came face-to-face with that man again, I'd kill him with my bare hands.

Dr. Mallory offered to run more tests but couldn't guarantee anything would change. We'd be no closer to a solution than we were now. He mentioned several times that given the events of my adolescence and what I described as happening now, I might benefit from seeing a therapist.

I wasn't sure how I felt about that particular opinion other than angry. Was the medical doctor pushing me off on a therapist because he couldn't do his job and figure out the exact physical thing that was wrong with me? Or was I just being a massive douche, refusing to accept there was really nothing wrong with me physically?

Probably the latter, and holy shit. Now I needed to add "hypocrite" along to "douche." For the past three months, I'd extolled the virtues of therapy to Rio. I'd read professional case studies and private testimonials on individual doctors and group grief counseling centers. You name it, I'd looked at something about it. But the moment a doctor suggested I take the same advice and seek counsel with a professional therapist, what did I do?

Well . . . fuck.

Thankfully I'd kept most of my struggle internal—so far. At least I didn't have to worry about eating crow on top of everything else.

That thought scrubbed my brain while I did the same thing to my face with both hands as Elijah sped down the road. He was cool about letting me sit in silence for a while, just looking out the window as Beverly Boulevard's designer strip malls, gourmet noodle houses, and chichi Pilates studios passed by.

"Which castle, young prince?" he finally queried.

I froze mid neck grab and slowly turned to look at my buddy in the driver's seat. When I opened my mouth to speak, I burst out laughing instead. The maniacal fit took a few minutes to settle down, and he didn't seem to mind.

When I finally stopped long enough to get some words

out, I asked, "What did you just ask me?" I swiped the tears rolling down my cheeks and sucked in my runny nose. "Holy fuck, man. That felt so good to laugh like that. Thank you."

I rested my large palm on his shoulder and squeezed with hope that he would give me a quick look when it was safe. Eventually he did, and I squeezed his shoulder again. "Thanks for everything. Honestly. I'm not sure what I would've done without you the last five days." I pulled my hand back, using it to cover my mouth with a brutal slam. I looked back up, hating that I was staving off real tears—and not very successfully. "Elijah, I'm so fucked up."

My friend accepted my confession as if he were relieved about it. Before I could express my surprise, he gave me a definitive nod. "Why don't you just tell me what's going on, Big G? You know I can handle it, right?"

I heaved a breath in and blew it out, punctuating the exhale with a quick nod. "I do, man."

"So do it, goddammit. Set yourself free, Grant."

"I don't think it will be that easy this time."

Now Elijah took a turn at the laughter, though it was more subdued than my sci-fi bad guy indulgence. "Bro, since when do we do things the easy way?"

"This is true. But I don't think putting it out into the universe is going to make it disappear."

"Try," he encouraged. "I mean, what do you have to lose? It's not like you're going to get *more* tense, right?"

I'd been waiting for an excuse for my own side-eye fun. Here it was. "Why are you so invested in this?" I groused. "Don't get me wrong. I'm lucky to have a friend so concerned about my well-being and stability."

Elijah shrugged. "I'd like to think you would do the same

for me. Holy shit, this traffic is out of control." He slammed on the brakes as traffic grinded to a halt near the T-section at Santa Monica Boulevard. As the momentum of the car settled, he took advantage of the chance to meet the full intention of my stare.

"You wouldn't even have to think twice about it," I declared. "I'd be there for you."

We bumped fists and then shook them out like our hands were burned from the contact. So immature, but we nodded in approval of our antics.

"Okay, before I miss a crucial turn, where are you staying tonight?"

"Would you mind if I stayed at your place? I realize I'm just inviting myself. If Shawna's coming over, just take me—"

"Nah, she's not coming over. At least, I haven't invited her. To be honest, I should've never started with her."

I snorted. "I seriously didn't want to say anything, but—"

"You should've said something," he bit out.

I winced. "Maybe I was hoping she'd mellowed about the obsessive stuff."

He groaned while glancing between the road and me. "The sub frenzy is strong in this one, Anakin."

"Yes!" I raised one finger in the air quickly like I was asking for the check at a restaurant. Just as fast, I dropped it. "Wait. How am I Anakin?"

"Don't get me wrong," he went on, deliberately sidelining my gibe. "The girl's a wild fuck, and sometimes that's exactly what I'm in the mood for. But I don't appreciate people just dropping by unannounced."

"Nope. You never have. Not even Bas or me."

"That's right. But like we were just saying, you know I'll

always have your back. I just want to have it on my terms. Does that make me sound like a giant dick?"

"You are a giant dick."

"*Pffft*. But fair enough," he said through a laugh.

"Speaking of your giant dick, though . . ."

"Sorry, honey. You'll never taste that goodness."

"Okay, now you're just pitching this down the center of the plate, asshole," I cracked. "But I was going to say, that's probably why she's sleeping in her car out in front of your house."

Thankfully, traffic jammed again. The guy flung a stunned gawk in his moment of navigational freedom. "She's doing what?"

"Hey, once you give them a ride on that freak-of-nature cock, they go all marry-me-eyes on you." I fanned the air in front of my eyes while batting my lashes. "Oh, Mr. Baaanks! What a beautiful, giant cock you have!"

"The better to fuck you with, my dear."

I tossed my head back in laughter.

Elijah joined in but sobered after a good half minute of our sophomoric antics. "Wow. That was some solid topic changing, Twombley. Good to know you haven't lost your game. You never were one to be pressured into talking about something you didn't want to."

While the compliment was backhanded, I pretended it wasn't. Once Elijah was parked in his garage, I gave a little curtain call just beyond the passenger-side door.

"I'm going to change and take a walk down by the water. Want to come?" he asked.

"Yeah, all right." The evening air was balmy for the first week in June, and the beach was relatively quiet because schools were still in session. Give this place another few weeks, and it would be at maximum capacity every day.

We walked on the shore, neither one of us wearing shoes. The beach at night was a completely different experience than the beach during the day. Some creatures that lived in the ocean and right at the water's edge were only visible at dusk, and others when there was just enough moonlight overhead. So many things were there to be discovered just by shifting the hour of day you went.

"Grant?"

"Yeah, man?" I replied quietly.

All afternoon, I could sense the guy working up the courage to ask me about my abduction. And damn it, after everything he'd done since dragging my ass back from Catalina, I owed him the truth. At least the best that I knew it.

"I've been trying to add stuff up about last week."

"I know. And I really appreciate that you haven't given me a ton of shit about it."

"How did you get to Catalina? Do you know?"

Fuck. Me. I had to chuckle because this was such an Elijah move. The man always dug right in on the hard parts. "Yeah. I know. The problem is, when I tell you, you're going to think I'm blowing smoke up your ass."

"Well, why don't you just spill it, and I'll decide what I believe and what I don't believe?" my friend responded. "At this point I deserve the benefit of the doubt, right?"

"You absolutely do."

I let the assurance settle between us for another handful of steps. White foam washed over my feet, becoming a strange but accurate analogy for the life I'd once known. The way I'd looked at all aspects of that life. All the shit I'd considered so important…now dissolved and washed out into the sea of new perspective. It was poetic and probably a little pathetic, but it lent a boost of fortitude that I was badly in need of right now. Especially in pushing volume back up my throat.

"So, you know all the training exercises you've always told me about?" I went ahead and asked him. "All those badass courses you've taken, including the dos and don'ts of being a prisoner of war?"

"Of course," Elijah murmured. "What about them?"

"They're bullshit." I chuffed. "All of that goes right out the window when it really happens."

"Like what?" he inquired. "What do you mean, specifically?"

For a few more paces, I scoured my mind for an example that wouldn't have my bloodstream feeling like a seething lava pit.

"I tried to pay attention to the direction we were heading by finding a star or a landmark," I finally said. "But a storm was forming that night, and I couldn't see a single star. Since it was the middle of the night, I couldn't see anything, actually."

We continued to walk along the water's edge, but I looked over at my best friend every few feet to ensure he was still beside me. I knew this would be hard to have to explain, but it was feeling even worse than I'd expected. No wonder I was having such terrible nightmares every night. I was around other people all the time but had never felt more alone in my whole damn life.

"Look how dark it is out there." With my chin, I motioned out to the wide-open ocean. "And we are here on land, so we have all this light pollution to create a glow."

I spun on my heels and looked back to the line of

beachfront homes. Many were lit up, life spilling out of the sliding glass doors and onto the back decks and private beaches just beyond. After a few seconds, I turned back to face the water.

"But out there?" I stared out beyond where the waves were breaking. "Man, it's so dark at night. When those bastards boarded our yacht, we were still in international waters. Out about two hundred miles or so."

Elijah kept quiet, nodding when appropriate but not saying much more. My guess was he didn't want to interrupt now that I'd started talking.

"I was so worried about Rio. And dude, I'm talking about being beside myself with worry. The look on her face when they dragged me out of our stateroom . . . it nearly broke me. We'd spent so much time on the cruise working to break down her walls. All of them. But her issues . . . they're so raw and new for her. I wasn't sure she would survive alone. I could barely keep my shit together."

We turned and walked on once more. I needed some time to gather my thoughts, and Elijah seemed to need some processing moments too, though I already knew he was readying more questions. Hell, I hadn't even answered his original inquiry. If I knew my best friend as well as I thought I did, he'd go right back to it when he worked through the stuff I did say.

Yet again, the man assessed me from head to toe. I wasn't sure he saw what he needed to, since the better part of a minute passed before he spoke again. "You doing okay?" he finally muttered. "Is this too much? Reliving this shit?"

"Nah, I'm solid. I'll let you know if it becomes too much at any point, though."

"Fair enough. So, you never really answered my question. How did you end up at the back side of Avalon?"

Dog meet bone.

Damn it, the man was so much like Rio, and that realization instantly fed me another.

Maybe the reason Elijah and Rio weren't getting along was because of how alike they were. They spent so much time arguing about who cared about me more, they couldn't see what was so obvious to everyone else. It was actually kind of sweet, if they hadn't put us all in more danger by obsessing over the wrong details. We were losing valuable time every second we stood around doing nothing.

"Do you think Bas would come over if you called him?" I asked, deciding to pop the top on this party once and for all.

His gaze bugged wide. "Now?"

"Yeah. I think so," I returned. "It's time. I'm pretty damn sure about that. We all need to talk. He needs to hear this shit as much as you do, and if I only have to tell it once, I'd be a happy man. Not talking about this shit at the office would be a great idea too. I don't know, maybe the girls should be here as well."

"Be serious, Grant. Now you're talking crazy, and you know it. Bas will never go for that."

"Well, I for one have not been thrilled about keeping Rio in the dark. And once Bas hears what I have to tell you guys, he may change his mind."

"Well, let's start here, with the three of us. Like it's always been. If he wants to tell Abbigail, he can do that. As far as Rio is concerned, I'm shocked you haven't told her everything already."

"I've been trying to get my shit together. And to be honest, my first instinct was that you two could help first. When we had to push off the meeting this morning, I guess I took it as a sign to keep rearranging stuff for a bit." I tapped at my temple. "And I think it helped—but still, I'm just not sure I want to drag her into the mire with me quite yet."

To that, Elijah gave up a thoughtful "Hmm."

"What do you mean, hmm?"

"Just be careful with her, man."

That answer seemed conveniently ready and waiting, and I wasn't sure what to make of it.

"Be careful?" I frowned. "What do you mean?"

"I just think that woman might be in way deeper emotionally than you are," he explained. "You know what I'm saying?"

I replaced the scowl with a smirk. "Sure. Says the guy with submissives lining up outside his front door?"

"All I'm saying is your cute little chef was ready to stir-fry my balls the last time she was at my house just because she didn't think I was shooting straight about your whereabouts."

My small smile grew into a satisfied—and proud—grin. I loved that passionate, protective woman. It was so damn official. "If you say something so stupid about my feelings for her again, you won't have to worry about her because I'll be the one castrating you. Are we clear?"

Elijah held his hands up in surrender. "All right. Easy, killer."

"Don't joke about that shit either." An icy shudder ran down the length of my spine. "Just call Bas. I don't think he'll even pick up the phone if I call him at this hour, let alone drive down here to have a nightcap and a chat."

"Come on. You know he's been worried about you. Let's

not drag him all the way down here so the two of you can circle around each other for a couple hours. I'll throw you both out if you start that bullshit." He stopped with such sudden fury, sand flew from his feet in damp chunks. "You with me? Because I'm tired of playing referee for the two of you."

Well, shit. It was rare to see Elijah get pissed, but there it was. I blinked a couple of times as he walked past me and toward the sliding glass door that led into the back of his house. But I breathed a little easier as he took out his phone and pressed it to his ear.

I stood on the beach and let him go because I wanted to try calling Rio again. But now that we were close to Elijah's house and I was on his Wi-Fi network, my phone dinged several times in rapid succession with notifications. Rio had called while we were strolling on the beach. Goddammit, I'd missed her. At least she'd left a voice message this time. After entering my password, I pressed the device to my ear and listened.

"Hey, it's Rio. I called a couple times before. I was hoping you'd pick up, but I guess you must be busy. I was calling to see how the appointment went today. You've been on my mind all day. So, well ... yeah. I guess I'll talk to you later. Well, not tonight. I'm going to bed. I didn't have a chance to tell you, but I'm going back to work tomorrow. I wanted to tell you in person ... or not on your voicemail anyway. All right, guess I'll see you around. Night, Grant."

I gaped at the phone, noting the time she left the message. It must have been right when we got back and went down to the beach, because it was nearly two hours ago. She would definitely be sleeping by now.

I'll see you around?

What the hell kind of crap was that?

Frankly, it was the exact kind of crap I deserved for leaving her in the dark this long and then not being available when she tried calling. Several times, apparently.

Awesome. More fires to put out to keep the peace with my beautiful Blaze.

CHAPTER TEN

GRANT

Perspective had always been a key thing for me, but it felt more important now than ever. It always gave me the ability to appreciate what I had because I knew what it was like to have things taken away. I knew how to be a good companion because I knew what it was like to be lonely. Lately, it was reminding me about the importance of family and friends, having to face the despair of thinking they'd been taken from me.

All right . . . the other way around.

Which was worse.

Much fucking worse.

With that thought still in the front of my mind, I watched Elijah shuffle to answer the doorbell. I heard Bas's low voice blending with Elijah's in conversation, so I sat up and tried to smooth out my shirt a bit. We were all in casual clothes since it was well past business hours, but that didn't give me permission to be a slob.

Our host beckoned us toward the breakfast nook in his kitchen. "You guys want some coffee? Tea? Something stronger?"

"Coffee sounds great," I replied. "But you don't have to wait on me. I can make a cup of coffee for myself. Point me toward the Keurig, man."

Elijah laughed and steered me in the direction of the round wooden table and matching chairs where Sebastian was getting comfortable. "I don't do that coffee grounds in a plastic pod crap around here." He shook his head with a disgusted frown on his face.

Sebastian and I just looked at each other.

"Who is this guy?" Bas asked me under his breath.

"Betty fucking Crocker, apparently."

Bas snorted an unrefined sound at my comment, but then we got serious.

"How's the boy?" I asked him, figuring the subject of Kaisan would be a good icebreaker. I was right. The smile that spread across his face...well, it was priceless. A truly unprecedented expression for my longtime friend. Pure joy was the only way to describe it.

"He's good," Sebastian murmured. "I think he grew while I was at work today. Abbi says he sleeps most of the day and just wakes up to eat, so it would make sense if he did."

"But he's so young. Can you tell that stuff already?" I asked. "I mean, is there a pattern or a schedule or whatever? Man, I know jack shit about babies."

"I was saying the exact same thing a year ago," Bas stated. "And even now, man, I just go along with what the mama says most of the time."

I laughed. "Seriously?"

"Seriously," he assured. "When Abbigail was pregnant, I was all into it, you know? Every doctor's appointment, every detail, every decision. Now, everything is constantly changing on the fly. So much happens in a day. I can't possibly be consulted on everything. I would never get anything done at work."

Elijah joined us at the table with a serving tray. He had coffee mugs, spoons, a French press that was filled to the top, and an assortment of creams and sugars. The coffee smelled so good, I perked up and my mouth watered just from the aroma. Still, I had to bust his balls a little.

"Are you wearing an apron?" I made a show of looking down his body like I expected to find some frilly protective wear tied behind his back.

"You're a real comedian today, Twombley," our host said while narrowing his glare in my direction.

"Yeah, you won't be saying that for too much longer." I busied myself with making a cup of coffee after making that remark.

Bas sat forward like an eager student. "Well, let's get down to it. I'm guessing you two didn't call me here at this hour so Banks could show off his Sur La Table purchases."

At least a dozen quips evoking inspiration from Giada De Laurentiis to all the British baking shows bombarded my brain, but Bas had taken time to leave his life and haul his ass over here for me. The man made that allowance for very few people in his world. He deserved more than continuing wisecracks about coffee foam and proper meringue.

"I saw a neurologist this afternoon, as you probably already know," I told him. "That's why I left work early."

"Right." Bas took a sip of his coffee. "Shit, Martha Stewart. This is really good coffee. I'm not joking."

Elijah narrowed his eyes and flipped him off.

Completely unfazed, Bas chuckled and then bade me, "Okay. Go on."

"The guy said I don't have a TBI."

"Traumatic brain injury," Elijah supplied.

"I'm aware of what it is, Wolfgang Puck." He looked back to me with another totally new expression. Holy shit. It was full-throttle concern. "What then?"

"Residual damage from repeated concussions. More or less."

"How did that happen?" Bas asked.

"Repeated blows to the head," I supplied. "Mostly pistol whippings, if that's what you call it when it's a rifle or a shotgun and not an actual pistol. I don't know. But there's stuff that happened on that boat that I haven't told anyone. I just . . . well, I don't like thinking about it or remembering it, but now . . . I don't have a choice."

"What do you mean?" Sebastian pressed.

"You don't have a choice?" Elijah finished the second part of the question.

Bas thumbed in Elijah's direction and said, "Yes. That."

"I've been having a lot of—shit—I don't know? Flashbacks? Nightmares, maybe? It's hard to tell the difference." I wrapped my hands around my coffee mug, trying not to fixate on my white knuckles. "What I mean is, it's hard to tell if I'm remembering something that actually happened or if my brain is making shit up. Sometimes there will be things that I know happened. Like things with Rio from before I was taken. And that will be mixed in with bad shit, so then I get really confused if it's real or not."

Elijah released a soft whistle. "Dude."

"How can we help you, Grant?" Sebastian asked in yet another mode. This side, I knew. It was his nerves-of-steel, take-no-shit CEO mode. And right now, it was everything I needed.

"I don't know. But some of what I'm remembering is bad.

Bad as in illegal bad." I stopped, ensuring I had the full lock of his gaze so there would be no mistake about how serious he needed to take me right now. "And I'm pretty sure it involves you."

He didn't answer right away. I didn't expect him to. The man hadn't gotten to his place in life with kneejerk reactions to announcements and accusations that came flying at him on the daily. After his gaze darkened and his posture stiffened, he nodded tightly and finally spoke again.

"I think you'd better start from the beginning and tell us everything you know, my friend. Even if you aren't sure if its real or a dream or whatever. Especially if you're going to hurl statements like that."

So for the next two hours, that was what I did. I gave my two lifelong friends the *Reader's Digest* version of the events I could remember. I started right where Bas ordered me to, with being dragged off the boat where I had made so much progress with Rio. It was the night Kaisan was born. Actually, it was after midnight by the time we got on the pirates' speedboat, so technically it was the next day, but it was a good reference point.

I glossed over the eight days afterward—about being held helpless and captive—despite how my friends attempted to hook more details out of me. Honestly, I wasn't sure how important it all was.

How important I really didn't want it to be, damn it.

Instead, I let them hear all about the ninth day.

That was when I had been dumped into the Pacific Ocean off the coast of Santa Catalina Island and told to swim for shore or drown. Thank God I had been dealing with a boatful of idiots and not actual seamen. If they had been, they would've known when the tide was changing that day. They would've also known that during a changing tide, I would have had the best chance of surviving a two-mile swim in my weakened condition.

I had ridden the current most of the way to shore because I'd had very little energy to swim. By the grace of some former lover's angel, I'd somehow stumbled up the sand on the back side of Avalon. I told them about the private resort on the far side of the island that most tourists never even see because they don't get farther than the harbor where the tourist cruisers drop everyone. I scared some rich vacationers half to death, but they were kind enough to help me once they realized I wasn't going to hurt them.

"How did they not call the authorities?" Elijah finally cut in. "Your luck was on a full tank that day."

"They may have been foreigners?" I ventured. "I don't have a clear memory of it, but I think so. Maybe German or Dutch." I shook my head after thinking for a minute. "Yeah, I don't know. One of them let me borrow a phone, and yours was the easiest to remember."

"Sure." Sebastian snort-laughed it. "His last four digits are six-nine-six-nine."

He and I shared a hard chortle, but Elijah went on like we were still just sipping his foo-foo brew with its high-end sugar. "That explains why you were so dehydrated when I finally got to you."

"Well, that swim was one part of it," I muttered and then really did take a swig of my java. But before I could finish, both Bas and Elijah were all but down my throat again.

"Stop doing that, damn it. We've had enough with you trying to build suspense here, man. Just tell us the details."

"Easy there, Betty Crocker. I was about to finish my sentence when you jumped my shit. How much of this caffeine have you gulped already?"

"He needs to get laid," Bas interjected, resulting in my shock that he didn't end up with the French press in the middle of his lap.

"I'm doing just fine in that department, thank you very much."

"He is. I can very much vouch for our brother," I asserted. "He and the monster have lady callers all the time. Well, one lady caller in particular."

I nodded enthusiastically, mostly because it felt so good to not be the one in the hot seat. When these two hadn't yet been on board with Rio and me seeing one another, they constantly gave me shit about spending time with her. Even when I had insisted that she and I were just friends, they'd continued to badger me about it.

Too bad, Mr. Banks. Turnabout's fair play, dude.

"Well, here we are with some classic Twombley," Elijah issued, scowling hard and folding his arms. "Anyone locate that remote yet? Because this channel has definitely been changed."

Sebastian pushed aside his coffee cup in order to fully steeple his fingers. "He's right," he growled. "Your tale is missing some key parts, G-man. Get on with it."

"Fine." I shoved aside my own cup now too. "You really want all the ugly details, kids? Then that's what you'll damn well get."

Before I could hit the reset button, Elijah put his hand on my arm. The action was probably meant in comfort, but it violently startled me instead. The memories were already starting to take over, immersing me so deeply that I jolted to my feet. My chair flipped backward, smacking into the pristine plaster of the kitchen wall.

"Hey, hey. All right, man. Easy." But Elijah's soothing tone didn't reach me.

"Those bastards starved me like they had a schedule they were following," I grated out. "One day I would have a very small meal and some dirty water, then two days with nothing at all. If they caught me trying to ration it for the off days, they took it all away."

A chill ran up my spine, and my whole body gave an involuntary shudder. Weirdly, that was when I finally noticed that Elijah was on his feet too. He stood in front of me but gave me plenty of space to breathe.

"Grant. Fuck. I'm so sorry, man."

At some point, I dropped my face into my hands and slithered down the wall until my ass hit the kitchen floor. I couldn't look at either of them in that moment, but I could feel their expectant eyes boring into me.

Worried, pitying eyes.

"Hey," Elijah tried again. "Dude—"

"Don't." I cut him off right there. "All right? Just don't."

"Don't what?" I watched his demeanor change, and I knew he was changing tactics. "I was going to say you're totally fixing that wall you just fucked up." Then he muttered, "Asshole."

Fucking Banks. Always knew the right thing to say and when to say it. I started laughing and shaking my head back and forth. I did it slowly at first but then a bit faster.

Finally, I lifted my face to look at the two best friends I could ever dream of having.

"God, you guys. What am I going to do? I'm so fucked in

here." I knocked on my head like I'd seen Rio do so many times and instantly stopped. I knew how alarmed I felt when I saw her do that to herself. I wasn't about to go down that path.

Elijah knelt down on the floor beside me, and Sebastian shifted over until he was straddling the closest chair backward.

"I think we need to get you set up with a therapist, my friend," Elijah proposed. "Probably the sooner the better. Maybe one who deals with PTSD, like Dr. Mallory suggested?"

It wasn't a bad idea. And neither was this sharing *shit* either. The more I talked about what happened to me, the more I knew that the lasting effects on my psyche weren't going to just go away on their own like I'd been hoping.

"In the meantime," Bas said, pinching the bridge of his nose, "I got the distinct impression, from your words specifically, that I'm somehow involved in this. Are you feeling stable enough to talk about that part now? If not"—he held his hands up in supplication—"I get it. And it's okay. We can hold off and do it with a doctor in whatever way they suggest. But if you can talk about it, I would like to know what's going on, because I have a family I need to protect. And, like it or not, that includes your girlfriend by extension."

Elijah choked on a laugh. "Don't let her hear you say that." Though he ultimately uttered it under his breath, it was loud enough for us all to hear.

"Wasn't anything I wasn't thinking," I assured him.

"So you're in agreement?" Bas urged. "Maybe it's best to get as much as possible out in the open?"

"Yeah, man," I said at once. "Right here and now. It's for the best."

"What's for the best is making sure you come out of all this with as few scars as possible," Bas insisted. "So if you're really not ready—"

"You know a better time and place?" I retorted. "It has to be here, man. It has to be now. It's not like we can break out this subject matter at work. Possible eyes and ears in the walls, right?"

Elijah cleared his throat roughly. "Dude has a point."

"More importantly, I can't continue to keep Rio hanging in the dark about all of this. We've been working hard with each other. And we made so much progress on our first portion of that trip. Honest to shit, you guys, things were going great." I took a moment to let the smile spread up from my heart to my face and let my friends see how truly happy I was with this woman. "But then the other night..." I gripped my neck and slid my hand up to rub the back of my head. "Shit."

"The other night what?" the guys said in tandem.

"Okay, that was just creepy," I said, giving them the side-eye.

"The two of you do it all the time!" Bas shouted.

Elijah cocked a brow. "Yeah, but our version is cool, man."

"For fuck's sake," Sebastian growled, dropping his chin to his chest. "I'm dealing with grade schoolers."

"Sorry, man." I knocked his leg with my foot. "I've been so stressed out. You have no idea how good it feels to just cut up today. And for some reason, this dickhead keeps making me lose it." I pointed at Elijah like everything was his fault.

That earned me another look full of missed impressions from Sebastian, though he was clearly back to business with his typical intensity. "Did you get the impression the people who took you had ties to the other pirates who took over those SE freighters a couple months ago?" he asked.

"Absolutely," I answered without hesitation.

The corners of his gaze went brutally tight.

Elijah was practically emulating the look.

"What makes you so sure?" Sebastian persisted.

"They underdosed whatever drug they used to keep me compliant. So a lot of times it made me tired but didn't knock me out. Pretty quickly, I figured that if I played possum, they'd talk freely in front of me. I probably heard a lot more than I would've if they knew I was still conscious."

"Good job, man," Elijah praised. "That was really smart thinking."

"Thanks," I said. "I mean, the first time it happened was a bit of a mistake, but after that, I just went with it and used it to my advantage."

"Twombley," Bas bit out. "Will you just spill it? I don't know why you're building all this suspense like you're writing a Helen Hardt novel here. Just fucking tell me what's going on."

I readied a good chunk of snark as a comeback but couldn't go through with it. Bas's agitation made sense. A shit ton of it. He knew his life was about to get complicated again, and he clearly hated having to accept it. Now he had Abbigail and baby Kaisan to protect too, upping the ante immeasurably on his overall vulnerability.

"On more than one occasion, I overheard these losers talking about the same shipping lane that you brokered the Malaysia deal for. Remember when you went there when you first started dating Abbi? I think you met with the minister of transport."

"Forgetting that isn't an option," he muttered. "As in, ever."

I reacted with a shaking head more from surprise than argument. "And you say I'm the one with a story to tell?"

"That trip almost ruined everything with Red. Let's just say that much. I was so lucky she saw the error of her ways. And damn..."

Bas got a far-off look then, and I knew him well enough to know he was remembering something. No. Realizing something. Okay, maybe both.

"What is it?" I finally asked.

"That situation? With Abbigail?" Now his voice was much quieter. Not somber. Focused. Brutally so. "Do you know why she finally heard me out? Gave me a chance to explain myself?"

"Nah, man. Why?"

He couldn't meet my gaze then, and I had a feeling his answer was going to be a doozy. This answer was the kind that could—and likely would—change things.

"It was Rio," he explained. "Rio told her to stop trying to control everything all the time. That love doesn't color inside the lines. Sometimes it's messy, and that's what makes it exciting."

He finally looked me in the eyes then, his blue meeting with my blue. The bottomless oceans of love we felt for these two women reflected back to each other. Finally. God, could I hope that *finally* our tides would ebb and flow together like they had for most of our lives? Because I missed him. I missed my best friend, and I really needed him right now.

"It was Rio," he said again, nodding with even more purpose.

I decided to leave it there because we didn't need to say anything more on the subject. The rest would be up to him as far as how he handled himself with her. She and I both felt like he owed her several apologies, but again, that was on him. Clearing some of the air between us felt so damn good, though.

Elijah brought us back to the subject at hand. "That shipping lane is one of the most used in the trade as a whole. It wouldn't be that uncommon for maritime pirates to be targeting that zone."

"Oh, there's more." I heaved in a breath but held up my hand. I didn't need to be nagged about being dramatic. This shit was legitimately hard to deal with. The worst memories still stuck in my throat like a wad of gauze I could neither swallow nor cough up. Recollections that strangled me in the night, causing nightmares that seemed more real than living through the actual events. Even worse, that shit followed me around during the day, as well. It lurked in shadowed corners, even when I was walking in broad daylight. It sneaked out from the faces of strangers who stared too long. In the wraiths they'd one day be . . .

I finally got up off the kitchen floor and stretched. I brushed off my pants out of habit and because I needed to do something with the nervous energy that was gathering while I thought of how to explain the next part to my friends.

"Twombley!" Bas's sharp shout called my attention from fussing with my clothes.

I wheeled back on him, going for the whole effect with my coiled fists and openly gritted teeth. "This is more difficult than you understand, okay?"

"I'm trying. Patience is not my best virtue. You know this about me."

"Wait," Elijah said. "You have virtues?"

Sebastian gave him the bird. It was the perfect pause I needed to tug on the ignition cord for my words. Thank every higher power there was for Elijah's uncanny sense about that. I owed this guy so much when this was all over with.

"The boat we were on wasn't very big," I started. "Smaller, I'd estimate, than even the one Rio and I were on for our trip. I think that was sixty-five or seventy feet. The one I was held captive on was a fifty-footer, if I had to guess. So the living quarters were cramped with that many men on board. Part of the boat was sectioned off for cargo on top of that, and that's where they put me."

Elijah's expression got even tauter. "So, no bed or bathroom or basic accommodations?"

"Well, the point is, I was in with their cargo. So..." I swallowed roughly. "I got a good look at what they transport."

"Drugs?" Bas guessed.

"No."

"Weapons?" Elijah inserted.

"No." I shook my head while answering.

"What?" they asked in unison.

"Bodies."

"Bodies?" they repeated like two parrots.

"Dead bodies. A lot of them. Piled on top of one another. And fuck me, the smell." I roiled from the memory but tried to keep my cool and continued to speak. "It will never get out of my nose."

So much for calm and cool. I had to hustle to Elijah's sink as a wave of nausea thundered through me. Beads of sweat dotted my forehead and rolled down my temple as I hurled with ruthless violence.

When it was over and the coffee was gone from my gut, Elijah thrust a bottle of water into my hand. "Thanks," I croaked. "This is really goddamned embarrassing."

"Dude," Banks said. "I'm so sorry you're dealing with this. We're going to get you some help, okay?"

What could I say? Seriously . . . what? So I gave a quick nod and splashed some cool water on my face.

"Hold up. Are you absolutely sure that's what was in there?" Bas asked hopefully as I dried my face with a clean kitchen towel. "It was probably pitch black, right? Maybe it wasn't actually human bodies?"

I gave up a dark laugh. I knew Sebastian was only trying to save my sanity in the best way he knew how, but I leaned against the kitchen counter, suddenly feeling every exhausting minute behind the hour of the day we were pushing. It felt like my adrenaline left my body along with the caffeine.

"Do you guys remember when we found my mom? And she'd been there, in the bedroom, for a day or two?" I looked at each of my friends and they nodded, so I continued talking. "I remember sitting and cradling her in my arms until someone came. The police? Maybe the coroner? They made me let go, and they took her body away."

"Yeah, man," Sebastian said. "That day was shit. We were too young for that kind of experience. We're going to do things so much better with our own kids."

"Point is, I know what a dead human body feels like, and that cargo hold was filled with them. And the smell?" I shuddered again. "It's a very particular smell."

"Ugh. Okay. I believe you." Now Bas looked green, too.

"So what does all of this mean? How do these pieces fit together?" Elijah demanded.

"I've had a lot of time to come up with a theory," I offered right away. This part, I could absolutely deal with away from the sink. "I think these assholes are probably undertakers for the criminal world. What better place to dump bodies than the middle of the ocean, right?"

Bas plunked his nose back into the clamp of his fingers. "Damn," he muttered.

"Double damn," Elijah seconded.

"But more than logical," I asserted. "We already know the government in that area of the world is as crooked as they come because of the deal they made with Bas."

"But how does this involve him?" Elijah asked.

"With Shark Enterprises using that shipping lane as much as we are now, we've increased freighter traffic in that area by—what would you estimate, Bas? Thirty percent?"

"At least," he concurred.

I nodded while slowly pacing the length of Elijah's kitchen. Thankfully, his automatic room spray kicked on to diffuse what I'd just subjected his poor sink to. "With the increased traffic comes increased attention from the authorities, for one thing," I continued. "Also, smaller freight lines want to copy what the big boys are doing, so they start using the same routes to offer identical service to customers." I stopped to spread my arms out, palms up. "More traffic means more law enforcement attention. All of that means less freedom to do bad, stupid shit—like use dead humans as fish food. I heard them bitching about why they still had a full cargo hold. They couldn't make the 'drop,' as they were calling it, in that shipping lane we've been using because there was too much boat traffic when they were there."

"So why did they commandeer our vessel a couple months ago? What do you theorize that was about?" Bas challenged.

"My guess is a factfinding mission," I suggested. "I think they were looking to see who the ship belonged to, what was on board, and most importantly, how quickly we would respond to the boat being taken over. Not just an answer from our internal operations, but what sort of media attention it would get. They needed to know the situation they were dealing with."

Elijah, now on the opposite side of the kitchen, angrily pounded both palms on the edge of the long counter. "So now what?" he bit out. "Where the living hell do we go from here? We definitely need a plan. If you think they're going to keep trying to bully Shark Enterprises out of that traffic lane just so they can go about their dirty business, those pricks can think again. We need to have a plan in place to protect our assets."

"And our families on the ground here," Sebastian added.

"Absolutely," I agreed. "That being said . . . Bas, we have to tell the girls what's going on. Rio can already tell something's going on, and I don't like lying to her by omission. I don't want to fuck shit up with her before we even get off the ground. I really want to make a life with her."

Sebastian gave me a sideways glance with one of those rom-com best buddy looks that I never thought he'd permit on his face. "Seriously? You're that into her?"

"I'm pretty sure I love her. No. I know I do. The thought of anyone hurting her, or doing anything to cause her pain, including me being stupid, just makes me ache in here." I rubbed the center of my chest with my fist. "Like I can't breathe right. I've never felt this way before, so I'm guessing it's love?"

Even though I posed it like a question, I didn't expect an answer. I knew I was in deep with Rio Katrina Gibson.

Both Elijah and Sebastian chuckled and shook their heads.

"Oh, man. Welcome to the world of feelings!" Elijah exclaimed.

CHAPTER ELEVEN

RIO

That was the worst night's sleep I'd ever had. I wasn't sure I could think of one worse. Even when three sheets to the wind, eventually I would pass out completely and log a few hours. Of course, there were the room spinners and the bouts with the hiccups that inevitably led to throwing up, but again, at least sleep came in between those joyous events.

No, last night was just hell. Torturous hell that nothing seemed to help. I employed every trick in the book except for sex, because who was I going to do that with? And I tried handling things myself, and after getting off the second time, I still couldn't sleep. I had, however, discovered a really great porn site by way of Pornhub that I bookmarked for future reference. They had some great links on their site for some really cute role-play costumes, so I made a few middle-of-the-night purchases too.

Credit cards should be time sensitive. I made the dumbest buying decisions between the hours of one and four in the morning. Seriously. Was anyone thinking rationally at that time of day? Why would a retail establishment even allow purchases to be made at those hours? They had to know people weren't making the best decisions.

Poor Robert only got about ten hours yesterday with all

my shifting around and up and down and in and out of bed. He would probably be a real bear this morning because of it.

Of course, the cause of all the insomnia was the tall guy. I missed him. It was one night apart, and everything seemed off in my world. It wasn't just that I hadn't seen him. I also hadn't talked to him. Not on the phone, not in person, nothing. Not one time all day, and he was supposed to have a really trying day.

Ideally, I would've been with him at the appointments he had so I could hear firsthand what the doctor thought was going on and what the plan was for treatment. In my experience with Sean, he never really listened to what a doctor said past the point if he was going to be getting medicine to take or not. It was very frustrating.

When I did finally get a phone call from Grant, I was away from my phone and he left a voicemail. I called him back within minutes, but he was already off to his next appointment with Elijah.

Even though I felt like my eyelids were lined with sandpaper and my back felt like I'd carried my Fiat a mile down the 405, I decided to go into work. It was a few days earlier than originally planned, but there was no way I could sit around all day and be ignored by the only person I wanted to see or talk to. At least at my business, people treated me like I was important. Never mind they were being paid to do so.

See? There *were* perks of being the boss.

I thought I would be nice and early as I turned into the industrial business park where Abstract Catering rented space. To my surprise, however, the parking lot was full when I arrived. It was nice to see the new crew was punctual, I guessed, but I felt like a slacker arriving last.

Walking in with my arms piled high with office supplies, I surprised everyone because I wasn't supposed to be starting until Monday.

"Good morning!" I said after setting down my load. I scanned the faces for Hannah but didn't see her. "Where is Hannah?" As soon as the question was out of my mouth, I heard her confident, alto voice come from behind me.

"Here I am!" she said cheerfully. "I was taking inventory for the day in the walk-in. I like to do that just to make sure everything we'll be using today is still fresh and wasn't used on the fly for something else. If we need to run out for an ingredient, I'd rather know now than in the middle of cooking. Am I right?"

"You scare me a little bit," I told my young friend with a suspicious look.

"Why?" She looked like she didn't know whether to laugh or be offended.

"Because that is so insightful and wise. Frankly, you intimidate the hell out of me. I'm very glad you work for me instead of my competition, let's just put it that way." I slung my arm around her shoulders and walked with her back into the refrigerator. "Do you need to get anything else in here? I'll help you."

"Are you staying all day? I thought you weren't starting until Monday? Don't get me wrong, I'm so happy you're here, and I hope you're staying all day. I've been looking forward to you coming back." She talked while shuffling through the produce on the top shelf.

"I'm here for the day. I'm going a little stir-crazy at home. Grant has gone back to work, and I've been tossed out with the bathwater." I made a dramatically sad face and slumped my shoulders down low in an attempt to look even more pitiful.

She stopped what she was doing and turned to look at me.

"Whaaat?" She gave her head a little shake and looked adorably confused. That combination was the first time I'd ever seen the girl act her age. She continued to chuckle while her one-word question hung in the air.

"You know the saying, 'Don't toss the baby out with the bathwater'?"

"I most definitely do *not* know that saying. What does it mean?"

"Ummm..." I put my index finger to my chin, thinking of how to explain the antiquated idiom. "It means you shouldn't get rid of something good while you are getting rid of something bad. So, I guess if taken literally, the author is dumping out the dirty bathwater, but oops! The sweet little baby was still in the basin."

"How bizarre!" She laughed.

"Not really when you think about it. Especially knowing that children bathed after the adults and everyone used the same bathwater. I think the baby was probably the last to get washed. Ewwww, right?"

We both wrinkled our noses at the idea.

"Okay, it looks like everything is in here that we need for today and in good shape. I was worried about the basil most of all," Hannah said, getting back to business.

"I can understand that. It turns quickly no matter what trick I've tried."

"That, and we had to snag a bunch of it yesterday as a sub for some chives that didn't make it from last week. You know the back corner there"—she pointed to the back quadrant of the walk-in refrigerator—"is consistently colder than the rest of the cooler. Have you noticed that before? I have stuff frost there all the time."

"Yeah, and I'm sorry Abbi or I never mentioned that before we just up and left you here on your own. I think I owe you an apology all around for that, though." I stopped walking and waited for her to turn and look at me. I really wanted her to hear my apology.

"Don't worry about it, Rio. I'm glad I could help."

"I'm serious, Hannah. I don't know what I would've done without you here. It made a huge difference knowing Abstract was in good hands while I was busy getting my shit together."

"Let me ask you this. If you don't mind, I mean."

"Shoot." And I didn't mind. Firstly, I liked Hannah. She was the first woman I'd met in a long time who I clicked with. To be honest, I really needed a female friend, too.

"Do you feel like you have your life on the right track now? Was the time away well spent?" She held my gaze while asking. Her blue eyes were such a deep indigo, I wasn't sure how I hadn't noticed them before. The dark color added to her seriousness and intensity.

"I do," I finally answered. "It really helped to go away with Grant. I faced some things I'd been running from since Sean's accident. Grant"—I looked skyward while trying to decide how to word my next thought—"is an alpha male. I'm not sure if you know what I mean when I say that . . ." I left my comment open deliberately, wanting her to supply if she knew what I meant without me having to define the term unnecessarily. I really liked this young lady, but she was much more innocent than I was used to being around. That was the impression I had, at least.

She settled the whole inner debate I was having with an

impressive eye roll. "Rio. I know what an alpha male is."

With a nod, I said, "Good. I didn't want to have to give you that lesson first thing this morning. But the reason I brought it up is because he was firm with me when I needed it and helped me come up with a plan to improve some bad habits I'd developed when I was a young girl."

I thought about what I was saying for a moment and then continued. "And that wasn't my late husband's fault either, because I hid a lot from him." I smiled, remembering how easy it was to wrap that big bear around my finger. "Plus, he was a big pushover."

Hannah took both my hands in hers and said, "Then it was all worth it. The time you took away from this place. I will help you anytime, in any way I can—in a heartbeat."

"God, woman. You're a saint. Do you know that?"

"No, I'm your friend," she said solemnly and simultaneously squeezed my hands a little tighter.

Her words and gesture were my undoing. Those two things combined with the lack of sleep set my emotions into action.

My tears came on like a stampede of wild horses. There was no way I would be able to wrangle them back today. So much emotion had been corralled over the past few days— really, ever since Grant came back. Now, the fence was trampled and the mustangs were free. Hot, burning tears galloped down my cheeks, and even though I did my best to lasso them before they ran completely wild on the wide-open plains, a few still escaped anyway.

Hannah hugged me fully when she saw my tears. Normally I would resist someone's affection outside of my man's. Previously, Sean's, and now, Grant's. Other than that,

I rarely allowed another person's physical intimacy. But she just enveloped me like it was so natural and acceptable that pulling away would've been awkward if not offensive.

My guess was the Farsey family was a touchy bunch. If you gathered in their home for any reason, you'd better have your hugging shoes on. It was going to be a full-contact-sport kind of occasion.

"You call on me anytime you need a friend, Rio. And I mean that, okay?"

I nodded a few times, gaining enthusiasm as I went. I didn't trust my voice after the stampede but needed to move this pony ride along.

"Are you ready to get cooking? Otherwise, we aren't going to make the lunch run." Hannah got a mischievous gleam in her eye. "Hey . . . do you feel like making the deliveries today? It's been a while."

"Hmmm, let me think about it for a minute. I'm not sure I want to deal with that madness on my first day back. I need to assess the mountain of paperwork on my desk. I may be chained to that chair all day."

"Shoot, I hadn't even thought of that. You probably will be. I know stuff has been piling up over there. Seems like every time someone comes in, they put something on your desk."

Hannah went to the service line to get everyone on track with their tasks, and I stepped outside to make a phone call. Once the kitchen got humming with everyone on their stations, it was nearly impossible to make a phone call.

I figured I would dial him one time. If he had a chance to talk, that would be great. If he couldn't talk, I'd leave a message. The last thing I wanted was for something little to snowball into something big. And really there wasn't even something little. Not really.

And now I was telling lies too. I shook my head and stabbed his picture in my recent calls list before I got myself all pissed off and spent another day stewing and another sleepless night alone.

One ring barely finished before his voice flowed through my device and right into my bloodstream and caused an explosion in my aching heart.

"Blaze."

"Hi," I breathed. Thank God I'd decided to come outside, because he would've never heard me inside the kitchen.

"Baby, I miss you. So bad. Please come back. Are you coming back today?"

"Grant." I smiled and waited to see if he'd give me a chance to talk.

"Sorry." He sighed, and I swore I could feel his smile across the phone line. "Yeah? You still there? I'm just so glad you called."

"I've missed you too. I'm so glad you picked up before your day got too busy. We're really spoiled, you know? I mean"—I laughed a little nervous laugh—"look at us."

"I know what you mean," Grant agreed easily. "But Rio, I don't want to let you go. It's that simple. It gets harder each time I have to say goodbye to you. So, the solution seems so obvious. To me at least."

I heard a hint of mischief in his voice, but just a hint. When his voice had that particular edge, I couldn't really guess his mood with complete accuracy. Sometimes I was right, sometimes I was wrong.

Better to just clear it up from the start. "What are you saying? What does that mean?" I was afraid to know the answer but wanted, no, needed to at the same time. Grant chuckled on the other end of the call, and then I was certain the bastard knew right where he had me with this game of cat and mouse he was playing.

Well, this mouse could play dirty too.

"Watch yourself, Tree. Paybacks are a bitch. Especially when you've been away from the only vagina you'd better be touching these days."

"Is that right?"

"Yes."

"Did you forget I know where you work?" he asked in a low, promising tone.

"What does that have to do with anything?"

"I'll clear that place out in less than a minute and have you beneath me on any number of flat surfaces in your establishment, Ms. Gibson."

"I don't think so."

"And as I recall," he continued as if I never spoke a word, "all those countertops you have there are just about hip height for me. Or did you forget that part too?"

"I think you're the one with memory loss here. I realize your heart has to pump blood all the way up to that thick skull of yours—like twelve feet off the ground—but we aren't having sex in my kitchen, where food is prepared for public consumption. Ever. I could lose my business license."

"Only if we're caught."

"Oh my God, you're crazy."

"About you, yes. But I will go categorically insane if I don't see you the minute I get off work. Where are we sleeping tonight? Or fucking and then sleeping, I should say."

"Jesus Christ, is this what happens after one day of not having sex? You're a basket case."

"You love me just the way I am. Admit it."

And although he was teasing, I wondered if he was inwardly wanting me to say those magic words to him. Were we getting to that point or already at that point? Or was it too soon? Our relationship had always been on some strange accelerated path. It was my understanding that was as victims of circumstance more than anything else. I guessed if I analyzed the what and when of our history, everything about us was.

One thing was certain, though. When I did say those three words to this incredible man, it wouldn't be over the phone. Hell no. I'd be lost in the magic of his ocean-blue eyes and enveloped in the safety and comfort of his strong, capable embrace. Then I would have the courage to bare myself to him emotionally.

Because even though he'd already told me he loved me once before, the circumstances weren't ideal for him either. A man was going to blurt desperate declarations while being led away to God knows where by God knows who. If he had never come back to me after that midnight raid, I would have had that memory to cherish, at least. It had been a going-away gift of sorts. Thinking like that now made me chuckle, and I heard Grant stir on the other end of the phone line.

Oh shit.

"Have you heard a word I said?" my easygoing tree asked not at all impatiently.

"No," I laughed lightly. "I'm sorry, though. I really am. I was daydreaming. But you know what? I was thinking about you." Hopefully that would throw him off my scent.

"Maybe you should go home, baby? That kitchen can be dangerous if you're not all-in."

"No," I said at once. "I'm so tired of being at home. Once I get in the swing of things here, I'll be fine. Maybe I'll scoot to the store on the corner and grab a Monster."

"Rio."

"Graa-ant," I whimpered his name in two distinct syllables. "Dude, why that voice? You know what that does to my lady parts. Plus, why are you on my ass right now?"

Now he was the affected one, judging by the growl that rippled into my ear and straight to my core. This new sound came in hot on the heels of the voice he just worked down there moments before. I was going to need a fresh pair of panties soon.

"Oh, Blaze, I'm not in your ass. But that situation can be rearranged."

Yeah . . . definitely both affected now. But the dirty flirting had to stop. I still had to go back inside and get work done, including dreadful bookkeeping. That stuff was difficult to concentrate on during normal workday conditions. What would it be like trying to concentrate with this fresh on the brain?

Grant must have taken my silence as a hint to keep going. "Because you shouldn't be drinking that garbage as a substitute for rest."

"Okay, Daddy," I mumbled under my breath.

"Woman, why do you want to call me that? You know what that does to me. Especially after twelve nights without sex."

I burst out laughing. "It's been one night"—I dropped my voice to a sultry whisper just to antagonize him before we had to hang up—"Daddy."

He groaned so low I could feel the vibrations in my pussy.

"You're going to pay for that, Blaze."

"Mmm, can't wait. Let me know where I'm seeing you later, okay? Because I have to get back to work."

"I'm thinking the Naples place. How does that sound?"

"Yeah, okay. I like it there. It's way nicer than my bungalow, but it still feels like home because it's not far from Seal Beach."

"I'll have Joel bring a key over to Abstract before you leave today. I'm sure you'll be heading home before me."

"Don't be ridiculous. I can swing by and pick it up from you. Please don't make a special trip."

"We'll see."

I didn't bother arguing about it further. He was as stubborn as Sebastian when it came to doing things his way, and I'd watched that man work Abbigail over so many times. I always wondered why she fought him on everything when he was just trying to take care of her, and I would think, God, you dumbass, just let him do it.

So now when I heard myself doing the same thing, I had to yank myself back by the collar and stop. And if I were honest with myself, it felt really good to be taken care of to the extent these men went to.

Sean took care of me too, just in a very different way. He and I did so much growing up together. With that came a lot of discovering who I was, what I believed at my core, and what I wanted from my partner. After I figured out what I wanted from a man, he did his best to be that man. It was completely ass backwards when I thought about it now, but that was what happened when you got married young. Neither of us wanted to split up, and inherently, we were very compatible, so it wasn't that big of a stretch. Especially since we were already committed to one another.

The difference with Grant was that I now knew so much more about myself and who I was fundamentally. I knew where I needed a partner to fit into my life and what I needed from another person.

Trying to force someone into being the things you needed when they didn't naturally fit wouldn't really work out for anyone.

★ ★ ★

As decided, Grant and I met at his home in Naples. This was my favorite place the man owned. The Brentwood condo had a lot of potential, if for nothing else but the location. But that place needed to be renovated in the worst way, and my man was a fancy guy and liked his fancy things, so we rarely stayed there.

"Hey, handsome," I said when he answered his phone.

"Hey, beautiful. Are you here?"

I smiled just hearing his voice. I couldn't wait to feel his arms around me. "Yes, just turned on your street."

"Perfect. I'll go open the garage door so you can pull right in."

"Now that's what I call service. I'll see you in a few seconds." I disconnected the call just as he came into view. My God, he took my breath away.

I barely had time to unfasten my seat belt before Grant opened my door and hauled me out of Kendall. The man swept me off my feet and up into his arms. He bumped my door shut with his ass, and I let out a schoolgirl giggle and quickly buried my face in his neck.

"Oh my God," I mumbled into his delicious-smelling skin.

I could just inhale near that spot for the rest of the night and be a happy woman. The distraction of smelling my favorite cologne worked, because my embarrassment morphed into arousal in no time.

When I completed a trail of kisses up to his ear, I whispered, "I can walk."

"No way. I don't want to let you go. Maybe ever." He watched my reaction very closely. Based on my history, I couldn't blame him. He probably thought I would knee him in the balls and make a break for the front door.

Instead, I wrapped my arms around his neck and squeezed a little tighter. With a contented sigh, I husked, "Mmm, okay."

Grant leaned way back to look at me.

"What?" I grinned.

"I don't know. I wanted to be sure you weren't playing a trick on me or that I picked up the right girl out in my garage."

"How awkward would that be right now?" We both chuckled at the thought. "But seriously, do you still have a lot of stray girls coming through your garage that you'd be worried you grabbed the wrong one?"

"Do you really have to ask such nonsense, Rio Katrina?"

"No," I answered quietly and scrunched my nose up. I didn't want to argue, fight, or disagree. Not even in the smallest degree. "I'm still working on me. You know that. I think, overall, though, I'm doing really good, Grant. And I have you to thank for that. I know I have work to put in, and I'm showing up for it. Every single day, I swear I am."

"Baby." He sat on the arm of the sofa and dragged me to stand right in front of him until our noses were almost touching. "You're breathtaking. God, sorry." He gave his head a little shake, and it was so adorable, and—I don't know?

Touching, maybe. To see a man react to my physical presence that way was really overwhelming. I didn't know what to say in response.

"Grant—"

"No, hear me out. Please." Scooping my hands up in his strong ones, he brought my fingers to his lips and delivered a few soft kisses to each hand before speaking again. "I get sidetracked when I look into your eyes because I swear I can see my own heart and soul inside you."

Oh shit. I could already feel the tears stinging the backs of my eyes. What was this all about? I swallowed roughly and pushed those suckers down with all my might and listened very intently. This was not the time to drift off. Even I could tell that.

Grant continued to speak, giving my hands periodic squeezes while he did so. "Rio, you've given me so much of yourself since you lost Sean. You've trusted me to protect you and care for you. You've allowed me to stand by you and support you while you demanded justice for your late husband's death. I've had the honor of being your friend, someone you can talk to, laugh with, and sometimes cry with."

"Grant—"

"Please. Let me get this out. Baby, I've had more than my share up in here lately." He tapped his temple with his index finger a couple of times and then held my gaze for a few moments more before starting to talk. The anticipation was nearly suffocating by the time words came out again.

"You've shared your fears with me and your hopes and dreams for your new, rearranged future. Last but not least, you've allowed me the privilege of touching this magnificent body and the rapture of bringing you pleasure, time and time again."

Grant stroked my bangs back across my forehead, and I let my eyes drift shut while his fingers were in contact with my skin. When he began to speak again, my lids shot open. "I don't know what I've done to deserve any of these things, let alone all of them, but for you to say you have me to thank for being the amazing creature that you are?" He huffed a disbelieving chuckle. "No. No, my beautiful queen. It's all you. I'm just basking in your glory. I don't want to push my luck right now, but this feels like the perfect time for me to tell you—"

"I love you." I blurted the words I'd been trying to tell him for the past ten minutes.

"What did you just say?" Grant asked with a hint of shock or maybe dismay in his tone.

"I love you, Grant Twombley. With every single beat of my heart." I wrapped my arms around his neck and pressed my forehead to his before saying the words a third time. "I love you. Please don't leave me again, though. That nearly broke me."

The smile on his face was so brilliant and pure, it could've illuminated the entire nighttime sky. "Holy shit! I didn't expect this day to end like this."

I climbed onto his lap and straddled his legs with my own. "Oh baby, the day isn't over yet."

CHAPTER TWELVE

GRANT

"Mmm, I'm so glad you said that. We have twelve nights to make up for, remember?" I hardly believed I got the whole tease out, considering she was meting a cruel version of the same with her sexy undulations across my crotch. And damn it, I loved every hot, pulsing second. If she ripped open my slacks and impaled her body on mine right now, it wouldn't be soon enough.

"Is that really how your brain works?" she snarked back. "One night off from having sex is equal to twelve? Christ, are you even going to remember what to do after twelve nights off?"

"Careful now," I growled, wrapping my arm around her waist to hold her close to me. But the little brat squirming against my dick just giggled again—until suddenly she wasn't.

"Oh!" She jolted in my embrace, pushing up from my chest like we were teenagers on the couch and she had to take another shot before we went on. "I have something to show you, mister. I can't believe I almost forgot."

Rio wriggled harder, trying to get some space between our bodies. The mischief of her mood changed the color in her eyes from the normal whiskey to a glowing amber.

"Should I be nervous?" I made my cocked brow as obvious

as the bulge in my pants. "You look like you're up to no good."

"Noooo." She dragged the word out across two beats. "I'm an angel and you know it. Wait here, though. I'll tell you when you can come into the bedroom, okay?"

She tried to get off my lap, but I couldn't bring myself to let her go. "The bedroom?" I drawled. "Well, that's the right direction, at least."

"I won't argue there." Finally, she smacked at my arms that were banded around her middle. "But first you have to let me up."

"Fine, fine," I grumbled and let her scurry off.

While she hummed and fiddled around in the bedroom, I absentmindedly scrolled through emails. I deleted obvious junk and opened a few that looked like I could forward to Reina to handle, not wanting to get involved in complicated communications at the moment. I had no idea what Rio was doing in the other room, but even her light bustling was making my balls clamor.

After ten minutes that felt like a decade, I huffed with impatience and surged to my feet. "Ready or not, woman," I muttered. "Here I—"

She cut me off by distinctly clearing her throat—just before appearing in the doorway with such a flourish.

My phone tumbled out of my limp fingers.

"Mr. Twombley?" she cooed. "You are Mr. Twombley, right?"

For a long moment, I didn't respond. I couldn't. My balls weren't just gentle little playmates in my pants anymore. The two of them were all but choking me.

"Jesus. Fucking. Christ. Woman."

Even then, that was the best thing I could formulate. I was

so glad I had gotten eloquent words out earlier, because now I couldn't be responsible for the piggish caveman words that were tumbling around in my brain. I started toward her, but she held her hand up and gave me a little shake of her head.

"Blaze, what is this?" With a hand gesture, I swept from head to toe and then back again. "You look incredible."

The one confusing part of the sexy outfit was the clipboard she cradled in her arm. Well, that and the pair of glasses.

When did she start wearing glasses?

"Good evening." She made a big show of flipping through some blank pieces of paper on her clipboard. "Are you Mr. Twombley?" Her new stare was gorgeous and wide, blinking expectantly at me from behind those adorable glasses.

Before answering, I walked over to stand a little closer to her. I absolutely had to get a better look at the skimpy outfit she had on. Christ on a caduceus, she'd given Nurse Naughty a magnificent upgrade. The red pinstripes on the thing followed her curves perfectly—at least until the barely-there skirt ended, not even a millimeter past the point of covering her pussy. Holy shit. I couldn't wait to see what was going on around the back side. It was why I'd finally found the strength to walk over— until I realized she was still waiting on my answer.

"Oh yeah," I said, thumbing back to myself with a rough jerk. "That's me."

"Good. You're right on time. Please come with me." She spun in the direction of the bedroom and took about two steps then stopped abruptly. I almost plowed right into her because I was so obsessed with her ass in that little, tiny, tantalizing skirt.

"Ohhh . . . sorry." She gulped when noticing the hungry look on my face. "I almost forgot. Did anyone collect your co-pay?"

"My co-pay?"

"Yes, for your office visit with the doctor today." She gave me a wink to let me know this was all her way of a little role-playing fun, just in case I'd missed the setup. But right now, I swore not to miss a goddamned thing. This was too good. So very good. Just the potent healing I needed.

"Ohhh, right. My co-pay." Thinking quickly, I motioned back toward the living room. "The other girl said I could take care of that on my way out."

Rio made a disapproving face and shook her head. With those sexy glasses on, she made my dick twitch in my boxers. These damn games of hers always got to me in the strangest ways.

"Well, she's new and doesn't know what she's talking about." She looked at her clipboard again, and all I could think about was spanking her ass with that thing. Hell, yes. It was so going to happen by the end of the night. "I need to collect your two hundred dollars right now."

She held her flat palm right under my nose and waited. I looked back, acting my way through incredulous ire. "Two hundred dollars?" I blurted. "I was just at the doctor's office yesterday. My co-pay was not two hundred dollars."

She gave me a sympathetic nod. "That was probably your primary care doctor. This is a specialist. This co-pay is different."

She thrust her hand in my face again, and I grabbed it, startling her to the point of squealing. The sound was so delicious, all I could think about was causing it again.

"Listen, lady." I twisted her arm around to the small of her back and spun her at the same time, pressing her face against the wall in the hallway just outside the bedroom. Her clipboard clattered to the floor beside our feet. "It's very rude to shove things in people's faces. Do you want me to show you how rude it is?" I pushed my knee between her thighs, and she whimpered. "Is that a yes? Or do you want my damn co-pay?"

She was already panting into the wall. And I thought the sound of her little yelp was the best thing I'd hear all night. "Just give me the money or I'll get in trouble," she snapped out, keeping up the game.

Without releasing her, I reached into my back pocket, pulled out my wallet, and slipped it into her free hand. "Take what you need while I see what you have under this skirt."

"No."

"Pardon me?"

"No. I can't let you do that. I could lose my job. Just get the money out yourself."

"When I tell your boss how rude you've been, you might lose your job." I relaxed my hold on her, then backed away completely. My cock was making an obscene tent in the front of my slacks, and I reached down into my waistband to rearrange things before opening my wallet. Rio's gaze was trained on every move.

"How much was it again?"

When she spoke, her voice was dry and scratchy. "Two..." She swallowed once, then again. "Two hundred." While I was flipping through the bills in my wallet, I heard her mumble, "Asshole."

I shot my eyes up to hers with lightning speed. "What did you just say?"

"Um...pardon?"

"Did you just call me an asshole?"

"Of course not, Mr. Twombley."

I narrowed my eyes at her. She narrowed hers back. I had to bite my cheek to keep from bursting out laughing. This little shit was going to be the death of me. In the meantime, I was going to live the best, happiest life I could've ever hoped to live.

"Do you need a receipt for this?" she asked when I finally handed her the money.

"Yes. My boss is a real jackass. He likes to know where all his money goes."

She picked up her clipboard and looked at her pretend paperwork again. "Oh, you work for Shark Enterprises." She whistled low and long and then said, "Swanky. But I've heard that guy is a real egomaniac. His second-in-command, too. It must be a shit show around there. Like, every day."

"You have no idea."

"So what brings you in today? You can sit here." She motioned toward the bed.

"Do you want me to get undressed?" I started unbuttoning the top button of my dress shirt.

"Pardon me?" Rio asked, shifting from foot to foot enough that the dress's hem began giving me a peekaboo at her pretty triangle again.

"You say that a lot," I volleyed but didn't bother meeting her gaze again. If the woman was going to wear an ensemble that showed off the gathering droplets on her sex, she was going to get men gawking at her crotch instead of her face.

"Well, you're very presumptuous," she cracked in return. "Do you normally strip down at the doctor's office?"

"I guess it depends what I'm there for. What does your cute little cunt—umm, clipboard—say the reason for my visit is? Just curious."

She pretended to scan her papers once again. When she

looked up, she was melodramatically somber. "Mr. Twombley, this is a very serious problem. I don't know if we can help you here."

I couldn't help but chuckle. "What is it?"

"This says you have a time shift problem, where one day seems like twelve. And that's not—"

I couldn't take it anymore. I grabbed her so fast around the waist that she shrieked as I threw her on the bed. At once, I covered her with my body. As I nuzzled my way into her cleavage, pushing down the costume's flimsy zipper along the way, she was a mass of soft limbs and intense laughter beneath me. All the better to raise my head and plunge my mouth over hers with all the arousal and adoration that brimmed from me like a jar of shot stickers in her make-believe doctor's office.

"You're a fucking riot, you know that?" I said to her between those consuming kisses. "But these glasses... Save these, woman. I'm digging these glasses."

She flashed me with a prim grin. "Whatever you say, Dr. Twombley."

"Ohhh. Dr. Twombley now, hmm?"

As my eyebrows leapt, she gave hers a good waggle. "If the promotion fits..."

I shifted my lips to the end of her nose. "What the hell makes you think of this stuff, I'll never know. Do you have a running inspiration list, or—"

"Are you going to keep talking or put your dick in me?"

I reared up, almost laughing yet again. But that'd ruin what her snarky, sexy syntax had just done to every inch of my clamoring cock.

"You know what? Maybe I'll just shove my dick into that sassy mouth of yours instead. And give me my two hundred dollars back, you little shit. Where did you put it? There aren't any pockets on this outfit."

I leaned back to look at the skirt that was all bunched up around her waist from her thrashing around beneath me. The prim white bodice was nearly ruined too—but I didn't imagine the manufacturer made this stuff for long-term wear and tear.

"You can have it back if you can find it," Rio said with smirking challenge. "How's that?"

"Hmm, okay." I sat back on my heels, pinning her legs down under me. With one side of her dress in each hand, I gave a solid yank. Most of the zipper, as well as several flimsy snaps, went flying.

"Grant!"

"You didn't say it still had to be wearable. Now be quiet. I've heard enough from you. Do you like this bra?"

"Yes! Don't you dare rip it, Tree! I swear to God, I will hurt you."

"That's funny, little brat. I mean, given your current position. Where's my money?" I dug my fingers into her ribs and tickled her, and she shrieked so loudly I worried for the integrity of my eardrums.

"Holy shit, woman! I've never heard a noise like that come from a human before." I fell to the bed beside her, laughing then as hard as she was. "Oh my God. I may be hearing-impaired from that. I'm going to need that co-pay for real now."

We both started laughing all over again.

When she finally calmed down, she hovered above me in her sexy white lace bra and shredded naughty nurse attire. "Do you know how much I love you?" she asked.

"Show me," I demanded, my voice husky because I was so ramped up by this woman. I lifted my hips and pulled my pants all the way down, then kicked them free when they were past my knees. "Hop on, girl. Put my cock inside your sweet body, right the hell now." I held my hard shaft straight up for her, staring without blinking as she swung her leg over and mounted me. "Fuck, Rio. So sexy, baby..."

"Oh my God, you feel so good," she said as she eased partially down my length.

"I swear, I'm never going to get tired of this cunt. You're so tight around me."

"You better not get tired of me." She sealed the dictate by leaning down and kissing me. At first, it was just a light kiss, giving way to her luxurious sigh as I filled her completely for the first time that day.

"Never," I promised, but I gave up on forming any more words as our movements picked up a quicker rhythm. At the same time, our kissing grew in intensity. Eventually I sat up, cradling her back in my arms as I swung my legs over the side of the bed to gain some leverage on the floor. The extra force helped me to fuck up into her, my strokes getting deeper and harsher by the second. She responded by bending her knees alongside my thighs and moved with me. It was heaven. I was so close to exploding inside her...

But not yet.

One of the best things about being so much bigger than Rio was I could just move her where I wanted her, and she couldn't do a whole lot about it. I didn't want to come yet, and if she kept squeezing me the way she was, I was going to end my visit at the doctor's office way too soon. So I moved my arms beneath her in order to cradle her ass before standing all the way up. The loss I felt the moment our bodies were no longer joined was more profound than I would've thought possible.

But I planned on fixing the situation fast.

Once I lowered her back on the bed, I knelt over her and removed my shirt. Then it was time to get her fully bare.

I took my time about the act, savoring every inch of her skin as I finally revealed it. When we were both completely naked, I got settled between her thighs.

"Grant," she protested. "You don't have to."

I stopped that ridiculous statement with one stern look up the length of her body. "No, actually, I do. For my own sanity, I do. You have no idea how much I think about your pussy when I'm not physically touching it in one way or another. It's a wonder I get anything done in a day." I spread her pink folds open and inspected the treasure before me. "In fact, I wanted to see if you could start coming to work with me?"

At once, she burst out laughing. "Yes, I think that can be arranged. And I don't think Sebastian would mind that at all. Do you?"

I met her gaze from my current location. "Are you kidding? Do you know how many times the entire floor has heard that man ejaculate?"

"No. Stop. Just stop. God, fuck." I felt her disgusted shudder beneath me. "For the love of God, Grant. I don't think I can recover from ohhh, oh-kay, never mind. Shit, that feels good."

Wisely, I buried my face in her pussy mid-rant or she would've gotten herself all worked up over Bas and there would've been no going back.

No going back.

All thoughts for a later time, though, because I had to focus to prevent my gorgeous little nymph from thrashing around so wildly. But while I banded my arm around her abdomen a little tighter, I didn't let up on relentlessly strumming her G-spot with my long index and middle fingers. "Keep up all that bucking, Blaze, and you're going to make yourself squirt," I chided.

"Me?" she spat. "Make myself—" She stopped again, panting hard. "Okay, then you need to—oh hell, Grant, please, just—"

"Just what, baby?"

She cut loose with a full scream-moan thing that had to be the most erotic sound I'd ever heard from the woman. "Stop! Just stop! It's too much!"

"My sweet, sexy Blaze. I'm not doing anyth—"

"Bullshit!"

"What? You're doing all the work. Be still and relax into it. You know it feels better."

"Lies. All. L-L-Lies," she stuttered.

"I wouldn't lie to you, baby. But I so know you need to come. I can see how ready you are. Look at all of this." I licked her from bottom to top, loving the entire experience. Her new high-pitched moan just made everything better.

"Please, Grant. Please. Why do you make me crazy like this? Finish me off, please."

"Sit up a little, Blaze. Just a little. Put this pillow behind you." I grabbed a pillow from close to the headboard and propped her torso up a bit higher. "Can you see me?" I asked but got no response. "Answer me," I demanded.

"Yes. I see you," she said, eyelids heavy with lust.

"Then watch me stroke myself while I eat your pussy."

"Grant! Oh God, yes. You're so hot doing that. Looks so good." She flopped back into the pillow.

"Keep looking at me," I snarled as heat coiled in my balls

and fought its way up my shaft. Getting to lap up the honey from her channel . . . it was damn near icing on the cake. Literally. "Look how hard I am for you."

I knew this girl better than she knew herself at this point. When she sat up again, I fisted myself a little tighter, moved my hand a little faster. And the whole time kept my mouth working her pussy the way I knew she liked. It was taking serious coordination, but she was going to have an epic climax, I was sure of it.

"Grant! I'm coming . . ." she barely breathed, but I knew she was gone. When she had those silent orgasms, they were far more intense than when she moaned and cried out. Sometimes the silent ones scared me, though, because she looked like she blacked out for a moment or two.

While she still had her eyes closed, enjoying the last of her orgasm, I quickly stood over her and pumped my shaft the last few times necessary and spurted my own release across the inside of her thighs. When I was done, I had to resist rubbing the fluid into her skin like moisturizer until it disappeared into her flesh, somehow making my essence a part of her. I knew it was a totally barbaric notion, but the intense feelings I had for this woman turned me into an animal, and I couldn't deny it. I wasn't even trying to.

We decided to order in and ate sushi out of temporary containers at the coffee table in the living room. Rio had a cooking channel playing on the television, but we had the sound down low because neither of us were watching it. We were more interested in sampling each other's dinner, laughing, talking, and just spending time together.

By bedtime, we were exhausted. With Rio just having gone back to Abstract this morning, she wasn't used to the alarm going off at fuck-me-o'clock. If I were honest, it had been difficult for me to get up this morning too.

"Ready for bed?" she asked after we traded a bunch of yawns. "I have to be at the kitchen bright and early, so I'm going to go in." She waved a hand toward the bedroom.

We weren't completely familiar with each other's workweek habits because we hadn't had many sleepovers while she'd been working. There had only been two or three that I could remember.

"Yep. I'll be right behind you. I just want to lock everything up and set the security alarm." While explaining, I turned off the television and put the throw pillows back in place on the sofa. "Do you want a bottle of water for overnight?"

"Yes, please. Thank you for asking," Rio called from the bedroom.

She was already pulling the covers back on the bed when I walked into the room, two water bottles in hand. Instead of handing her one, I pulled her against my body for one last upright embrace before we said good night. I didn't think I would ever be able to stop touching her. This was why newly dating couples were so sickening to be around. Now I was that guy, and I still couldn't stop myself from doing it. In fact, I just grinned and buried my face in her short hair and held her against me that much longer.

I was asleep the moment my head hit the pillow. And it must have been a deep, unconscious sleep, because before I knew it, I was waking up to get ready for work. Rio was still fast asleep beside me, but if she didn't get up, she would be late as well.

"Morning," I mumbled.

I didn't hate mornings, necessarily. But I didn't love

them either. It usually took me an entire cup of coffee and a hot shower before I was ready for meaningful conversation. Somehow, I already knew that was okay by her. But not okay? Her still refusing to budge at my gentle nudge.

"Babe. Come on, we have to get up and get to work. You want to shower first? Or we could together?"

Well, that idea had me perking up a little quicker than usual. Normally when I woke up with a woman beside me, I just wanted her to leave. Morning shower sex was rarely an option I entertained. With Rio, everything was a whole new world. A brilliant set of possibilities. In this case, a little better than brilliant...

I slipped my hand beneath the covers, hoping to rouse her in more than the conventional sense. If I could get her body on board with the shower-for-two idea first...

But something wasn't right. I knew it as soon as I touched her.

"What the fuck?"

I whipped the covers back. Panic was both an ice storm and forest fire in my blood. My chest pumped, battling for air. Massive fail. Oxygen was as rare as coherent thought.

I was on my feet in a flash. They were sweaty—yeah, my goddamned feet—and I slipped but recovered before falling. Frantically, I glared from one side of the room to the other.

What the hell was happening?

The room. I was examining my bedroom, but nothing was familiar anymore. The furniture... it was all nearly gone. The walls... the very air... smelled metallic and cold. And that definitely wasn't my gorgeous Blaze lying so still in the bed.

I rushed to flip on the lights, but nothing happened. The room stayed dark and damp.

"What the fuck?"

My words had no volume. I couldn't even hear them as echoes in my head.

Wait. Why is it so cold and damp in here?

We must have left the slider open on the third floor last night. We'd sat out on the deck before dinner and must've forgotten to close it when we came in. Being this close to the Pacific, the whole place got dewy overnight. I'd made that mistake once before, and it took days to dry the place out. The housekeeper lectured me for three weeks afterward.

But . . . that still didn't explain . . .

Rio. My God, Rio!

"Rio!" I felt my way back to the bed and found the side where I had slept. I put my knee up on the mattress to crawl over to her. Only . . . it wasn't a mattress I knelt on. It was so damn dark in the room, I couldn't see anything. I felt around beneath me, and nothing made sense.

Until it did.

"No!"

I could hear my voice now. A roar full of sorrow and horror and devastation.

"No! This is not happening!"

I was frantic to move whatever it was—an arm, a leg—I couldn't tell, but I knew it wasn't her because it was big. Much bigger than Rio's body at least. And I knew the feel of her body, and she had been right beside me all night. I'd felt her there. I swore I'd kill those motherfuckers if they hurt her. If they took the one amazing thing I finally had in my life and hurt her . . .

I'd kill those goddamned barbarians. I'd haul them off their pathetic boat and kill them with my bare hands. First, I would get her back, then I would end them. Each and every one of them.

But there were more bodies now. They were getting harder to move because they were stacking up faster than I could maneuver on my own. But I had to help her. If Rio was still on the bed beneath all those bodies, she'd be buried alive. She'd die of suffocation beneath an avalanche of dead bodies, and I'd never be able to save her.

"Someone help me! Help me!"

I shouted it into the darkness while pulling on the leg closest to me, fighting to move it out of the way. Then I went for the next one, and the next one. I must have worked for hours that way, but for each corpse I moved to get to Rio, another two layers were added on top.

I was desperate. Devastated. For the first time since my mother's death, I openly sobbed. Rio was going to die right in front of me, just like my mother, and there was nothing I'd be able to do to save her.

Just like my mother.

In the distance, I could hear her. Her screams were muffled, but she was calling my name. I launched myself on top of the closest body, tugging and yanking the thing by the neck.

"Grant! Grant!"

"I know, baby." And once more, my mouth was moving but making no sound. Not carrying a decibel of volume. "I'm coming for you. I promise, Blaze..."

"Stop!" she called out. But that made no sense at all.

"Rio?" I yelled back. "Where are you, baby? Just hold on—"

"Grant! Damn it, stop! You're hurting me. You're going to break my neck!"

"No. No. I'm going to get you out of there, baby. I promise."

"Let ... go ... of me!"

There was something different to her protest now. In the pauses ...

The moments she gave herself time to gasp for air ...

"Asshole. Get off me. Wake the fuck up and get off me!"

A bolt of lightning struck me right between the legs. I flew across the cargo hold of the ship and landed on my back, staring up at the ceiling. My breathing was so erratic, it sounded like a woman's crying. Blinding sunlight came through the portholes. The crew must've felt generous and allowed fresh air and light in for the day.

"What the fuck was that?" Rio's voice was scratchy at half the volume it normally carried.

Cold water soaked my clothes, jolting me fully awake. I sat up and looked around, dazed and confused on the bedroom floor of my Naples condo.

Rio loomed above me, looking madder than I'd ever seen her. She held an empty water bottle in her hand, water still dripping off the rim. "Well? What do you have to say, damn it? Answer me."

"Huh?" I sputtered, scrubbing a trembling hand down my soaked face. "Answer? About ... what?"

"I said, what the fuck was that all about?"

"And I'm saying I don't know," I retorted. "Just calm down, okay? We'll figure this out."

She threw the water bottle aside. "Gee thanks, Sherlock. I feel a hell of a lot better."

I circled my gaze around. "What the hell is going on? Why am I on the floor? Why is all the bedding on the floor? And Jesus Christ, baby. What happened to your neck?"

I surged to my feet and rushed to her, but she skittered

back until she thumped into the wall. The terrified look on her face told me everything I needed to know.

I froze right where I was but couldn't stop my concern. "Holy fuck. Oh, baby..."

On pure instinct, I reached out to her again. With a shivering yelp, she flattened herself against the wall even more.

"Are you okay?" I whispered, finally dropping my arm. She just stared at me. "Please, Rio, just tell me if you're okay." I clawed the back of my neck and held on for dear life but never took my eyes off her. "Do you need medical attention? I understand why you don't want me near you right now."

Tears flooded my eyes, but the last thing she needed to see was me falling apart on top of everything else. I swallowed roughly and tried to get a handle on the emotional pain choking me like a vise.

Not about you right now, man. Not about you.

"I'm fine."

The small voice that emanated from her was more terrifying than her fury. At once, I hated it. And I hated myself for being the cause of it. I hated looking at how she scooped up the water bottle from the floor and then clutched it like a damn life preserver.

Because now she needed saving. From me.

"I'm going to call Elijah to come stay with you so you feel safe. I'll leave when he gets here." I studied the weave of the soaked area rug beneath my feet while I spoke. I couldn't bear the thought of leaving her, but I didn't know what else to offer her right then. The way she kept cowering... It was tearing my heart out, vein by painful vein.

"No. You'll do no such thing." She raised her chin in defiance, even though her voice was hoarse. I tossed all my vital organs into the shredder as soon as her desperate tears began. "Don't you dare leave me, Grant Twombley. You said you would never leave me!"

"I'm so sorry, Blaze." I took one step toward her but forced myself to stop. That was enough for now. "Please," I begged. "Do you at least hear what I'm saying? You don't have to accept my apology, but please at least hear me giving it."

One hot tear rolled down my cheek, and I dashed it away, hoping she hadn't seen my weakness. "Please, Rio. Know that I am so sorry. I would never willingly hurt you." But that fucker of a tear was joined by another. And then another. I put my whole face in the cradle of my hands and then fought to wipe the damn things away. I couldn't keep up with how fast they were falling, and I loathed the fact that she was seeing me like this.

When I finally looked up, all I could do was stare at her. I felt as terrified as she looked.

How did the best night I could remember in my whole life go so wrong?

"Can I get you some tea? It might help your throat feel better." I made some awkward gesture toward my throat, as if she wasn't aware where I just tried to strangle her while she slept beside me. "Please . . . let me do something for you." Anything. Just some sort of penance that would start healing the gaping wound in my chest.

"Grant, stop," she rebuked. "You don't have to wait on me. I'm not going to be able to go into work like this unless I leave right now and go home for different clothes that will cover my neck."

She winced after saying it, but why bother hiding the facts? We were going to have to stare at the reality of what I'd done until the marks healed anyway.

"Can't you just take the day off?" I asked in what I thought was an innocent suggestion.

"No, I can't just take the day off!" she barked suddenly, and I fought not to noticeably recoil.

It wasn't that I was that sensitive. I just wasn't used to her biting my head off. But I couldn't say I didn't deserve it.

Rio sighed heavily and let her shoulders drop. "It's only my second day back. What would that look like if I was already taking the day off? Everyone already thinks I'm a flaky basket case. I don't want to always prove them right, you know?"

I huffed. "Damn it, Rio. People don't think—"

"Just don't, okay? Not right now. I'm going to head out so I can go by my place and get some different clothes. I'll check in with you later in the day."

While I was trying to figure out the safest way to say goodbye to her, she had already turned and walked out. I heard her punch in the code to disarm the security alarm, and then she slipped out the door that led to the garage. I'd completely forgotten she'd parked her Fiat in there when she'd come over.

How had that been less than twenty-four hours ago?

My fucking God, what a difference a day made.

CHAPTER THIRTEEN

RIO

The garage door closed, and I put Kendall into first gear. Clutch out, pressure down on the gas pedal in equal measures, and pull out of driveway. Thank God it was all second nature at that point, because I was blinded by the tears swelling my eyes and the emotions clouding my thoughts.

The streets of Naples Island were quiet at the early hour, but I was still mindful of the low speed limit. While the neighborhood was perfectly manicured and meticulously groomed, the residents here did not tolerate rule breakers.

But did they tolerate heartbreakers? Because one of those lived among them, and he might have been the biggest thief I'd ever met. Grant Twombley stole my heart in just under a year, and now, possibly my sanity as well.

I'd begged him not to leave me. Not to hurt me. Begged. Him. Yet here I was, driving to my house in the early dawn's light, basically a rolling version of the walk of shame. Oh yeah, complete with tear-streaked cheeks and puffy raccoon eyes.

But I wasn't heartbroken about how he'd marred my neck. Yes, that episode was scary as shit and had earned him a spot on his therapist's couch as soon as possible—but I was able to wake him up, and I was, for the most part, physically okay. The marks on my skin would fade.

The dents in my heart were much deeper.

Dents that felt more like gashes. Hurt I'd never seen coming.

So where did we go from here?

The answer felt too huge to digest—even taking an eat-the-elephant-a-bit-at-a-time approach. All that accomplished right now was breaking everything down into other questions.

Was Grant going to take his mental state more seriously now? If so, did that mean we were on hold until he figured shit out? Would he only be satisfied seeing me if we had supervised playdates? Did I get to have any part at all in his recovery from this trauma? Did he respect me at least that much?

Only one thing was certain right now—and that was the uncertainty of it all. I didn't have a single answer for any of those and certainly wouldn't have them by the time I got to work. So I switched on an audiobook and focused on the things I could control: starting with navigating traffic as I got on the freeway to make sure I got to my destination in one piece.

By the time I arrived at the kitchen, the couple starring in my romance novel convinced me there were much worse things that could go wrong in a relationship than one bizarre nightmare. Maybe, just maybe, I was overdramatizing things. Hopefully Grant would call in a few hours, and we'd trade one-liners until laughing ourselves free of this morning's dismal cloud.

Yeah, I liked that attitude as much as the old, comfy Chucks into which I slipped my feet before going inside.

The place was already bustling, just like yesterday morning. For a second, that had me curious. Had Hannah decided we needed to staff-up at an earlier time and forgot to tell me? Abbi and I used to open the doors at four fifteen a.m.

It had been plenty of time to have everything ready and out the door for the lunch deliveries. If something had come up at the last minute, we were running around like chickens with our heads cut off, but there was no way to predict those situations no matter what time we came in. Eventually, we decided that it didn't make sense to be coming in any earlier. I would talk with Hannah about it and listen to her thought process. That didn't necessarily mean we would continue to do things the same way, but I would hear her out.

"Hi, Rio!" someone called when I came in the door.

"Good morning, boss lady!" another person shouted.

"Morning, Rio Grande," called the youngest member of our team, Jorge. He was an adorable guy, originally from San Juan, in LA on a work visa and hoping to apply for citizenship in the United States. Everyone at Abstract got along with him really well, and Hannah told me he'd asked her out, but she'd politely declined. That was probably for the best—only rare people could be both work friends and lovers—but the more I got to know the woman, the stronger I hoped that fate had true love up its sleeve for her.

I still had mountains of paperwork to get to, so I got situated at my desk and dug in. I knew Hannah had her routine, and I would see her when she came out after she did her daily inventory in the walk-in cooler.

About a half hour later, I finally caught sight of her. More accurately, Hannah was eyeballing me. Intently. Determinedly. Unhappily. While making a direct beeline for me.

Well . . . crap.

I sat up straighter, forgetting the pile of invoices in front of me. This was probably—no, definitely—the first time I'd seen an expression on the woman's face other than upbeat cheer.

"Hey. Morning." I kept my voice very low and very unassuming. "You okay? You look upset."

"Hi." She forced a smile, and I didn't like the feeling in my stomach. At all. "Do you have a sec?"

"Of course. Always. Have a seat. Just put my purse on the fl—"

"No. Not in here."

"Okay." I extended the word, grateful that it gave me a chance to push in a light laugh. "Then in your dome of silence, Special Agent Farsey?"

I wasn't congratulating myself for the humor when she darted her eyes from one side of the room to the other as if expecting danger to spontaneously appear. "Can you come outside to my car?"

I found myself looking around too but quickly nodded. "Yeah, sure."

Hannah expelled a rush of air before pulling aside a staff member with a blond-and-pink ponytail. "Hey, Brinn? Rio and I are going out to my car to go get some stuff I brought from home. We'll be right back in, okay? Answer the phone if it rings."

Once outside, I could barely get a look at my normally amicable friend. My nerves were really frazzled. Hannah never acted so cagey. Maybe it was me. Maybe it was the morning I'd already been through. So admittedly, I could've been reading the entire situation wrong.

"Hannah?" I had to power walk to keep up with her. Of course, she was parked in the last row of cars, too. By the time we rounded the back of her cute little BMW 1 series and she popped the trunk, I was close to panting. "Hey, is something going on?"

My friend bent down, ostensibly to get something out of her trunk, but then gestured for me to follow. Well, hell. Was her *something* actually my fault? Was she going to stuff me in that trunk too?

I gave my head a firm shake. My word. Grant and his strange dream were rubbing off in all the wrong ways.

Unless…they weren't. Before he fully woke up, he'd been babbling shit about my safety. He hadn't had a chance to explain everything to me yet either. Maybe I should've let him. Based on his behavior, I was definitely skittish too, even if I didn't understand why. On my way to work, I'd put it all in a neat little box with a tight-fitting lid so I could get through the day. There would be plenty of time to unleash the beast later.

"Hannah, tell me what the hell is going on or I'm going back inside. Right now." I said it firmly and felt a little bad about my tone when she straightened and I caught sight of the new look on her face. Something had her spooked too.

"Okay. Okay." She took a deep breath and then exhaled through pursed lips. "Maybe this is nothing and there's a very logical explanation for these things I'm about to tell you."

"Hannah, please."

"All right." She seemed to mutter it more to herself than me. "You're right, you're right. I just need to—" After fortifying herself with another deep breath, she looked ready to move on. "Yesterday, I went to the walk-in after we were finished for the day. Everyone else had left, so I made sure the main doors were locked, like I always do if I'm here alone. You and Abbigail really drilled that into me when I first started here." She nodded soundly like she was proud of the fact.

Intuition had me adding an approving dip of my head. "Good, I'm glad you do that. Better safe than sorry."

"But I remembered seeing some canned goods up on the top shelf of the walk-in that needed the expiration dates checked?" She presented it like a question, maybe to make sure I knew what task she was talking about.

I nodded again, indicating that I did. There were so many things that had to be done around a commercial kitchen. The chores never stopped.

"And I knew if I didn't do it then, while nothing else was going on, it would never get done. You know how it gets around here—"

"Hannah!" I had to stop her or she would continue justifying her actions for ten more minutes. Clearly my young friend was a nervous rambler.

"Okay, sorry. Sorry." She took another deep breath, exhaling through her mouth so she could continue at a much calmer pace. "So, I got the stepladder out and climbed up to the shelf."

"All right. But why did you bring me out to the parking lot to tell me this? I'm really lost."

"Okay." She tried to take another deep breath but ended it on a weird wince. Before I could even begin deciphering it, she said, "While I was up on the ladder, someone locked me in the walk-in. I was stuck inside there for about forty minutes."

"Wait. What?" I sagged against the car behind me. Fortunately, it was Kendall. "Who?" I demanded at once. "Did you see exactly who did that? They will lose their job immediately. That's not something we take lightly, Hannah. It's very dangerous."

"Wait. There's more." She stepped over and grabbed my forearm, drawing me to finally focus on her face. Tears were flooding her eyes, despite her best efforts to clamp them back.

Of course, her effort was a giant fail. They spilled down her cheeks in mascara-tinted streaks.

I pulled her into my embrace and held her there while she cried softly. Her whole body was trembling, but I needed to hear the rest of this story. After a few more minutes, she straightened up and swiped under her eyes, removing any smudged makeup. Cry time was over for Miss Farsey, apparently.

With a very steady voice, she said, "Something very fishy is going on, Rio."

"Okay," I said slowly. "Tell me all of it, then. Everything that happened. How did you get out of the cooler? Did you call someone? And why the hell didn't you call me?"

"I didn't have my phone on me." A sheepish flush suffused her high cheekbones. "It was setting on Abbi's desk. I usually put it there during the day. I mean, right now I do. You know, while she's not here?"

"Of course. Of course."

"After this, though, I'm going to get a chef's jacket with bigger pockets so I can keep it on me." She nodded in approval of her own plan, and I had to smile a little at her sweet habits.

"Okay, so how did you get out of the cooler?"

She shrugged. "Someone eventually unlocked the door again."

"Huh?" I folded my arms. "Okay, so who? And didn't you say everyone had gone home for the day?"

"Which is true, to the best of my knowledge," she asserted. "And before you ask, I totally checked all the outside doors first. You and Abbi have ingrained that part into me. They were all still locked when I got out of the cooler."

"Are you absolutely certain it was locked when you were

inside? Did you try your hardest to get out?"

Well, that pissed her off. Her twisted features told me as much. "I'm not a freaking idiot, Rio. Of course I tried to get out." And then the biting syllables of her verbal assault. "I was freaking out and yelling and pounding on the thing like a maniac."

She closed her eyes before a maverick tear ran down her cheek. When I reached out and wiped it away for her, she popped her eyes back open.

And . . . wow.

Gone was the capable, talented chef that worked for me on any other given day. The woman before me looked more like a seven-year-old little girl freshly woken from a bad dream.

"I was so scared," she admitted with a shivering, tiny voice. "I almost had a panic attack until I remembered all my training and calmed myself down. It was truly terrifying."

"All right, all right. I didn't mean to insinuate you were dumb. I'm sorry. What are you talking about, though, remembered your *training*? Do you have a panic disorder?"

"I shouldn't have said anything about that. It's not what's important here." She waved her hand carelessly, like swatting away a fly.

"Hannah," I insisted. "It is important, just like the rest of the story is. You're trying to pull one over on the wrong person when it comes to a mental health challenge. I'm just saying." But as soon as it was clear she wouldn't elaborate further on the panic topic, I went back to the original issue at hand. "So someone has a key to our building who shouldn't. I'll have the locks changed on all the doors. We rent this space, so it could be any number of past occupants. I don't know if the landlord really changes the locks between tenants, you know?" Now

I was the one looking to see if I made sense—a feeling that worsened as soon as Hannah spoke up again.

"Wait. There's more."

"You've got to be kidding." I groaned, feeling suddenly stuck in that damn *Groundhog Day* movie. But this version wasn't cute or funny. "All right. What else?"

"When I came out of the cooler, I ran to my desk to get my phone. But it was already opened past the lock screen. I don't know how, because I have a password on it."

"Odd," I muttered as I had to force my next question out. "Was it just basically open to your home screen? If that's the case, maybe it was just a strange glitch from a provider update or—"

"Oh, no," she interjected quickly. "It was open to my photos app."

I gulped, though it did little to ease my suddenly dry throat. "Well, shit. Someone was looking through your pictures?"

"Not the pictures," Hannah stated. Her throat convulsed, emulating my nervous action. "There was a video pulled up on the screen."

"Of what? God, I'm already afraid to know." I narrowed my eyes, knowing damn well it was going to be bad. The rush of fear to my brain and the pounding pulse in my throat already told me so.

"The video was of me, inside the walk-in. Whoever locked me in there was somehow videotaping it too."

And damn my raging instincts for being so right this time.

"Do you still have that video? Is it still on your phone?" I asked.

"It should be. I didn't delete it."

"Okay. Don't touch your phone at all. Don't do anything

with your phone at all. I realize you have since then, but don't do anything else, now, okay? I'm going to call someone to come and get it."

"Rio."

"Yeah?"

"There's more."

"Oh, for fuck's sake." I sucked in a deep breath through my nose, praying to God and anyone like him that I had strength to deal with more. "Okay, tell me."

I endured about twenty seconds of her skeptical stare, like she debated if I could really handle her new information bomb, before letting the wind have a good chunk of my cool.

"Hannah, stop fucking around and tell me. You have no idea the kind of morning I've already had." But when hearing my own voice, I winced. "Shit. Sorry. I'm really sorry."

"Well, I might understand the kind of morning you've had," she replied.

"What do you mean?" Now I really didn't like where this was headed. At all.

"After the video footage of me in the walk-in, there were still shots of Mr. Twombley. Like a slideshow."

"Mr. Twombley?" My echo was strained, having to make its way past the disbelief that stormed my senses. I almost repeated it again, as if a third incantation was going to render the reality—and my terror from it—invisible. "Pictures . . . of Grant?"

"Yes. And Rio . . . those shots didn't look good. I mean . . ."

"What?" I was demanding but at least not a bitch about it now. "They didn't look good . . . in what way, exactly?"

She raised her head, exposing her blue eyes at their fearful widest. "Do you know where he is right now?" she rasped.

I didn't hide my double take. It was such a strange and personal question. Of course I knew where he was and told her so with a shaky nod. Thankfully, she didn't need more than that to continue.

"Oh, thank God. Because in these photos, it looked like he was being held prisoner or something. His hands were bound behind his back, and he was blindfolded." Unbelievably, her gaze flared bigger. The rest of her expression was a combination of dismay and fear. "But Rio, as disturbing as that all was . . ." She shook her head and covered her mouth with a shaky hand. When she finally lowered it, she uttered, "It wasn't even the creepiest part."

I wrapped both arms around myself. It was galling not being able to hug my friend instead, but I couldn't think about trying to keep her together when it felt like my own pieces were about to crumble into a huge pile on the sun-drenched asphalt.

"Tell me." I had to order it at her. I didn't have any room for polite requests now.

"In every picture . . . it looked like there were a bunch of dead bodies all around him."

For about ten more seconds, I didn't move. Then I promptly turned away from Hannah's adorable car and threw up.

With my body folded in half at the waist, I lost every single thing that had been in my stomach. Thankfully there wasn't much, but the retching went on for long after the contents had been evacuated.

Once I calmed down, I told Hannah to go back inside so the rest of the employees didn't start wondering what was going on. I reminded her not to touch her phone until I came to get her. I needed to make a few calls.

The first number I dialed was Grant's.

He picked up after the first ring. I felt terrible for calling him at the office because I knew how busy he was.

"Blaze. Baby, how are you? I'm so glad you called." I heard a door close in the background, and his voice changed to one I recognized from other events in our history. The one he used just with me when he was caring for me with his careful compassion and love. "You doing okay?"

"Yeah, I'm all right." Shit. I could feel the damn tears coming on already. Just the sound of his voice gave me unspoken permission to lean on him. "Well, no, I guess I'm not."

"What's wrong? Is it your throat? Baby, I'm so sorry. I can come get you, and we can go have it looked at."

"No, no, it's not that." I swiped the tears off my cheeks before getting into my own car. I needed to sit down while I talked to him.

"I really don't mind," Grant offered.

"Grant. Hey. You need to listen to me."

"I *am* listening."

"Something's happened at the kitchen. But I don't think I should talk about it over the phone, okay?"

"Oh." He paused for a few seconds while he processed what I was saying. Finally he asked, "Are you okay?"

"Yes, I'm fine. But I think it has something to do with that dream you had. Well, in a way. Maybe more than one. I mean, scary ways, Grant. At least I think..." I huffed and palmed my forehead. "I don't know! Maybe I'm just being melodramatic again."

"I'm not follow—" He stopped midsentence and was quiet for a few beats again. "Baby, stay put and hold on for me. I'm not taking any chances right now. Not with any of this."

"Okay." I offered it willingly. I was so relieved to just be listening to the steady resolve in his voice that I'd agree to walk inside and slurp down a jar of pickles if he asked.

"I'm texting a friend of mine right now," he stated. "As soon as he gets his ass in my office and I can fill him in on what's going on, we are going to come to you. I don't hear the kitchen. Are you outside right now?"

I nodded but realized he couldn't see that. "I'm sitting in Kendall. I'm not just out in the op—"

"Well, get inside and wait until we get there," he decreed. His voice gentled at once as he queried, "How many people are there right now, baby?"

There must've been a reason Grant wasn't using Elijah's name, but I couldn't quite figure it out. If this whole mess were in relation to Sebastian Shark, I was sure the bad guys who were after him knew every one of his friend's names too. Exactly like they'd known to go after Grant in order to get to Bas.

But how did Grant's abduction hurt Bas? Had the bastards even made a single demand to Sebastian during Grant's captivity? They'd eventually released him, but had they even contacted Sebastian?

More answers I needed from my tree.

But he and I would deal with that later. This moment was about taking care of my team, and he was offering to help. "I think we have about six or eight on the crew now," I told him. "I didn't get a good look before Hannah took me outside to talk to me."

"This involves Hannah?"

"Yes. Deeply."

"Motherfuck."

"Grant?"

"Yeah, baby?"

"You really need to tell me what's happening."

"I will. I promise. The minute I see you and we can safely talk, okay?"

"Okay."

"Now go inside the kitchen and wait until we get there."

I nodded again and then tamped the urge to call myself a clueless fool. "All right," I croaked. "Please hurry. Someone besides us has a key to the building."

"My friend just walked into my office." Grant was using his obey-me-or-else tone now.

How I wished I was listening to it in any other situation. How I longed to be searching for any reason to sass him, just to sit and grin as he detailed how he'd use his body to discipline mine because of it. How I wished . . . *how I wished* . . .

"It won't take us long to get to you," Grant growled. "Go inside, please."

"Okay," I said again, though now it wasn't more than a whisper. "I love you, Grant."

"I love you too, Blaze."

I pressed the End button and held my phone against my chest for a couple of seconds. What the hell was going on? How had we gotten mixed up in this? Oh! I almost forgot. Sebastian Shark, of course.

Inside the kitchen, Hannah came over to my desk, and we acted like we were going over some menu options. Everyone else was too busy getting components ready for the lunch service to notice what we were doing, so we were able to talk quietly. I explained that Grant and one of his best friends were on their way over and they would take care of things.

"Just like that?" Hannah asked, getting agitated at a more rapid rate than before. "You just trust them to handle everything? Don't you think we should be calling the police?"

I pulled my hands down in a calming motion. While my friend couldn't be blamed for her nervousness, she had a low alto voice that gained volume instead of pitch in her excitement. There was no actual whisper module for this girl, but I needed her composure right now more than anything.

"I trust these men implicitly," I told her right away. "This is definitely not something the police should be involved with. You can speak with Grant and his friend Elijah when they get here, and I think they will be able to help you understand why that is, okay? Please, Hannah, you have to go with me on this. I'm positive we don't have all the pieces of this puzzle yet."

She scowled. "Frankly, Rio, I don't want to be involved in this at all."

"I don't either, believe me. But it might be too late for that. Let's just go about our normal routine and try to get some food out the door."

But my rah-rah was all for show. I slapped on a confident face only through supreme force of will. Inside, I obsessed about Hannah's persistence to take this to the police. How would Elijah and Grant handle it if she kept insisting? Were they willing to do things I didn't even want to think about?

We were busy helping with lunch preparations when Grant and Elijah walked in the door. Hannah was working on peeling apples beside me at the stainless-steel countertop when I heard her mutter, "Jesus, Mary, and Joseph."

I looked up and couldn't stop the smile that spread across my face. It was so good to see my man standing there, looking so incredibly handsome. Unbelievably, this golden god of a male was interested in me. How had I not scared him off with all my crazy? How had I not driven him away with all my strange habits, intensity, and passion for the odd things? Somehow, he had stuck by me through the worst time in my life. He saw the dark side of my psyche and still loved me in spite of it. And I hoped like hell he was going to let me return the favor. The new strength of his stare was a damn awesome encouragement. I truly had to be the luckiest girl on the planet.

Wiping my hands on a towel, I walked toward him and Elijah. Grant opened his arms, and I stepped right into his embrace. It was always a little awkward with the height difference, but we made the best out of the situation.

"Hey, beautiful," he said while finger-combing my bangs off to the side.

"You are such a liar. But that's okay because I needed to hear that."

"Why are you saying I'm a liar? You wound me." He put his hand over his heart like he was protecting the vital organ from damage. I expected Elijah to chime in at that point, ready with some remark that'd have me resisting the urge to punch him despite his willingness to drop everything to get here, but the man had been uncharacteristically quiet up to that point.

I sucked up my pride, peeking around Grant's tall frame to say hello to the guy. He and I both knew we were never going to be best friends, but I could at least be cordial.

"Hi, Elijah. Nice to see you again. This is my head chef, Hannah Farsey." I turned to where Hannah had been standing, but she was no longer there. I looked on the other side. Nope, not there either. I looked up to Grant, and he just shrugged.

"She the blonde? All-American-sweetheart-looking

chick?" Elijah asked, and I couldn't help but narrow my eyes at his rudeness. Why did everything that came from his mouth have to be so crass?

"What?" he asked incredulously. "What's wrong with saying she looks like America's little sister?"

"Did you see which way she went?" I figured I'd just move on to a new topic. "I'm going to clear everyone out of here, and then we'll be able to talk a little more freely. Can you guys step outside with me for a quick second?"

I didn't wait for their reply. I just squeezed between their large bodies and right out the side door that led to the parking lot. After I moved far enough from the building, I turned around to wait for Grant and Elijah. Thankfully they were right on my heels.

"Okay, I'm not going to tell you every detail of what happened here in the past twenty-four hours until everyone's gone, but there's good reason to believe someone has the place bugged in some way. I'm not really sure how much you even want to talk inside there." I gestured back to the building with my chin. "Maybe when the lunch delivery crew leaves, I can send the rest home and we can go somewhere else too?"

The men looked at each other and had some sort of wordless conversation. No lie. It was like witnessing a telepathic discussion between two Vulcans from *Star Trek*.

"Okay, you two. What the hell is that all about? Do you have a secret handshake, too?"

They both grinned, and I knew that was a yes.

"Oh, for Christ's sake. Are you going to teach it to me?"

Elijah answered immediately. "Umm, no. It's only for the guys."

But then the man blew my proverbial socks off. He

actually winked and grinned, letting me know he was teasing.

Wait. What?

This guy had a sense of humor? I didn't know how to process that information, but it didn't really matter. Because while I was picking my jaw up off the ground, they both turned and headed back toward the building.

When Grant realized I wasn't in tow, he dashed back to where I was rooted. Without a word, he dipped low, planted his shoulder into my belly, and hoisted me over his shoulder.

"Oh my God!" I laugh-shrieked. "Put me down, you—you— giant tree! Holy Christ, I think I'm going to get a nosebleed at this altitude."

"Brat," he chuckled and swatted my rear end.

"Hey, ow! That hurt."

"I'll kiss it for you later. How does that sound?"

This time, when his voice dipped to that sexier register that I loved so much, I let the sound zap me right between the thighs. I sighed as it bounced around like a pinball until I was ready to tilt.

"Promise?" I whispered as he brought me back over his shoulder to slide down the front of his body, never breaking eye contact with him as I went. More of the electric pinballs pinged through me, flying up and down my limbs now, as the man bent low and lovingly brushed his lips across the sensitive surfaces of mine.

"Always," he uttered back.

CHAPTER FOURTEEN

GRANT

Rank this right up there with trips to the dentist and having my taxes prepared. Yeah, that was fair. Oh, maybe scooping Robert's cat box, too. I didn't want to know what other bullshit had rained down on my brand-new girlfriend's life because of my best friend.

In theory, she'd already lost her husband because of Sebastian. Well, there was no theory involved. That was straight-up the reason Sean Gibson was gone. Now, I was about to hear an account that would detail how her employee and young friend, Hannah Farsey, had unknowingly been put in harm's way too.

Damn it.

How soon until Rio realized there was nothing about me redeeming enough to stay with me? Why would a woman want a man like me in her life when all I did was bring a black cloud of problems?

And these weren't problems like a hangnail or leaving the house with one navy-blue sock and one black sock, thinking they were a matching pair. These were big problems. Big, deadly problems that seemed to be getting bigger by the day.

Sure, our sex was amazing. Off the freaking charts was more like it. I could make Rio come three different ways just by talking to her about it. Once my cock was involved, she didn't stand a chance. But we had to have a life outside the bedroom too. Or so I was told.

But I had to cross that dismal bridge when I got to it. For now, all that mattered was focusing like I had blinders on, seeing nothing but the pertinent facts as Elijah stepped free from Abstract's massive cooler. I even ignored being surprised by his subtle shiver. The man was usually a walking furnace.

"Okay," my friend stated with a decisive clap of his hands, which drew Rio and Hannah out from where they'd been huddled and silent near her desk. "Grant and I have swept the place and can't find any bugs or cameras. If there was something in here, it was likely temporary, and whoever put it here took it out with them when they left. Needless to say, I think we're pretty safe to talk here. It will save us the risk of being overheard in public or being followed to our private homes. Which brings up another question. Hannah, bring me up to speed since you are new to the group here. Where did you say you live currently?"

This bastard didn't need to be taking notes the way he was playing it at the moment. God, I knew this guy like the back of my hand, but I just sat back and watched him work his magic. Later, when I told Rio and pointed out all his techniques, she'd be outraged on Hannah's behalf. He actually had a smart pad out and was jotting stuff down, but it was all for show. The man had a photographic memory.

"I live with my parents and sisters," Hannah replied in a voice so small, it was almost impossible to hear her over the hum of the commercial-grade appliances. She started fidgeting with the cuff of her chef's jacket, but damn it if Elijah wasn't staring like she'd started a full striptease. And the girl was so engrossed with her nervousness, she had no comprehension of his attention.

Finally, when she realized no one was talking, she looked up. My buddy simply shifted his eyes to the screen in front of him, then up to her as though he just did so for the first time and hadn't been mesmerized by her the entire time.

Well, damn.

If I had to place a cash bet on the table right there, it'd be on the odds that my best friend was sporting an erection for this young woman. While true, she wasn't his usual type. But maybe my estimations were getting rusty. I hadn't seen Elijah Banks this transfixed with a female since—well, since Hensley Pritchett.

There! I said it!

And I hoped like hell the witch's name didn't work like Beetlejuice, because Hensley was the last piece of trouble any of us needed to deal with right now. Least of all the friend I had to keep laser-focused on the glaring mystery at hand.

"And where did you say your parents live, then? Exactly?" Elijah persisted with Hannah.

Normally I'd be backing up the guy with at least some visual high-fives, affirming how deeply I valued his tactical commitment, but it was now coming across as raw douchery. And I definitely wasn't the only one to notice.

Poor little Hannah was sizing up my friend with folded arms and a tight glare. "And how does that possibly concern you, Mr.—I'm sorry, did you say—Barks?"

"Oh, shit," Rio sputtered, thankfully under her breath. Still, I squeezed her leg under the counter. I really didn't want to see her and Elijah at each other's throats constantly, and he didn't always have the easiest sense of humor.

"It's my concern because we may need to set up a security detail for you, and I need to know where to station my team."

"Okay," I swiftly interjected, "Hannah, why don't you just finish telling us what happened here, and we'll deal with all that afterward? I'm sure Rio has that information in your employment records. We can look it up and let you get on with your afternoon." I turned to Hannah with a look of genuine care. "I know you've already had a long day, and I'm sorry it's been that way."

Thankfully, my manners garnered a polite nod from Hannah in return. She centered her composure before explaining what happened yesterday when everyone else had gone home. The poor girl was so increasingly upset while telling the story, Rio went and put an arm around her for support.

Wisely, Elijah maintained his quiet attention during the whole account. When Hannah rolled around to the part about seeking Rio out this morning, he finally asked, "Do you have your phone here?"

"Yes, right here." Hannah pushed the device across the stainless-steel counter, barely touching it along the edges, as if it were contaminated.

"Have you used this phone since yesterday?" Elijah inquired. "For anything at all?"

"No. I went straight home last night and just left it in my purse overnight. I didn't tell anyone about it until informing Rio this morning."

"I need to take this with me and have someone who is better at the tech side of things look at it. Are you okay with that? Is there a password on here?"

"Yes, there is, on the lock screen."

"I'll need that."

Hannah grabbed a sticky note from the desk, jotted her password, and gave it to Elijah. He looked at it before folding the paper and putting it in his pocket.

"Word of advice? That's a terrible password. Not secure at all. If you use that on other things like websites and social media, you should change them all to something with at least ten characters. And not in numerical or alphabetical order."

"I thought you just said you aren't a tech guy?"

"Ms. Farsey, that is just common sense." Elijah closed his smart pad cover and stood and looked at me. "I think we have everything we need here."

"What about the locks on the doors?" Rio demanded.

"What about them?"

"Someone came right in here!"

"Call your landlord or a handyman. I have other things to deal with, Ms. Gibson."

Rio looked at me, and if a person could really have steam coming from their ears like in cartoons, she would have. I didn't know why Elijah insisted on antagonizing her.

"Baby, I can deal with it later, or like Elijah said, call your landlord. Maybe it would be good that they know someone broke in here? What do you think about that, Banks?"

"No," Elijah said at once. "I don't think the authorities should get involved yet. And if there is a report of a break-in, that's what will happen. Let me see what is on this video and see if there are any clues. There may be a message from our friend on here that the women didn't pick up on when they watched it because they don't have all the pieces to the puzzle. Make sense?"

"Yeah, I hear you. I'm going to hang here and talk with Rio

while you deal with that phone. Let me know what you come up with?"

"All right, my brother. Stay vigilant, though."

"Of course."

"Ms. Farsey, can I offer you a ride home? I would feel much better knowing you got there safely," Elijah said to Hannah, and Rio and I just gaped at the comment. The two of us waited with bated breath for her reply.

"I—I have my own car here." She just stared at him for a few beats—maybe trying to figure out his angle. Motive wasn't easy to guess with Elijah because he played every hand so close to the vest.

"My driver will follow you home, then. Again, just for safety. That will allow me to get the lay of the land in your neighborhood for my men."

"Is all of this really necessary? I mean, what am I going to tell my family as to why a crew of burly men are hanging around our house?" Under her breath, Hannah muttered, "Although my sisters might find them interesting."

"If my men are doing their jobs the way they've been trained, you won't even know they're there."

"Oh" was the only comeback she could offer.

They left soon after, Elijah's driver navigating the dark SUV right behind Hannah in her little silver BMW. Typically, the man didn't indulge in the extra convenience of a driver like Bas did, but when he had a lot of work to do, it was nice to not lose valuable time stuck behind the wheel in LA traffic. On a bad day, that could suck up half a person's time.

Finally, I was alone with Rio. Our morning came rushing back over me like a herd of panicked cattle. I wanted to take her in my arms, bury my face in her neck, and feel the comfort of her presence. But the memory of the morning's events made my brain seize up and my emotions switch directions.

Maybe she still didn't want me to touch her. Maybe she was still afraid to be alone with me. It seemed like I stood in the middle of Abstract Catering's kitchen watching her watching me, each of us trying to figure out where our relationship existed in the order of those sort of things.

But nothing had changed inside my heart from the moment I'd confessed my love to her. I needed to stop these ridiculous, damaging thoughts and switch direction again.

She hadn't been standoffish since I arrived. In fact, she was the one who called me to come over and help figure out what was going on with Hannah.

But as my overactive brain reminded me, if it weren't for me and my best friend, Sebastian Shark, none of this would be happening in the first place. Especially at her place of business.

First her late husband, now her livelihood.

Holy shit . . .

Maybe these pirates were trying to get even with me and not Bas this entire time. Why had they struck my figurative house so many times and not his?

Sure, there were the piranhas, but that mess with Tawny Mansfield could've been a local small-time hit on a street urchin woman just to get even with Bas for embarrassing Viktor Blake at the Edge groundbreaking. And when Terryn Ramsey took her life, that had nothing to do with anyone other than the little nutjob herself.

But the dangerous hits so far had only involved me or people I loved.

I swallowed roughly and made eye contact with my beautiful Blaze, who had been watching me like an animal in a manmade habitat at the zoo.

See the tall man in the industrial kitchen, ladies and gentlemen. What will he do next?

"Grant?" Rio said my name in the most vulnerable-sounding voice I'd heard from her in some time.

"Yeah, baby?" I answered in nearly a whisper because I didn't trust my own voice to sound confident right then. Not in the slightest.

"Can you hold me? Just for a little while?"

She didn't have to say another word. With my long gait, it only took one purposeful stride to reach her side. I bent over to hug her and lifted her so her feet left the floor. Instantly, she wrapped her legs around my waist and her arms around my neck. I didn't bother to look at what was in the way. I just sat on the edge of the counter with my face nuzzled into the crook of her neck and shoulder. It was my favorite spot on her body to press my nose and lips while we were wearing clothing. Her natural scent was so potent right there, I could not get enough of her.

"I want to put you in my pocket and take you everywhere I go all day."

I could feel her cheeks get tight with her smile at my suggestion.

"I think I would like to be in your pocket all day. Can you imagine the fun I could have in there?"

"That's a dangerous fantasy to have right now. Especially with you rubbing on my cock the way you are."

"Mmmm. Is that what's going on beneath me here?" She sat up taller and ground her pussy into my lap.

"Goddammit, you're a troublemaker." I pinched her ass cheek, and she yipped. "You and I need to have a serious conversation. And as much as I would love to do that with my dick buried inside you, I don't think either one of us would be able to pay attention for very long."

"Can we just sit like this a little longer? I'm so tired of serious conversations. This day sucked. These arms feel so good wrapped around me."

"Of course we can. And these arms are here for you anytime you need them, Blaze. Anytime. In fact, consider these arms your arms now."

She hummed against my neck and then said, "I like that. I could be really productive with four arms. Plus, with those arms, I could finally reach things on top shelves without getting a ladder or chair to stand on."

"You're funny. Do you know that?"

"Yes, but you love me. You said you do, and there are no take backs."

"You couldn't make me take those words back if you tried."

Eventually, Rio dropped her arms down from around my neck, scooted out of my arms, and led me over to her desk. I repositioned myself, parking my ass against the thing, while she scooted close once more with her cheek on my chest. I leaned back on her desk with stiff arms. My torso created an inclined plane for my girl to rest on, and it was oddly intimate without being sexual.

I had a feeling life with Rio would be like this. So many new discoveries, all with one incredible woman.

Before, I thought I needed to have a different woman in my bed all the time to experience fresh and exciting things, but somehow life had gotten to be duller and more predictable than ever. Turned out, the answer wasn't rotating the faces that came in and out of my bedroom. The answer was finding the right face and keeping her. Period.

Now, I stared down at that very right face and stroked her cute little bangs to the side of her forehead. She smiled but didn't open her eyes because this had become one of the little things I did to show affection for her.

Quietly, I told her something I hadn't told her before. "Do you remember the night I was taken from the yacht?" Then I sort of chuckled and choked at the same time, because of course she remembered. It was a night neither of us would ever forget.

She sighed. "Yes, of course."

"I know, that was a dumb question. But we had showered after that mind-blowing fuck on the deck, remember? You were so sleepy."

She smiled the sweetest smile, still keeping her eyes closed. Maybe if she stayed like that, this would be easier to talk about. "That may have been the best sex of my entire life. You were a maniac."

"I used your shampoo when we showered just to be quicker because you were so tired. So for the first two days, if I closed my eyes, I could smell you. I could escape the nightmare I was in because your smell was right on my body with me. Who would've known?"

Rio finally looked up and put her palms on my face. "I'm so sorry. I'm so sorry. I'm so sorry. I'm so sorry." She rushed the words out over and over while tears streamed down her cheeks.

I took her hands in mine and held them. "Blaze. I didn't tell you that so you'd feel bad. It was something good I had, in the middle of that shit storm. You helped me get through those days. You weren't there, but you were. You know?"

"I was so scared. I thought they'd taken you from me and I'd never see you again. I didn't know how I'd survive." She dashed the wetness from her face in angry swipes. "I want you to tell me what happened though, when you're ready."

"Have I ever told you the story about my mother's death?" I watched her face twist a little with confusion, probably wondering why I'd bring that up when we were just talking about the abduction at sea.

"Umm, no. You've made a few comments about her dying from a drug overdose, but that's about it. But I'm—"

I held up my hand to stop her. "There's a reason I'm bringing it up. Just hear me out. I was young. Just a teen... fifteen. I was friends with Bas and Elijah already. Actually, Elijah was with me when I found her. Sebastian came right away. You know, for all the shitty things she did in the way of mothering, I still loved her the best I could. So when I found her body, it was hard. Up to that point, I'd never seen an actual dead body before, so it took me a couple of minutes to realize what was going on. I mean, shit, she was so cold. Her skin, you know? And not stiff, but I don't know. Firm? I don't know how you describe that. Anyway, it took a police officer to drag me away from the body so they could take her away. I didn't want to let go of her. She was all I had." I shrugged. "I mean, she was a super shitty mother, but she was all I had."

"I'm sorry you had to go through that when you were that young. And where did you go after that? To live, I mean."

I looked away. I don't know why I felt so self-conscious all of a sudden. Everyone knew my story by that point. So many stories had been written about Bas and me—how we'd come up from nothing to where we were today.

"Bas and I lived on the streets. We took care of ourselves. Well, he had his sister, Pia, too. But yeah, we squatted in his dad's place for a long time after that old boozer died. As long as the rent got paid, old man Blake never came around. The neighbors all knew what was going on, but we kept out of trouble." I rolled my eyes and grinned. "For the most part, at least, so no one told the authorities."

"That's incredible. I mean, you realize how incredible that is, right?"

"I don't know about all that. We were just doing what we were doing. We didn't want to go into the system. We'd heard enough horror stories about what foster homes were like from other kids on the streets, so we knew we didn't want to be a part of that. And Bas would've rather died than be split up from Pia, so he did what he had to do."

"I don't understand, though, how the authorities just let children roam around on the streets, knowing it's going on. I mean, they have to know, right?"

"Well, sure, they know. We used to talk to the CPS case worker that would've been assigned to our cases if we would've been in the system, but they are so overwhelmed with cases. If they see older kids are doing okay on their own, they look the other way. They don't want the extra work any more than the kids want to go into the system."

"That's unreal. And a crime on its own." She shook her head but didn't meet my gaze. "That's so fucked up."

"Baby, you can't fix everything in the world, you know?" But I loved her kind, generous heart that wanted to.

"I know that. But I think about all the years I wanted a baby so badly. Sooo badly, Grant. And they make it so difficult to get a baby in the foster care system. Believe me, Sean and I tried."

There wasn't a good response to that. All it did was bring up memories of her deceased husband, and honestly, I didn't want to think about Sean Gibson at the moment.

"Okay, so let's go back to you finding your mom. That must've been really hard for you, I can only imagine. Does that somehow relate to your time on that pirate vessel? Did those people kill your mother?"

I laughed. Hard. I just couldn't help it. Now that took an active imagination, connecting those two things in that way. "No, baby," I finally chuckled out. "The two things aren't related. Not like that, at least. I told you that story about my mom because that was the first time I'd ever seen or touched a corpse. It's just not something you ever forget." With eyes closed, I sucked much-needed air in through my nose, desperate to stay grounded in the here and now. Still, I forced myself to say, "It's a particular feel—the skin, the smell, even. Everything about it is . . . distinct."

I looked at her directly to make sure she was still with me. But this Rio was so different from the woman I dealt with in the days before my abduction. The one who was unpredictable, unfocused, and vacant at times—and wholly capable of scaring the daylights out of me with that empty stare. But for the time being, she was gone—and I rejoiced in that because I needed her full attention now.

We all needed to be on the same page with what was happening, because lives were at stake now. Playtime was over. I had a feeling whatever Elijah found on that video footage on Hannah's phone wasn't going to be a bunch of teenagers trying the cinnamon challenge.

Rio nodded that she understood my intention now, so I continued. "Onboard the thugs' boat, most of the space was used for cargo storage. They tossed me in with the cargo. No nice stateroom for the prisoner, of course."

I gave her a wink, trying to keep it light, but she immediately frowned. Nothing about this was remotely lighthearted, and I knew the effort had been a long shot.

"Did they tell you what they wanted? Why they came onboard our yacht and took you?" she asked.

"Not directly. Over time, I figured it out—which leads me to think that these pricks aren't done playing games with us yet. That's why we're thinking we probably need to move—"

I stopped that train of thought before it could even pull into the station. Rio would hit the roof if I told her I was taking her to a safe house like Bas did with Abbigail last summer. But damn it, my girl didn't miss a trick. She caught that slipup and now had her chocolate glare pinned to my forehead like a sniper rifle's sight.

She slammed her hands to her hips before declaring, "Oh mister, if you think you're stashing me away like your fish friend did to Abbigail, you have another think coming."

"We can talk about all of that later. There hasn't been an actual plan decided on." I dropped my voice to the dominant tone she responded to without question. The one that warned her not to fuck with me on this. To be extra sure she caught my intention, I leaned over and said right beside her ear, "Because if your safety becomes an issue, you absolutely will do what you are told, Blaze. I don't care if I have to hog-tie you and carry you there myself. Clear?"

She shivered, and when I sat up straight again, I watched as her mouth dropped open as if she were going to rail on me, but then she thought better and closed it. Opened again and closed. Finally, I spoke before she could launch into a tirade.

"Baby, listen to me." I tried to scoop up her hands, but she pulled away from my grasp. I narrowed my eyes at her and held my hands out for her.

After making me wait there like that a few beats, she finally placed her hands in mine. I needed that connection with her. Right now, more than ever. She just didn't understand that yet.

"These men are cruel, evil excuses for humans. Filthy animals who don't deserve the space they take up. They won't go easy on any woman they get their hands on. Do you understand what I'm saying?"

I waited for some sort of response, and finally my stubborn queen nodded.

"None of us would recover from it, Rio. Not your team here, not your sweet friend Hannah, not Abbigail—and especially not me. None of us could handle you being taken away from us."

I gripped the back of my neck again and held on for at least a minute while Rio and I stared at each other. If she thought she was going to intimidate me with the dirty looks she was surfing my way, she had another think coming. Why the hell would self-preservation be where she chose to dig in? It didn't make sense to me.

"I was kept in their cargo hold the entire time, never taken above deck or to any other part of the boat. They came in on a few occasions to give me food and water." I cringed, but she needed to hear this part too, so she understood how deplorable the conditions were. "If I had to relieve myself, I had to do it in there too. In the corner. Like an animal."

"There wasn't a bathroom in there?" she asked, horrified.

I just shook my head, disgusted and embarrassed by the admission.

"Oh." She thought about it for a few beats, then twisted her face when she realized what that really meant. She hugged me carefully and said into my chest, "Babe, I'm so sorry you had to go through all that."

Nuzzling into the top of her hair, I smelled her floral shampoo and smiled. That damn jasmine smell would forever be my comfort smell now that this woman ruled my world.

"Yeah, well, that's not the worst of it."

"Oh no. Grant, what else?"

I explained how they cracked me in the head and drugged me repeatedly. "Dr. Mallory at Cedars said it will take some time to get back to normal," I concluded. "Things like my memory and temper. But it should all be okay in time."

But Rio came back with more questions. "What about therapy? What about some sort of trauma or PTSD support group or something? I mean, Grant... after that dream last night... there has to be more to this story." She looked at me skeptically.

"Yeah, unfortunately, I'm just getting to that part." I gripped my neck and rubbed up into my hairline. God, the tension stacked up, brick upon brick, until my muscles felt like a solid wall.

"Oh no." She cradled her face in her hands. "I was afraid of that." After she looked up, she waved both hands toward her body. "Okay, lay it on me."

"The cargo they were transporting..." I paused, unable to think of a gentle way to say it, so I just blurted out the truth. "Well, these folks were moving bodies out into the middle of the ocean and dumping them where no one would ever find them."

"Bodies," she repeated.

"Yes, bodies. Dead human bodies."

"Grant." She paled and shook her head. "Fuck."

"I know. Trust me, I know."

"So were there bodies in that cargo hold with you while you were in there? Oh God, please tell me they had already dumped their load."

"No, it was pretty full. I was the only living thing in there. Well, me and the rats." I shivered and my stomach roiled.

"Oh my God. I am so sorry. I don't know what else to say. I keep saying that, and it sounds so stupid now."

"It's fine, love. I know it's not easy to listen to all of this. It's not easy to tell you. Trust me. If I could've gotten by without having to put this shit into your mind, I would've. But last night—well, yeah. Last night." I waved my hand through the air as if that helped explain it.

"Please don't keep things from me. Ever. Life isn't always easy. It isn't always neat and tidy with a pretty bow on it. But if we're going to do this"—she motioned back and forth between her heart and mine—"then we have to promise to be open and honest. I can't be in a relationship where it's any other way."

"I understand that." I nodded solemnly.

"Do you?"

"Yes."

"Okay, because you just tried to play it another way. So, your instinct is to not be open and honest. And seriously, Grant, that's concerning."

She walked away from me then and started shuffling papers on the desk beside me. I waited for her to look at me again, but she just kept doing the mindless busywork.

"Hey. Blaze, look at me, please."

She turned toward me, still mid eye roll while doing so.

"What the hell is that for?"

"What?" she snapped.

"The sassy thing? Are you looking for a red ass?" I growled in response to her open glare. "Oh, you're all full of it, now. What's going on?" God, the woman could turn on a dime.

"You know I'm all-in here, right? I'm standing here, giving you everything I have, Grant. Every. Damn. Thing." She put her hands on her hips yet again, and her ireful pose spiked my desire for her in the most intense way.

"And you don't think I'm doing the same thing?" I heard how I was raising my voice and also knew I needed to bring it way down. But seriously, she was pissing me off. How much more did she want from me? What else was even left?

"Well, I'm not sure. I hear you telling me you'd rather lie to me than be open with me, and, well, that's not a super comforting notion."

"No. You're hearing what you want to hear. I'm telling you my instinct is to protect you. I wanted to keep all that shit from you because it's a damn horror movie. Why would I want to share that with the woman I want to protect from all the bad things in this fucked-up world? Why would I want to bring the monsters into our home myself?"

Yep. Now we were yelling.

If she just weren't so damn stubborn and would just admit there might be another way to look at something.

"Because partners slay monsters together, Tree! What about that don't you get?"

"I don't want to see you get hurt, damn it! And I don't want to be the one to hurt you. I would never forgive myself. Do you have any fucking idea what seeing those marks on your skin did to me this morning? Marks I'd inflicted? And then that look of absolute terror on your face?"

I gripped my hair, but even that sharp pain wasn't enough. I wanted to cut off something vital to prove to her how much it hurt me to see her like that.

"In that moment, I wasn't your partner, baby. You get that, right? Not by any stretch of anyone's imagination. In that moment, I was the monster."

My voice completely broke on the last word, and I dropped my chin to my chest. I didn't even have the courage to hold her gaze. When I looked up, I knew what I was about to say was going to be brutal, so I sucked in a deep breath first.

"If that happens again, I think we'll have to go our separate ways."

"What?" Her voice was hushed and shivery. Tears immediately filled her eyes. "Wh-Wh-What did you just say?"

"I don't think you need me to repeat myself."

"So that's how you deal with the hard stuff? Like that? You run, when you've yelled at me so many times about not running? Are you fucking kidding me?"

"No. I've never run away from anything in my life. But I don't know what else to do, Blaze. I can't hurt you like that again." It was agony to have to say these things. How did she not understand?

"Have you even considered seeing a therapist? Like a non-egomaniac would do?"

"I'm not an egomaniac."

"Okay," she said in the most condescending tone. Coupled with the way she patted my arm while she said it, I wanted to put her over my knee and take it out of her backside right the spot.

"You're pushing the wrong buttons with me righ

woman. I can't warn you strongly enough," I said in a lethally calm voice.

"Is that right?" She smirked. "Maybe something will finally get through that thick tree-trunk head of yours. My God, are you that dense? Why would you throw away something this good instead of going and talking to a professional first? You've suggested—oh no, pardon me—you've insisted I see a therapist how many times now? So how hasn't it crossed your thick skull for you do the same thing?"

I watched her closely while she spoke. Her point was a good one, I had to admit. But something else was going on with her, and I really hoped I wasn't reading her wrong. All the tension that had built up between us was cracking something in her, and a mischievous glint twinkled in her eye. One more smart remark, and I'd know she was pushing me on purpose. I just needed to lay the bait and see if she'd bite.

"All right, Blaze. You make a solid point. And you're right, we are good together. In fact, I've never had better." I went to stand in front of her, next to her desk. Then I pushed in closer, crowding her back until her thighs were up against the edge of the thing.

At once, her nostrils flared. She gave my body a quick once-over, starting down at my wingtips and finishing at my Adam's apple. No way did she miss the erection in between. Probably not my rough swallow when her attention was there, either. It was as though her body sent out a command and mine responded.

Her answering throat undulation was the confirmation ...eeded. Inside her tight little body—and throughout mine— ...rgument had turned to full arousal.

...ooking my fingers into two of her front belt loops, I

tugged her body forward until it *thunked* into mine.

"What's on your mind now, Blaze? You look like you're burning up inside."

"What?" She nearly choked, and I chuckled. "What are you talking about?" she asked, trying to sound nonchalant, but the red flush creeping across her chest gave her away. It always did.

"I don't know, baby. You have this firestorm look in your eyes. And shit, girl, if that's for me, I'm going to take advantage of it." Theatrically, I looked at the desk behind her, as if checking out my flat surface options, and then back to her. "Right here, on top of your desk."

"We can't. That old thing will break. No way." She huffed.

"Well?" I asked, looking around. "Where? You said we can't fuck on the counters in here—your rules, not mine. And that damn clown car you have is way too small for anyone to have a good time in."

She smacked my abdomen with the back of her hand, and I grabbed it so quickly, it shocked her.

"Pardon me, miss. I don't appreciate being struck."

"Well, don't talk shit about my car."

"That's not a car. It's a toy."

"Fuck you!"

Promise?

"Come over here. Sit." I dragged her a few feet from her desk and pushed her down into the nearby chair. She was panting and flushed, her gorgeous gaze wild with desire.

"Grant. What are you doing?"

"No. It's what you're going to be doing." I unbuckled my belt as she looked up and watched. "Let's keep that sassy mouth busy so I don't have to listen to it for a while. Yes?"

She squinted and pressed her lips together.

"You know I love your dirty looks, baby. Look how hard I am for you." I stroked my cock a few times before stepping right up to her. "Open," I said, but she held her mouth closed tight. "Don't make me force you, Blaze. You won't like my tactics."

Rio opened her mouth but just slightly, so I took her chin in my palm and bent down so we were eye to eye. "Are you the comedian now? Suck my cock the way I know you love to, and you'll get off too." While I spoke to her, I put pressure on her face with my hand, increasing it as I talked. "Keep fucking around, and you'll be aching for it for two weeks. Maybe three. Including touching yourself. And yes, I will know and can prevent you from doing it."

Her cheeks were red from where I squeezed them. It made her face all the more gorgeous when she jerked her glare back up the length of my body.

"So you have a chastity belt just hanging around?"

"Do you really want to find out?"

When I stood back up to my full height, she followed me with her stare. I couldn't remember a time I'd seen her more aroused. Holy shit, maybe I'd run over to my favorite kink place in Hollywood and pick up that chastity wear just for fun. Why not? Every day with this woman was truly going to be a new adventure ...

But as for right now ...

"Do it," I barked at her. "Suck me good and deep, woman. No drop left behind."

And Christ, did she. If there were still cameras in that place, we gave someone a real show or were probably going to find ourselves on an amateur internet porn site.

Rio drove us home, and we were both relaxed and hummed along to the radio the whole way.

CHAPTER FIFTEEN

RIO

"What's wrong?" Grant shouted from the downtown condo's living room as I scowled at myself via the bedroom mirror for at least the hundredth time.

"I hate this bathing suit." I pouted at him, despite how my insides flipped when he moved into the doorway and filled it with his large, golden frame. "It looks ridiculous. I feel like a bean pole." Especially when I'd appear in it next to the man who looked like Pool Bash Ken, sleek and beautiful in his tight tee and board shorts. "I think we should just stay home. Or I'll stay home, and you go. But take that pasta salad I made last night. It's in the refrigerator in the Tupperware container."

"No." He took my hands down from where I was tugging at the stretchy material of the suit's top. "Stop." Then he kissed each knuckle before setting my arms by my sides. "This bathing suit is amazing. You look mouthwatering in it."

He leaned down and kissed a hot, wet trail up my neck, finishing with a hard bite just below my ear. I moaned and leaned back into him, wanting to forget all about this stupid pool party and stay home for our own special game of Marco Polo instead.

"And I'm not taking the pasta salad, nor am I going without Get your little ass ready and let's go, or we're going to be late. You know how shitty the traffic can be to Calabasas." He spun me back toward the master bathroom and gave me a little shove.

"Whose stupid idea was this again?" I called out to him.

"I guess Abbi wanted everyone to come over. I have to say, it's not a bad notion. I think if we go into the day with a good attitude, it will be a good one."

"What? You're fucking Deepak Chopra now?" I rolled my eyes and leaned closer to the mirror. Robert was waiting to see if I'd turn the water on for him for the seventh time, so I groused to him, "Shit, send the guy to two therapy sessions, and he's crashing little cymbals on his fingers." The cat just rubbed his face on the faucet, so I gave him a quick pet. "The answer is no, big boy. Daddy is being a meanie and says I have to hurry up and get ready to go to some stupid pool party."

Grant, on his way back out of the bedroom, whipped his head around the corner again. "Did you just call me Daddy to that cat?"

"No," I said too quickly, but the jig was up. We both knew I had, and I burst out laughing. "So what! Aren't you kind of his adoptive pet Daddy-O? Plus, you like him! I see you pet him and hear you talk to him."

"What choice do I have when he's waving his ass around in my face when I'm trying to shave at the sink?"

"See? You do love him. Just like I knew." I grinned and turned on my heel, going into the closet to find something to put on over the hideous bathing suit.

It would probably be too warm for my usual black band T-shirt, so I roughly swiped from item to item in the closet. A little yellow-and-white-striped trapeze dress from one of the boutiques in Hawaii was the perfect answer. I grabbed my denim jacket for later, in case it got cold, and my daisy Chucks, and I was a done deal.

We made our way out of downtown and up into the rolling hills where Bas and Abbi lived with their new baby. I was anxious and nervous to see Abbigail and meet the baby, especially since the last time I'd seen them had been when she'd walked in on me trying to set the yacht on fire.

I wasn't sure if she'd ever told anyone about that incident, but no one had ever said anything to me about it, including the boat rental company. Hopefully—please God, please—Abbi wouldn't bring it up today in front of the others. Oh my God, I'd be mortified.

No. What came after mortified? Okay, yes, that awful day was firmly parked in my past, but the last thing I needed was something like that coming between Grant and me—especially after I'd damn near read him the riot act about being open and honest with me.

There was yet another reason I didn't want to be going to this stupid pool party. Of course, the one time in my life that I wouldn't have minded a gigantic traffic jam on the freeway, it was smooth sailing. Grant insisted we have a driver come pick us up and take us so we could both drink if we wanted to. So we sat in the back of the car, snuggling like teenagers on our way to the prom. A prom with a beach theme, given my bikini and Grant's sexy shorts, but it was a fleeting thought anyway.

"What time are we meeting your Realtor tomorrow?" I asked my favorite tree.

With my head tucked under his chin, Grant stroked the exposed skin on my arm. "She's meeting us at your place in Seal Beach at ten. Is everything squared away there? The way you want it when she sees it? We could sleep there tonight if you have things you need to do still."

"Well, that won't work because now Robert is downtown and we didn't leave him enough food and water to be on his own for that long. I'm sure the bungalow is fine. There may be a few things out of place, but if we scoot down there an hour before you expect her, I can have it straightened up. You've seen the place. It's very small."

"But I think you'll get top dollar for it. The market is really hot right now, though it's never really tame that closed to the water. People love that little community."

"It's a great town," I said wistfully. I would miss living there.

"Hey. Don't sound sad." He bussed the top of my head. "You don't have to get rid of it, you know. You could rent it out on a long- or short-term basis."

"Nah. I don't want to deal with that. I don't want to watch a home I once loved go through that kind of abuse. Spring breakers and what have you. Plus the constant cleaning and repairs."

In no time at all, we were giving our name at the guard shack at Sebastian and Abbigail's exclusive neighborhood. I took a deep, calming breath and blew it out.

"You doing okay?" Grant asked for about the fifth time, which made me want to throat punch him.

"If I say no, will you take me home?"

"Probably not, but I can have the driver circle the neighborhood until you calm down a little bit."

I blew out a long sigh. "You know it's not going to get better until I just go inside and get this over with."

He shot over a tender glance. "Is this about Abbi or Ba⸱

"Yes!" I said with mock enthusiasm, inspiring him⸱

new chuckle. I was so happy that he and Bas had patched up their friendship. I'd hated seeing them out of sorts after being brother-close for most of their lives.

"Have you and Abbi ever been at odds before?" he asked, but we were nearly there, so I tried to keep my reply at general fly-over level.

"Not at odds, necessarily," I said. "Sean and I did a lot of parenting of that woman when their mother died. Even though we were young too, Sean was the oldest sibling of the family, and he already was out of the house. We followed the plentitude of work he found out here and quickly fell in love with California. Abbi came to visit us as a graduation gift from their dad, and she didn't want to go back home either. Mr. Gibson wasn't happy that he was losing his little girl then too, but he couldn't hold her back. So, we promised to look after her. Sean took that very seriously. A promise to his dad was everything."

Grant listened very attentively, and I felt terrible for going on about the Gibson clan. But there really was no reason I shouldn't. For one thing, he'd asked. And additionally, I wasn't pining for my late husband anymore. There was part of me that would still mourn Sean a little until the day I died. It just wasn't every day now. He understood that. I felt him telling me that. We were at peace about it.

Still, I felt compelled to apologize and didn't know why. "I'm sorry."

"For what, Blaze?"

We pulled into the grand, circular driveway of the Shark ome. Every time I arrived at this place, I was stunned by its gnificence.

"For going on like that. Holy shit, this place is really ible, isn't it?"

"It's unreal. Have you ever been here at night?"

"I don't think so. Why?"

"I swear, on a clear night, you can see one hundred miles in every direction. It's breathtaking. Would you like a home like this?" he asked as we slid out of the car. But I didn't have time to answer because an adorable hurricane of a child came bolting across the driveway and attached herself onto Grant's legs.

"Uncle Grant! Uncle Grant! I haven't seen you in twelve whole months!"

"Vela!" Grant bent down and scooped the girl up, tossing her into the air and catching her in a big hug. She squealed with delight every single second. I just watched in awe. The love these two nonrelated people had for each other was going to make me tear up—this time in all the best ways.

Grant leaned back while still holding the little girl in his arms. She rolled her eyes, sensing what was coming next. "Let me get a good look at you."

The driver handed me the dish of pasta salad and set our beach bags near the front door since Grant was busy with Vela. Finally, Sebastian and Abbi came out to see who'd arrived.

"Uncle Bas, look who's here! Uncle Grant! It's been forrreevvveerr!"

The adults laughed, and Pia came out through the front door next. "Okay, Uncle Grant, you're spoiling her rotten. Vela, stand on the legs God gave you, please."

"Oh, now you've done it," Grant whispered loudly to Vela, but she was already shaking her head.

He set her down on the ground, but she tugged him down so she could whisper just as loudly, "Uncle Bas says maybe if she had a man, she wouldn't be so grumpy all the time."

"Sebastian!" Pia smacked her brother in the shoulder. Grant hooted, and Abbi and I even had a laugh. It was the perfect icebreaker for the tension I'd been feeling when we drove up. Leave it to a child to inject some humor exactly where it was needed.

"You're in so much trouble." Grant laughed, pointing at Sebastian after Pia followed Vela back inside. I was still chuckling behind my hand at their antics when Abbi came over to where I was standing.

"They remind me of my brothers when they're like this," she said with an indulgent smile.

I nodded. "I was just thinking the same thing."

We automatically fell into each other's arms. I knew she would be crying because, well, of course—it was Abbigail. But I had to admit, I was choked up this time too. I missed my sister and my business partner and, for the longest time, the only female friend I'd had.

"Let's go around to the pool ... or inside at least." Abbi looked at me cautiously. "There's someone here I'd like you to meet, if you're up for it?"

"Are you kidding? I'd be devastated if I didn't get to officially meet him. Is the little guy awake?" I asked hopefully.

"He is. Just got up, actually. Dori has him out back for a little bit to say hello to everyone. His cousin wants him to go in the pool more than her next breath, but I don't know if I'm ready for that yet. I think I would like that to be a quiet event between just the three of us for the first time, you know?"

"But does anyone ever tell Vela no?" I laughed. "About anything?"

Abbi chuckled too. "Definitely not her uncles, but Pia runs a pretty tight ship. So if she picks up on my feelings about something, she shuts her down pretty fast. I just need to outright say 'not today,' and it will be the last we hear about it."

"Well, there you go, then."

"I know, but I hate to be the meanie. The boys are always the fun ones, you know?"

"Isn't that always the way it goes?"

We were laughing and strolling arm in arm when we finally made our way onto the pool deck. It would have been comical to have had a camera at the ready, as every head swung our way, and then every mouth fell open as every set of eyes took in our physical embrace. Even better was how everyone tried to play it off as if they saw this kind of reconciliation every day—Grant included.

"Holy shit," I muttered with a snicker.

"Okay, so that wasn't me?" Abbi mumbled back.

"Don't think so. Wow, that was pathetic."

"Oh, why don't I ever have my camera ready when I should?" she moaned out. "Seriously, when will I learn?"

"You might want to get better at that," I gibed. "Because I understand babies do adorable things all the time. You certainly don't want to miss a trick."

"Maybe I should just ask Bas to hire a photographer to follow Kaisan around all day."

She issued the comment so seriously, I looked at her out of the corner of my eye first to see if I could gauge if she were joking around or not. Her expressionless face gave nothing away, though, so I turned at the waist and gawked at her.

The brat burst out laughing, and I was so tempted to push her into the pool, but she had the cutest shoes on. I couldn't bring myself to do it.

"You should thank the shoe gods right now. They saved your ass from getting tossed into that pool. You all are sleep-deprived and crazy up on this hill these days! Jesus, Mary, and Joseph!"

"Girl, that is the truth. I don't know what I would be doing without Dori's help, because even with it, I feel like a zombie most of the time. Bas tries to help when he can, but he has to get up so early for work. So what am I going to do? Make him get up in the middle of the night to change a wet diaper? That's just ridiculous. Plus, I'm trying to nurse as much as possible, so he's not much help there, either."

I just smiled sheepishly. What could I possibly add to the conversation at that point? How my lady-in-waiting was a godsend? Or that I knew anything about midnight feedings or wet diapers? But hey, I could regale her about the time my boyfriend was kidnapped by maritime pirates. Wait, that was no good either—not unless she wanted to hear about how they'd done it to settle some sort of score with her baby daddy.

"I'm going to see what Grant's up to," I said abruptly before walking away as casually as possible. I knew I'd left Abbigail just standing there like a fish out of water and even felt a twinge of guilt about it. But just a twinge.

I could still feel her stare drilling into my back as I made my way over to Grant. And Christ, it was a far distance from one side of their goddamn pool to the other.

When I finally got to where Grant was sitting, I looked around the chairs for our bags but didn't see them. He was talking with Sebastian and Pia but wrapped his arm around my waist.

"What's up? Whatcha looking for?"

"Have you seen our beach bags? I want to slather on some

ANGEL PAYNE & VICTORIA BLUE

sunblock ASAP. Don't want to burn." I scrunched my face at him, nearly touching my nose to his. "I'm told I'm pasty."

He pulled me down on his lap and tipped me back so fast, I laughed until I nearly snorted. Luckily, he blocked the sun with his big frame, or I would've been blinded since I was looking straight up into the sky.

"Oh my God, Tree. Put me back up."

Finally he tilted me upright, and I was so winded, I just shook my head at him.

"Jesus. I haven't laughed that hard in a long time." I turned to see what he had in a tumbler on the table, but it was clear, so it could've been a number of things.

"Are you thirsty?" he asked. "Do you want me to get you something?"

"Let me," Sebastian said. "Otherwise, what kind of host would I be?" He looked at me expectantly.

"I'll have what Grant is having."

Bas turned slightly to Grant. "Another?"

"Sure."

"Two waters, coming right up."

I looked at him and grinned. "You're full of surprises today. Water, huh?"

"Not a fan of drinking in the sun. It makes me feel like shit. And if you hop up for a minute, I'll get your sunblock. I put our bags over there in the shade because I didn't know if you had anything that could melt in yours. Makeup or lip stuff or whatever."

"Now see, Twombley? That's why you get paid the big bucks!"

I intended to add a kiss as his extra reward, but Grant wasn't looking at me anymore. His gaze, wide and bewildered, was fixed all the way across the pool.

I joined him, my own breath catching hard as Elijah Banks emerged onto the deck. But that wasn't the shocker sight of the hour. That part belonged when I observed his date for the party. Hannah, my head chef from Abstract Catering, was lingering about two paces behind him like his current submissive.

What. The. Hell?

I prevented myself from blurting those words by murmuring, "Stop gawking, baby, and put some of this on my back, please."

"Sure. Yeah," he said absently, accepting the sunblock tube from me. "Are you going to take your dress off, hot stuff?"

"Yes, smarty pants. Do you want to swim with me?"

"I would love to. But only if I get to feel you up under the water."

"I was hoping you would," I purred back. "But only when no one's looking."

"Fuck that. I don't care who sees me touching what's mine. This suit, baby." He leaned back a little to fully take me in. "And now you've done it. How am I supposed to even stand up now? These board shorts do nothing to hide anything."

He adjusted his cock in his swim trunks, and he wasn't kidding. I could see every shadowed outline of his glorious shaft.

"Think unsexy thoughts for a couple of minutes so you can settle things down in there. I'll be in the water." I pushed my way between his legs to give him a quick kiss and said very quietly, "And you can tell me what the hell is going on with Elijah and Hannah."

"I was hoping you knew."

I shook my head and pulled away, swatting his hand so we wouldn't keep getting worked up. As I walked away, I heard the pained groan when he finally saw the back of my bathing suit. The bottoms were very cheeky, so he was getting a good eyeful of my derriere as I walked.

At the shallow end of the pool, I took advantage of the steps to work my way into the water. It wasn't cold by any means, but it took a little getting used to. The women were chatting there in a group and called me into the circle to join them. Pia, Abbigail, Dori, and another woman I'd never met worked me right into their conversation.

"Rio, I don't think you've met Wren, have you?" Abbi asked. "She's Pia's assistant."

"And lifesaver more times than I can count," Pia added.

"Stop. You would get along just fine without me. Vela is old enough now. You don't really need a nanny anymore. And the work you do for Shark Enterprises... well, you have everything so streamlined."

Dori touched the girl's arm. "I think you should be quiet because you're kind of talking yourself out of a job. Unless that's what you're trying to do?"

"No! Of course not," Wren answered. "I love working for Ms. Shark."

"All righty, then," Pia added, clearly wanting to change the subject. "Who's hungry? Maybe we should dry off and work on bringing the food out from the house." She looked at our hostess to see if she had a different plan.

"Sounds good to me," Abbi said just as Grant dived into the pool at the deep end and began swimming underwater toward the group.

"Hold on to those tiny bottoms, sister," Abbigail teased.

"He's coming up right behind you."

I giggled and turned just in time for Grant to swim right into my crotch. I yelped and grabbed on to his cheeks while he came up from beneath the surface. "Oh my God! I can't believe you made it all the way across the pool like that."

He tugged my body against his, and I automatically wrapped my legs around his waist. Grant must have been on his knees in the shallower depth to keep us submerged as much as we were.

He growled when we rubbed against each other in the most delicious way. "Baby, I have so many talents you don't know about."

"Is that right? And I thought I'd seen all your tricks by now."

He gave me that wolfish grin that usually rushed moisture between my thighs. Damn, I was so into this guy. It exhilarated and scared me on every single level.

"No, Blaze. We're just getting started. I spend hours thinking of new ways to light your fire."

"I think you might need a more challenging job or something. It sounds like you have too much free time." I grinned.

After that comment, he dunked us both under the water. I came up sputtering and laughing, shaking out my hair to get the longer strands out of my face. Thankfully I'd gone with waterproof mascara this morning, or I'd look like a crack whore.

"You'll pay for that. When you least expect it." I tried to sound sinister, but we both knew he'd always have the upper hand. He knew how to dominate me in every way.

I wrapped my arms around his neck and rested my chin

on his muscular shoulder. His skin was already picking up a golden glow from the sun, and I was jealous. I never tanned, only burned. White to pink to red—that was my sun-kissed fate.

"I love holding you so close like this. You feel so perfect in my arms here." He murmured it for just my ears. We had moved away from everyone else in the water, but still, it was a tender moment just between us. A respite I desperately needed.

"It feels good to be held by you this way. I feel safe, and . . ." I searched for the word for a moment. "I think the word 'cherished' fits. Like a child, actually, but not in a creepy way."

That made Grant chuckle. "Good. Creepy is not what I was going for."

I laughed a little too. "You know what I mean. You do, right?" Christ, if this man didn't get me by now, he never would. He had seen every deep, dark corner of my psyche, personality, and physical body. Grant Twombley knew me better than any man—or woman—had ever known me. The connection we shared because of that was unique, special, and so beyond words. I held him even closer while he rocked our bodies through the warm water.

"Of course I do," Grant responded. After a few minutes— and several kisses that all but permanently curled my toes—he said, "What I don't understand . . . is that."

He turned so I could get a direct look at where Elijah lazed on a lounge chair like a damn Greek God, shirtless and golden. Hannah was beside him on her own chair, though I already wondered if the thing were actually a bed of tacks. I'd made several attempts to wave hello to her, but the woman hadn't returned a single one. She simply sat upright, cover-up buttoned to her neck, trying to look like she was reading the dystopian sci-fi book in her hands.

"Yeah, I'm not sure what's going on there. I thought you said he was banging some girl from some sex club you all used to frequent?" My voice was still very quiet and for my lover's ears only.

"As recent as last week," Grant confirmed. "Not that it meant anything or does anymore. That other girl's just a shag. I mean, I saw the way he was looking at this one at the prep kitchen the other day"—he gestured to Hannah with his chin—"but I thought he was just feeling protective of a helpless female."

I snorted heartily at that.

Grant just scowled, but it didn't take him long to get the bee out of his bonnet.

"I need to talk to him about what was on that video on her phone. That might explain more of this." He did the chin thing again in the new couple's direction. But then he looked around the whole pool area, making a whirlpool effect in the water around us as he turned. "I'm wondering if maybe Bas knows more, but I don't even see that bastard. Where did he go? This is his shindig."

My head spun a bit even after we stopped moving, so it took me a few seconds to catch up with a comment. "I don't see Abbi either. Maybe they went to get the baby? Are you ready to get out? We could go sit by Banks and Hannah. She's been too uncomfortable to even return my waves. And of course, he's being his usual charming self and ignoring her."

"Yeah, I'll go with you. Let's grab our towels, though. You need to cover your ass. That suit is ridiculous."

I batted my best innocent eyes at him. "You don't like it?"

"Don't."

"You asked for it, buddy. You were the one who said I should wear this suit."

"Yeah, but that was before I knew the bottoms were ass floss."

"Oh my God." I snorted again, this time in laughter. "I can't believe you just said that."

He stayed practically glued to the back of me as we went up the ladder and over to our beach bags. After I pulled my dress over my suit, we carried two chairs closer to the new odd couple.

Grant kicked Elijah's leg. "Hey, man. Mind if we join you guys?"

Setting my chair on the far side of Hannah, I said much quieter, "Hey. Hi. How's it going?"

I didn't miss the way she shifted her eyes back and forth to Elijah a few times to see if he was paying attention to our conversation before answering.

"Okay," she finally said. The normally upbeat, spunky, spirited friend of mine was completely gone, and in her place was a nervous and, I thought, sad young woman. But why sad? How did that even make sense?

"Hey, I was going to see if I could find a restroom in this palace." This time, I uttered it loud enough for the guys to hear. "Will you come with me?" I asked her.

"I can show you where it is." Elijah was on his feet in a matter of seconds, crowding between Hannah and me. "Do you need to use the restroom?" he asked her directly and followed the question with a one-word command. "Come."

"Come?" I repeated.

"Rio," Grant called to me, but I was too occupied at the moment to answer. I was locked in a stare-down with his buddy, Mr. Asshat Banks.

"Come?" I said again, my voice gaining gusto.

The sun was completely blocked out when Grant stepped in front of me.

I looked up, fucking furious enough to spit nails.

"I'll walk up to the house with you, Blaze. I know where the restrooms are."

I looked up the length of his chiseled torso until I got to his expressive blue eyes. At the moment, those eyes were all but begging me to just go along with him and not make a scene.

For once, just don't make a scene.

"I would like that, thank you," I said as calmly and sincerely as possible given the fact that I was seething inside. He was going to have some mighty explaining to do the minute we were out of earshot.

About twenty yards from the house, I said through gritted teeth, "Explain yourself, Tree."

"Baby, that's something you don't want to get in the middle of, unless your friend wants to explain it to you."

"What?"

"You have to just trust me. And trust Elijah. He knows what he's doing. He knows what she needs. And she's trying to figure out what she wants."

I narrowed my gaze before retorting, "And you know that exactly...how?"

"It's best if we all just stay out of it right now until they come to an agreement."

"I have no fucking idea what you're talking about."

"That's exactly why you should stay out of it, okay?"

"Wait. Is this..." I lowered my voice dramatically. "A sexual thing? Is he forcing her to do something she doesn't want to do? So help me God, Grant, I will castrate him. She is so fucking pure and naïve. She's such a good girl. She shouldn't be tangled up with a man like him."

He just listened to me dog his best friend and then stared at me. And stared some more.

Finally, he said, "You done?"

"I think so." I tugged my dress down. Smoothed the hem. I couldn't meet his stare now for some reason. But then after a few moments, all my ire came rushing back. "Grant! You don't—"

"Stop." The stare.

He pulled me into the tightest embrace, and I wished we were back in the water, blissfully floating with no cares in the world.

Grant held me at arm's length and bent forward to look me in the eyes. "Do you trust me? After everything we've been through, do you trust me?"

"Yes." That was the easiest answer I'd ever given in my whole life. "Grant Twombley, I trust you more than I've ever trusted anyone. Ever."

"Then hear what I'm saying. Stay out of that." He looked over my shoulder and down to the pool area where we'd left Elijah and Hannah sitting together. "Unless your friend wants to talk to you about it, stay out of it. That's between them. Okay?"

"Fine. Okay."

"Now, are you ready to go? I have something I want to show you, and it's only there for a certain amount of time, so we have to leave now if we're going to see it."

"You know I'd follow you anywhere, anytime, to any place."

He tucked his head down and gave me a gentle kiss. "Perfect answer, little Blaze."

CHAPTER SIXTEEN

GRANT

With a quick thump on the roof before I got in, I signaled to the driver we were ready to shove off. We said our goodbyes, which were delayed significantly when Abbi brought baby Kaisan out for everyone to *oooh* and *ahhh* over.

Rio held the infant for about five minutes, maybe less, then promptly handed the swaddled boy off to the next pair of anxious arms. We would definitely have to discuss that later. I wasn't sure which detail of the experience had her up in her head, but something definitely did.

Not that I fully blamed her for her heightened nervousness. The entire visit was a strain on her nerves. Socially seeing her former sister-in-law for the first time since the woman had her committed to an in-patient mental health facility, and then being able to mend their rift, was enough to call the day a win.

She and Abbi hadn't spent any time together lately, but they were smiling and talking when they were near each other today. It was the beginning of their healing, so I was claiming the visit as a success.

Holding the baby might have been the straw that broke the camel's back of her nerves, but so far, Rio didn't se overly agitated or angry as we drove toward my s destination. She lay across my lap in the back of the ca lumbered through downtown Los Angeles traffic. She probably assumed we were returning to the condo, but I had another plan in mind. A special visit that I sensed we both needed.

"Tired, baby?" I asked as I draped her denim jacket over her as a makeshift blanket. "Close your eyes until we get there."

"Get where? Are we going far? I thought we were just going...home..." Her voice drifted off, taken over by a long yawn. Already, she had me chuckling.

"No, not far at all, actually. But if you're that tired, any little bit of rest will help."

"I always get sleepy when I've been out in the sun. I think you were smart to not drink on top of everything else. There were a lot of emotions today. Some I expected. Others...well, those were surprises."

"Seems like it always goes like that when family is involved, doesn't it?" Not that I actually knew. It just seemed like the right thing to say.

"Where did you say we were going?" Rio asked again, changing the subject.

"Nice try." I dug my fingers into her ribs and made her squeal. "It's a surprise and you know it. But we are only blocks away. You're in the perfect spot, though, on my lap like that. That way you will see part of the surprise all at once, so stay there. And, if you're really quick and want to suck—"

"Grant Twombley, stop it right now."

"No fun," I whined, but I knew if this night ended the way I hoped it would, she'd be giving me more than a quick blow job in the back of a car.

My phone vibrated on the seat beside us, and I took a look without Rio seeing the screen. The message was the word I was hoping to see.

Ready!

With perfect timing, the driver pulled over to the curb.

"Look at me," I said to Rio as she sat up.

Her hair was sticking every which way from being in the pool, and still, she had never looked more beautiful to me. When she met my gaze, I put my palm alongside her jaw and cradled it when she leaned into my strength.

"I love you so much, Rio Gibson."

She smiled with dreamy, creamy perfection. "As I love you, Grant Twombley."

"Now come," I bade gently. "I want to show you something."

The driver opened the passenger-side door, and I sat and watched Rio's reaction before I got out on my side. I asked the driver to park so when he opened the door, as much of the Bunker Hill staircase would be visible from the street level. It was a little difficult because it curved and went up between the buildings, but she would get the idea the moment she got that first visual.

"Oh. My. God." She got out of the car in slow motion, gripping the door with one hand for balance and her other hand over her mouth in disbelief. "Grant." She turned to look at me. "You did this?"

"Yes. Do you like it?"

"It's beautiful. Does it go the whole way up?"

"Come on," I said, tugging on her hand a little. "Let's find out."

The location had been the site of a friendly lunch for us back when we were both lodged in each other's friend zo But even then, I was already smitten with her. Maybe r than smitten. I just couldn't admit it to anyone, especially myself.

Holy shit, had life thrown us on a crazy roller coaster since that day. It only seemed right to bring her back here tonight.

I had some help making the place extra special for this date, though. White tea lights in lanterns lit the way up the steps, from the bottom to the very top. Rio gushed the entire time about how beautiful it was and how she couldn't believe I had arranged this.

"Do you remember our lunch date here?" I stopped on one of the steps near the very top to ask her. Like that day, I went back down a few so she and I could be eye to eye.

"I do," she said, and her smile was shy.

With a finger beneath her chin, I lifted her face back up so I could look into her expressive mocha gaze. "What? Why are you being bashful? I don't think I've ever seen this look on you before." I leaned in and kissed her pert little nose. "I kind of like it. I think this would be what our daughter would look like if she got caught being naughty."

"Our daughter?" She gulped and then asked, "So . . . you do want to have children?"

"Sure. I mean, I guess. You do, right? And I want to give you the moon, Rio Katrina. I want to give you everything and anything your heart desires. If you want a baby, then let's make a baby."

For many long, magical moments, she just stared at me. Her mouth fell open, and her chin started to wobble. But before she completely lost it, I held up one finger.

"But first," I teased in a murmur. "Are you hungry? cause I'm starving. They barely fed us at that damn party. e on." I took her hand again and tugged her up the last few steps to the promenade at the top. I'd paid the woman with the empanada cart to stay late tonight just for us.

"You have got to be kidding me," Rio said when she saw the woman standing behind her counter, smiling and waiting for our arrival.

"My treat!" I swept a courtly bow. "I'm an old-fashioned gentleman, after all."

"Hmm. I believe it's my turn to pick up the tab, Mr. Twombley." She tapped her foot, picking up on the scene I'd already started to re-create. All the bantering we'd shared that amazing afternoon. All the laughter. All the connection. All the magic that was solely, wonderfully us.

"No way," I said—again, exactly as I had on that day. "Your money's no good here, lady. Tell the woman what you want, please."

We ordered our food and waited, and Rio beamed up at me the entire time. "You are really something, Grant. This is so special."

"I think that day I already knew I was falling in love with you. And yeah, I knew it was so wrong. You were a married woman, and I couldn't stop the feelings that were careening around inside me." I put my hands over my heart because I remembered how much it hurt. It physically hurt to want her so badly and not be able to have her.

We took our food and sat at the same table, although now it was set with a pretty white tablecloth. The lanterns cast a dancing, flickering shadow on our meal, which we consumed with real silverware. I couldn't deal with that maddeni~ plastic crap again.

"My God, these really are the best in this city. I w~ if she sells these to bake at home?" Rio said after che~ first bite.

"We could find out. Or . . ."

"Or what?"

"We could do this regularly. Like, every year. Make it an annual tradition."

"Like a birthday thing or something?"

Or an anniversary date.

But aloud, I only said, "Yeah. Something like that."

Plain and simple, I wanted to build a life with this woman. I wanted to start writing our history together, making our memory book. So when we looked back at the things we'd done, the places we'd been, and the adventures we'd shared, we would remember there were way more good times than bad. Yes, there were already some dark clouds that we'd weathered, but that didn't mean there wouldn't be more. I wanted to remind her—always—that life was about seeing the silver lining, not the stormy seas.

"Oh boy. I don't think I can eat another bite," my beautiful Blaze finally said, nudging her plate back a bit. She was so enthralled with the delicious street food, she hadn't noticed that I'd been staring at her—practically without blinking—for the past several minutes.

"What's on your mind, Tree? You've been looking at me like I'm about to pop with some nocturnal bloom."

Okay, so she had noticed. Why would I even be surprised? Still, I chuckled at her question.

"Nothing in particular," I said. "Well, that's not true. A lot of things, really. I just can't take my eyes off you. I'm raptured."

"Enraptured?" She met my gaze and grinned, preparing something cheeky to come next. But not if I cut her off nversational pass.

"Yes. Enraptured. I have something to ask you. Here"—I held out my hands—"come sit with me here." I pulled her over to the same concrete bench upon which I sat because I wanted to be touching her perfect skin, her perfect body.

"Hmm-kay," she drawled. "I'm not going to lie, Twombley. You're starting to freak me out a little bit." The confession came with the eager darting of her bright gaze, bouncing from feature to feature on my face, trying to settle on one place but then quickly moving to another.

"I know you don't love all this talk about feelings, and I'm hitting you pretty hard with it here tonight. But as you know, I had a lot of time to myself recently." I gave her a wink, making it clear that shit storm wasn't going to encroach on this scene in any further way than that. "And as I've been processing it all, I realize that I thought about you more than anything or anyone else. I thought about how I didn't want to live without you. How my life would be so incomplete without you in it, Blaze."

As I talked, Rio's eyes were wide and attentive. It was such a difference from the lost woman she was only a month ago.

She put her hands on my face before leaning in and kissing me. "You know I love you, too, right?"

"Yes, I do. You have no idea what that does to me inside, right here"—I patted my chest—"when you say that. I didn't think I would ever find a woman who would love me . . . for me."

"Grant. How can you say that? You are an extraordinary man. No. You're one of the most amazing people I know. Period."

"Rio, when I was a teenager, I was homeless. There were days—*days*—that I couldn't even take a shower becau I didn't have running water. A bed and a meal seemed li pipe dream." I bought myself a second to pause by running a hand back through my hair. "So a wife and family... Shit, that wasn't something I thought would ever be a part of my life. But Bas, that bastard"—I chuckled and shook my head—"he wouldn't settle for that life, and he dragged me into all his schemes and dreams, and before I knew it, we were bicycle couriers and making actual money. And then we just kept growing from there because we got that fire in our bellies for more. Always more, you know?"

Rio nodded along as I spoke because she'd heard the story before. "And look where you are now. Look at all you've accomplished."

"You're right. I have so much to be grateful for. But none of it matters, baby, if I can't have you by my side to share it with me. I don't want to be alone anymore, Rio. I don't want to be without you. When I call out in the night for my mate, I want you to be the one who answers."

I backed off the bench and dropped down on one knee, and shit, this patio was hard on bare skin, but I pulled the ring out of my pocket and looked up to Rio's huge stare.

"Rio Katrina, will you be the one who answers when I call? Will you marry me?"

"Oh, Jesus, Grant. Look at that thing!" She let me slide the kite-cut diamond onto her finger.

"Wait." I held her hand in mine. "Is that a yes?"

She flung her entire body at me and toppled us both to the ground. "Yes! That's a yes, you crazy tree. I'll marry you. I love you."

"I love you, too, Blaze. Forever. I promise, I will."

CONTINUE READING
THE SHARK'S EDGE SERIES

WITH
ELIJAH'S WHIM

Coming Soon!

EXCERPT FROM
NO PERFECT PRINCESS

BOOK THREE IN THE SECRETS OF STONE SERIES

MARGAUX

Fashion icon. It was a dirty job, but someone had to do it.

Even if all I saw outside the window of San Diego's most exclusive couture bridal shop was a parade of last year's jeans and ugly Christmas sweaters.

Ugh. The humanity.

I turned away from the horror show, sighing as I stopped in front of a mirror to readjust my beanie. It was a bold choice of accessory, running the risk of tumbling from damn-she's-fabulous to oh-no-she-didn't inside five seconds. The trick was the backside dangle. If that fell right, you were golden.

Perfect.

I sat on a couch and thumbed impatiently through a magazine. China patterns, honeymoon locales, reception favors, more china patterns...

I threw the thing down, pretty damn sure I felt a migraine coming on.

"Claire!"

For the love of Louboutin, how long did put

one wedding dress take? Okay, so she was my sister. Sort of. Technically, my soon-to-be sister-in-law—even if only a handful of people on the planet knew that. I wasn't sure I wanted the news expanded past those boundaries either. It had been sheer hell working out the bullshit surrounding the family everyone did know about.

No. Today wasn't a day for moping about Mother. Or the way she'd used my birth like a bargaining chip. Or the fact that she'd kept that truth from me for twenty-six years—and not felt a moment of remorse once I did find out.

Christ almighty. What was Claire doing in there? Sewing the damn thing by herself? Since there were three attendants with her, that was the *mystère du jour*.

"Claire!" I repeated. "Honestly, I'm growing roots from standing in the same—"

My derision died as my doe-eyed stepsister stepped out of the small room, silk and lace trailing behind her in a wave of tulle and princess-bride splendor. If I were a weaker woman, which I most certainly was not, I would cop to a lump in my throat at the vision standing before me, eyes aglow, dimples bracketing a shy smile, red hair tumbling into the gown's regal neckline.

Holy hell. Wait until Killian saw this. He thought he was head over heels before? Brother of mine, prepare your gut for a real train collision.

"Claire Bear. Wow."

It was all I could manage. And no, the tightness at the base of my throat had nothing to do with it.

The sales bitches beamed like they'd just birthed the ing Baby New Year. They had this one in the bag and knew exact reason why I pulled a full ice princess, glaring just enough to let them know the real bitch would come next. In an instant, they rushed forward to fuss around Claire once more.

"This dress was made for you, Miss Montgomery."

"Mr. Stone's eyes are going to fall out of his head."

"Amazing. Simply amazing."

It went on for fifteen minutes, one blah blah blah after another. I tuned out, my stomach turning on the latte I'd subbed for breakfast this morning.

This would never be me.

Never.

I would never walk down the aisle into the controlling clutches of a man. Ha—I didn't even have a father to walk me down the aisle. Like it was even a big deal anymore. Until ten months ago, I'd written off the dad angle from my life, with no reason to disbelieve what Mother always asserted—that my father had run out on us and didn't deserve a moment more of my attention. That all changed in a Chicago hospital room, where Josiah Stone had confessed to something much different—before taking his last breath.

Never knowing that his death had also killed off one of the most enduring fantasies of my life.

That somehow, my father would realize what a huge mistake he'd made in running from me—and return to embrace me with tears of grateful reunion. He'd tell me he didn't care about my makeup or clothes, that he only wanted to know what I was really like, on the inside, before sweeping me off to his mountain cabin, where—

Like going any further down that road was going to help right now.

Thank you, Mommie Dearest.

I officially hated that woman.

No, you don't.

Hmmm. I was pretty sure I did. Though I was too damn afraid of her to ever say it to her face, which was...unnerving. At really deep levels.

"Margaux? Are you okay?"

Claire's enormous brown eyes were fixed on me through the mirror. This chick didn't miss a beat with her attention or her concern, which pounded the unnerving right down into disturbed.

Christ, I was a mess lately. And the kicker? I was actually aware of it. Puke. Life had been much simpler when all I thought about in the morning was digging into someone else's dirt—and how fabulous I'd look while helping them with it.

"Have you seen the back of this one, Claire?" I flashed more daggers at the bitches. "Did any of you think to show her the back? It's stunning, Bear. Truly."

My diversion tactic worked, at least on the sales flock. They flurried again, turning Claire so she could see, erupting into more gibberish about the gown and its perfect fit, flare, and hemline. But damn it if my sister didn't keep her eyes fixed on me, silently—and unashamedly—trying to probe. I finally rolled my eyes and gave her the Margaux salute, jabbing my middle finger when the attendants weren't looking. She suppressed a giggle, but that didn't fool me. She'd be all over me the minute we were alone—because that was simply the kind of girl she was. Observant. Intuitive. And caring to the point where it was her damn superpower.

Lucky, lucky me.

The morning from hell transitioned into afternoon. ⸻ after dress. Perfection upon perfection. Okay, some ⸻ much. The lavender one had to go. Who the hell wore a lavender wedding dress? I suspected Claire tried that one on to see if I was still paying attention. Thank God I'd paused between emails, which had become my new obsession lately. Now that I was on the full-time roster with Stone Global, I needed to be serious about shining there.

The idea of continuing on with Mother—with Andrea—had seemed impossible when we returned from Chicago. After all her secrets had been unveiled, I couldn't even stand being in the same room with her. Even a simple explanation might have helped, though I never gave in to the illusion of receiving a full apology. That kind of thing happened in worlds where unicorns descended from heaven to save humanity from the zombie apocalypse.

She'd never come. Never called. Never said another word. And with her silence had wrecked whatever connection we'd had, however dysfunctional. I sent a formal letter declaring a leave of absence, but she and I both knew I was never coming back. Too many lies, too much deception. I was tired of Andrea Asher's games and refused to be a pawn in them anymore. Or so I told myself on the good days.

I'd barely had a chance to realize that woman of leisure wasn't a role I enjoyed playing, when Killian approached with the opportunity to stay on permanently with Stone Global's expanded PR department. It made perfect sense from a couple of angles. The Asher and Associates team had already been working exclusively with SGC, so everything already felt like my home turf. And as they say, blood is thicker than water. Or did it form the ties that bind? Or coagulate if you used hot honey? Whatever. It was irony at its best, however you phrased it. Killian, only a Stone by adoption, hired the real Stone, for the family business. To add a ha atop ha, Killian's lineage was now full public knowledge—and mine still a carefully guarded secret.

Because I demanded it that way.

I'd had a first-row seat for the media's last feeding frenzy about Stone family news. It had driven Killian Stone, one of the finest men I knew, into months of hiding. Well, last time I checked, my name wasn't Shark Chum. I'd be damned if I'd voluntarily splash into that same tank.

When Killian opened SGC's San Diego branch and brought me on, my friendship—and unique sisterhood—with Claire was forged deeper. Sure, we had less in common than most typical besties, but somehow it worked in our favor. With unanimous backing by the board, Killian named her the director of the new public relations department, with me as her tight wingwoman. She was the first to admit that she still had a lot to learn, so my experience had come into play in ways that made me feel, for the first time in a long time, like my contributions mattered.

So far, it had been a pretty cool gig.

So far...

This story continues in
No Perfect Princess: *Secrets of Stone Book Three*!

ALSO BY
ANGEL PAYNE & VICTORIA BLUE

Shark's Edge Series:
Shark's Edge
Shark's Pride
Shark's Rise
Grant's Heat
Grant's Flame
Grant's Blaze
Elijah's Whim

Secrets of Stone Series:
No Prince Charming
No More Masquerade
No Perfect Princess
No Magic Moment
No Lucky Number
No Simple Sacrifice
No Broken Bond
No White Knight
No Longer Lost

ALSO BY ANGEL PAYNE

The Blood of Zeus Series:
(with Meredith Wild)
Blood of Zeus
Heart of Fire
Fate of Storms

Suited for Sin:
Sing
Sigh
Submit

Lords of Sin:
Trade Winds
Promised Touch
Redemption
A Fire in Heaven
Surrender to the Dawn

ALSO BY VICTORIA BLUE

Misadventures:
Misadventures with a Book Boyfriend
Misadventures at City Hall

**For a full list of Angel's & Victoria's other titles,
visit them at AngelPayne.com & VictoriaBlue.com**

ACKNOWLEDGMENTS

The world of the Sharks and their friends was born during one stormy afternoon during a book convention, and now, thanks to the brilliance of Victoria Blue's heart and soul, has grown into this vibrant, ongoing story. From the depths of my soul, I'm so grateful to have been part of this really cool journey. Can't wait to see where you take it next! #SharkFanNumberOneForever!

My love and constant gratitude to Thomas and Jessica: the rocks of my soul, the fires of my heart, the centers of my existence.

Never-ending gratitude to Scott Saunders, editor god extraordinaire. Your patience, wisdom, and insights are deeply—and always!—the perfect touch!

A billion thank-yous wouldn't be enough for the incredible team at Waterhouse Press, always there with the blessings of your talents and encouragement: Meredith Wild, Jennifer Becker, Haley Boudreaux, Dana Bridges, Keli Jo Chen, Yvonne Ellis, Jesse Kench, Robyn Lee, Jonathan Mac, Amber Maxwell, and Kurt Vachon.

Special gratitude to the amazing Martha Frantz and Kika Medina, for helping out with the details when I need them most.

Also, many hugs from Victoria for her team, Megan, Amy, and Faith.

This job isn't possible without friends who know where

every body is buried and have all the frantic midnight texts and phone calls to prove it! Thank you for your constant love and support in my world: Carey Sabala, Jenna Jacob, Shayla Black, Dylan Allen, Jodi Drake, Corinne Akers, Rebekah Ganiere, and Tracy Roelle. We love you amazing goddesses!

ABOUT ANGEL PAYNE

USA Today bestselling romance author Angel Payne loves to focus on high-heat romance starring memorable alpha men and the women who love them. She has numerous book series to her credit, including the action-packed Bolt Saga and Honor Bound series, Secrets of Stone series (with Victoria Blue), the intertwined Cimarron and Temptation Court series, the Suited for Sin series, and the Lords of Sin historicals, as well as several standalone titles.

Angel is a native Southern Californian, leading to her love of being in the outdoors, where she often reads and writes. She still lives in Southern California with her soul-mate husband and beautiful daughter, to whom she is a proud cosplay/culture con mom. Her passions also include whisky tasting, shoe shopping, and travel.

Visit her at AngelPayne.com

ABOUT VICTORIA BLUE

International bestselling author Victoria Blue lives in her own portion of the galaxy known as Southern California. There, she finds the love and life-sustaining power of one amazing sun, two unique and awe-inspiring planets, and four indifferent yet comforting moons. Life is fantastic and challenging and every day brings new adventures to be discovered. She looks forward to seeing what's next!

Visit her at VictoriaBlue.com